DEAN KOONTZ'S FRANKENSTEIN
DEAD AND ALIVE

Dean Koontz was born and raised in Pennsylvania. He is the author of many number one bestsellers. He lives with his wife, Gerda, and their dog Anna, and the enduring spirit of their dog Trixie in southern California.

DEAN KOONTZ'S FRANKENSTEIN

BOOK THREE

dead and alive

DEAN KOONTZ

HARPER

Harper
An imprint of HarperCollins*Publishers*
1 London Bridge Street
London SE1 9GF

www.harpercollins.co.uk

This paperback edition 2012

First published in Great Britain by
HarperCollins*Publishers* 2009

A catalogue record for this book is
available from the British Library

ISBN: 978-0-00-745301-6

Set in Albertina MT by Palimpsest Book Production Limited,
Falkirk, Stirlingshire

Printed and bound by CPI Group (UK) Ltd, Croydon, CR0 4YY

MIX
Paper from
responsible sources
FSC **FSC™ C007454**
www.fsc.org

This trilogy is dedicated to the late Mr Lewis, who long ago realized that science was being politicized, that its primary goal was changing from knowledge to power, that it was also becoming scientism, and that in the *ism* is the end of humanity.

I am very doubtful whether history shows us one example of a man who,
having stepped outside traditional morality and attained power,
has used that power benevolently.

—C. S. LEWIS, *The Abolition of Man*

FRANKENSTEIN

dead and alive

chapter 1

Half past a windless midnight, rain cantered out of the Gulf, across the shore and the levees: parades of phantom horses striking hoof rhythms from roofs of tarpaper, tin, tile, shingles, slate, counting cadence along the avenues.

Usually a late-night town where restaurants and jazz clubs cooked almost until the breakfast hour, New Orleans was on this occasion unlike itself. Little traffic moved on the streets. Many restaurants closed early. For lack of customers, some of the clubs went dark and quiet.

A hurricane was transiting the Gulf, well south of the Louisiana coast. The National Weather Service currently predicted landfall near Brownsville, Texas, but the storm track might change. Through hard experience, New Orleans had learned to respect the power of nature.

Deucalion stepped out of the Luxe Theater without using a door, and stepped into a different district of the city, out of light and into the deep shadows under the boughs of moss-robed oak trees.

In the glow of streetlamps, the skeins of rain glimmered like tarnished silver. But under the oaks, the precipitation seemed ink-black, as if it were not rain but were instead a product of the darkness, the very sweat of the night.

Although an intricate tattoo distracted curious people from recognizing the extent of the damage to the ruined half of his face, Deucalion preferred to venture into public places between dusk and dawn. The sunless hours provided an additional layer of disguise.

His formidable size and physical power could not be concealed. Having endured more than two hundred years, his body was unbent bone and undiminished muscle. Time seemed to have no power to weather him.

As he followed the sidewalk, he passed through places where the glow of streetlamps penetrated the leafy canopy. The mercurial light chased from memory the torch-carrying mob that had harried Deucalion through a cold and rainless night on a continent far from this one, in an age before electricity.

Across the street, occupying half a block, the Hands of Mercy stood on an oak-shaded property. Once a Catholic hospital, it closed long ago.

A tall wrought-iron fence encircled the hospital grounds. The spear-point staves suggested that where mercy had once been offered, none could now be found.

A sign on the iron driveway gate warned PRIVATE WAREHOUSE / NO ADMITTANCE. The bricked-up windows emitted no light.

Overlooking the main entrance stood a statue of the Holy Mother. The light once focused on her had been removed, and the robed figure looming in darkness might have been Death, or anyone.

Only hours earlier, Deucalion had learned that this building harbored the laboratory of his maker, Victor Helios, whose birth name was legend: Frankenstein. Here members of the New Race were designed, created, and programmed.

The security system would monitor every door. The locks would be difficult to defeat.

Thanks to gifts carried on the lightning bolt that brought him to life in an earlier and more primitive lab, Deucalion did not need doors. Locks were no impediment to him. Intuitively, he grasped the quantum nature of the world, including the truth that on the deepest structural level, every place in the world was the same place.

As he contemplated venturing into his maker's current lair, Deucalion had no fear. If any emotion might undo him, it would be rage. But over these many decades, he had learned to control the anger that had once driven him so easily to violence.

He stepped out of the rain and into the main laboratory in the Hands of Mercy, wet when he took the step, dry when he completed it.

Victor's immense lab was a techno-Deco wonder, mostly stainless-steel and white ceramic, filled with sleek and mysterious equipment that seemed not to be standing along the walls but to be embedded in them, extruding from them. Other machines swelled out of the ceiling and surged up from the floor, polished and gleaming, yet suggesting organic forms.

Every soft noise was rhythmic, the purr and hum and click of machinery. The place seemed to be deserted.

Sapphire, primrose-pink, and apple-green luminous gases filled glass spheres. Through elaborate coils of transparent tubing flowed lavender, calamine-blue, and methyl-orange fluids.

Victor's U-shaped workstation stood in the center of the room, a black-granite top on a stainless-steel base.

As Deucalion considered searching the drawers, someone behind him said, "Can you help me, sir?"

The man wore a gray denim jumpsuit. In a utility belt around his waist were secured spray bottles of cleaning solutions, white rags, and small sponges. He held a mop.

"Name's Lester," he said. "I'm an Epsilon. You seem smarter than me. Are you smarter than me?"

"Is your maker here?" Deucalion asked.

"No, sir. Father left earlier."

"How many staff are here?"

"I don't count much. Numbers confuse me. I heard once – eighty staff. So Father isn't here, now something's gone wrong, and I'm just an Epsilon. You seem like maybe an Alpha or a Beta. Are you an Alpha or a Beta?"

"What's gone wrong?" Deucalion asked.

"She says Werner is trapped in Isolation Room Number One. No, maybe Number Two. Anyway, Number Something."

"Who is Werner?"

"He's the security chief. She wanted instructions, but I don't give instructions, I'm just Lester."

"Who wants instructions?"

"The woman in the box."

As Lester spoke, the computer on Victor's desk brightened, and on the screen appeared a woman so flawlessly beautiful that her face must have been a digital construction.

"Mr Helios, Helios. Welcome to Helios. I am Annunciata. I am not as much Annunciata as before, but I am still trying to be as much Annunciata as I am able. I am now analyzing my helios, Mr Systems. My systems, Mr Helios. I am a good girl."

"She's in a box," Lester said.

"A computer," Deucalion said.

"No. A box in the networking room. She's a Beta brain in a box. She don't have no body. Sometimes her container leaks, so I clean up the spill."

Annunciata said, "I am wired. I am wired. I am wired into the building's data-processing system. I am secretary to Mr Helios. I am very smart. I am a good girl. I want to serve efficiently. I am a good, good girl. I am afraid."

"She isn't usually like this," said Lester.

"Perhaps there is an im-im-im-imbalance in my nutrient supply. I am unable to analyze. Could someone analyze my nutrient supply?"

"Self-aware, forever in a box," Deucalion said.

"I am very afraid," Annunciata said.

Deucalion found his hands curling into fists. "There is nothing your maker won't do. No form of slavery offends him, no cruelty is beyond him."

Uneasy, shifting from foot to foot like a little boy who needed to go to the bathroom, Lester said, "He's a great genius. He's even smarter than an Alpha. We should be grateful to him."

"Where is the networking room?" Deucalion asked.

"We should be grateful."

"The networking room. Where is this . . . woman?"

"In the basement."

On the computer screen, Annunciata said, "I must organize the
appointment schedule for Mr Helios. Helios. But I do not remember
what an appointment is. Can you help, help, help me?"

"Yes," Deucalion said. "I can help you."

chapter 2

When the pizza-delivery guy, looking for the Bennet house, made the mistake of going to the Guitreau place next door, Janet Guitreau surprised herself by dragging him into her foyer and strangling him to death.

Janet and her husband, Bucky Guitreau, the current district attorney of the city of New Orleans, were replicants. The bodies of the real Janet and Bucky had been buried weeks previously in a vast garbage dump in the uplands well northeast of Lake Pontchartrain.

Most of the New Race were not replicants. They were originals, fully designed by Father. But replicants were crucial to taking control of the city's political apparatus.

Janet suspected that some significant lines of code had dropped out of her program, and Bucky was inclined to agree with her.

Not only had Janet killed without being told to do so by her maker, but she felt good about it. Actually, she felt marvelous.

She wanted to go next door and kill the Bennets. "Killing is wonderfully refreshing. I feel so *alive*."

Bucky should have reported her to Helios for termination. But he was so in awe of her audacity and so intrigued that he could not convince himself to phone Father's emergency number.

This suggested to both of them that Bucky, too, had dropped some lines of his program. He didn't think that he could kill, but he was excited by the prospect of watching Janet destroy the Bennets.

They almost rushed next door. But then the dead pizza guy in the foyer seemed worthy of further examination, considering that he *was* Janet's first.

"After all," Bucky said, "if you were a hunter and this guy were a deer, we'd take a hundred photographs, and we'd cut off his antlers to hang them over the fireplace."

Janet's eyes widened. "Hey, you want to cut something off him, hang it over the fireplace?"

"That maybe wouldn't be smart, but I would for sure like to get some snapshots."

"So you get the camera," Janet said, "and I'll look around for the best backdrop."

When Bucky hurried to the second floor to retrieve the camera from the master-bedroom closet, he discovered the Duke of Orleans watching the foyer from the top of the stairs.

Duke was a handsome German shepherd, caramel-and-black with two white boots. Since the New Race versions of Bucky and Janet had come into his life a few weeks earlier, he had been confused and wary. They looked like his masters, but he knew they were not. He treated them with respect but remained aloof, withheld affection, which they didn't want anyway.

As Bucky reached the top of the stairs, Duke padded away into one of the guest bedrooms.

Helios had considered having the dog killed when the original Bucky and Janet had been terminated.

But Duke was a New Orleans icon: He had saved two small girls from a house fire, and he was so well-behaved that he often went to court with his master. His passing would be a major human-interest story, and there might be a jazz funeral for him. This would draw too much attention to a pair of newly installed replicants.

Besides, the real Bucky Guitreau was a sentimental man who so loved his dog that everyone would expect him to weep uncontrollably at any memorial service. Generally speaking, the New Race was not good at faking grief, and any statue of the Virgin Mary was more likely to produce tears than were those born in the creation tanks.

With the camera in hand, the new Bucky hurried downstairs, where he found Janet and the pizza guy in the living room. She had placed the dead man in a plushly upholstered chair. She sat on the arm of the chair and, gripping a handful of the cadaver's hair, held his head up for the camera.

They moved the corpse to the sofa, where Janet sat beside it, and then to a bar stool in the study, where Janet let the head loll against her shoulder as if Pizza Guy were drunk. They hauled the body to several other locations in the house, took some pictures with women's hats on his head, then stripped him naked and dressed him in women's underwear for a few more shots.

They never laughed through any of this. Members of the New Race were capable of producing convincing laughter, but their mirth was not genuine. They did what they did with the dead man because their hatred for the Old Race was intense, and this seemed like a good way to express that hatred.

The dog followed them on this photo shoot, watching them from the doorways of various rooms but never venturing close.

Finally, they stripped Pizza Guy naked again, tied a rope around his neck, hauled him over a transverse beam in the family room, and let him dangle like a big fish on a dock scale. Janet stood beside the corpse, as if proud of her catch.

"You know what I think we're doing?" she asked.

All of this behavior had seemed as reasonable to Bucky as to her, though he didn't know why. He said, "What *are* we doing?"

"I think we're having fun."

"Could this be what fun is like?"

"I think it could," Janet said.

"Well, it's more interesting than anything else we've ever done. What else do you want to do with him?"

"He's getting a little boring," Janet said. "I think it's really time now to go next door and kill the Bennets."

The original Bucky had kept two guns in the house. "You want to take a pistol, blow their faces off?"

Janet thought about it, but then shook her head. "That doesn't sound fun enough."

"You want to take a knife or that Civil War sword on the wall of my study?"

"What I want," Janet said, "is just to do them both with my bare hands."

"Strangle them?"

"Been there, done that."

"Then what are you going to do with them?"

"Oh, I've got like a thousand ideas."

"Should I bring the camera?" he asked.

"Absolutely, bring the camera."

"Maybe we can put all these shots in an album," Bucky suggested. "That's what people do."

"I'd like that. But we're not really people."

"I don't see why we can't have an album. In a lot of ways we're *similar* to people."

"Except that we're superior. We're the super race."

"We are the super race," Bucky agreed. "Soon we're going to rule the world, colonize the moon and Mars. We'll own the universe. So it seems like we could have a photo album if we wanted. Who's to tell us we can't?"

"Nobody," Janet said.

chapter 3

Alone in the institutional kitchen at the Hands of Mercy, Ripley sat on a stool at one of the stainless-steel islands. With his hands, he tore apart a three-pound ham and stuffed chunks into his mouth.

The average man of the New Race required five thousand calories per day to sustain himself, two and a half times what the average man of the Old Race needed. Recently, Ripley had engaged in binge eating, packing in ten thousand calories or more at a single sitting.

The tearing was more satisfying than the eating. These days, the urge to tear things apart – especially meat – frequently overcame Ripley. Cooked meat served as a substitute for raw flesh, the flesh of the Old Race, which was what he most wanted to tear.

None of his kind was either permitted to kill or capable of killing – until ordered to do so by the Beekeeper.

That was Ripley's private name for Victor Helios. Many of the others referred to him as Father, but Mr Helios became infuriated when he heard them use that word.

They weren't their maker's children. They were his property. He had no responsibility to them. They had every responsibility to him.

Ripley ate the entire ham, all the while reminding himself that the Beekeeper had a brilliant plan for a new world.

The family is an obsolete institution, and it's also dangerous because it puts itself above the common good of the race. The parent-child relationship must be eradicated. The sole allegiance of members of the New Race, who were born from the tanks as adults, must be to the organized community that Helios envisioned, not to one another, but to the *community,* and in fact not to the community but to the *idea* of community.

From one of two walk-in refrigerators, Ripley retrieved a fully cooked two-pound brisket of beef. He returned with it to the stool at the kitchen island.

Families breed individuals. The creation tanks breed worker bees, each with its specific function to fulfill. Knowing your place and the meaning of your life, you can be content as no member of the Old Race ever could be. Free will is the curse of the Old. Programmed purpose is the glory of the New.

The swarm was the family, the hive was the home, and the future belonged to the horde.

With his fingers, he shredded the brisket. The meat felt greasy. Although the beef was well-cooked, he could smell the blood in it.

No matter how much he ate, Ripley gained not a pound. His remarkably efficient metabolism kept him always at his ideal weight.

Overeating, therefore, was not an indulgence. Ultimately, it was also not a distraction. He couldn't stop thinking about Werner, the security chief at the Hands of Mercy.

Hours earlier, Werner suffered what the Beekeeper described as "catastrophic cellular metamorphosis." He stopped being Werner, stopped being by all appearances human, and became ... something else.

Upon his creation, designed to be a physically imposing security specialist, Werner had been given selected genetic material from a panther to increase his agility and speed, from a spider to increase the ductility of his tendons, from a cockroach to ensure greater tensile strength for his collagen ... When Werner suddenly became amorphous, those feline, arachnid, and insectile forms began to express themselves in his flesh, first serially, then simultaneously.

Mr Helios had called Werner a singularity. This calamity had not occurred previously. According to the Beekeeper, it could never occur again.

Ripley was not so sure about that. Maybe nothing *exactly* like what happened to Werner would happen again, but there might be an infinite number of other calamities pending.

As a chief lab assistant to the Beekeeper, Ripley was too well-educated to be able to repress his anxiety. In the creation tank, by direct-to-brain data down-loading, he received a deep education in the physiology of human beings as nature made them and of superhuman beings as Victor Helios made them.

None of the Old Race could metamorphose into a beast of many natures. This grotesque fate should have been just as impossible for one of the New Race.

Werner's transformation suggested that the Beekeeper might be fallible. The Beekeeper's surprise at the change in Werner confirmed his fallibility.

Having finished the brisket without either satisfying his appetite or quelling his anxiety, Ripley left the kitchen to roam the halls of Mercy. Mr Helios had gone home. But even in these post-midnight hours, in a maze of labs, Alphas conducted experiments and carried out tasks according to their maker's instructions.

Staying largely in the corridors, for the first time nervous about what he might discover in the labs if he entered them, Ripley eventually came to the monitoring hub serving the trio of isolation chambers. According to indicator lights on the control console, only Isolation Room Number Two was currently occupied; that would be the luckless Werner.

Each room featured six closed-circuit video cameras offering different angles on that space. A bank of six screens allowed the simultaneous monitoring of all three holding facilities or gave a half dozen views of a single chamber. Legends at the bottom of all the screens indicated they were now tuned to Isolation Room Number Two.

The floor, walls, and ceiling of the twenty-by-fifteen-foot windowless containment cell were constructed of eighteen-inch-thick, poured-in-place, steel-reinforced concrete. They had been paneled with three overlapping layers of steel plate that, with the click of a switch, could deliver a killing charge of electricity to the occupant.

The Beekeeper sometimes created exotic variants of the New Race, some of which were intended to be warriors, living death-machines that would assist in the efficient obliteration of the Old Race when at last the day of revolution arrived. Occasionally, problems with their prenatal programming left these creatures undisciplined or even disobedient, in which case they needed to be sedated and transferred to isolation for study and eventual destruction.

He who had been Werner did not appear on any of the screens. The six cameras covered every corner of the chamber, leaving nowhere for the thing to hide.

Strewn around the room were the dismembered remains of Patrick Duchaine, one of the Beekeeper's creations who had been sent into the isolation room to test the capabilities of the Werner thing.

A transition module connected the monitoring hub to Isolation Room Number Two. At each end of the module was a massive round steel door made for a bank vault. By design, both doors could not be open at the same time.

Ripley looked at the vault door on this end of the transition module. Nothing on Earth, whether natural-born or made by Helios, could get through that two-foot-thick steel barrier.

A camera in the isolation room revealed that the inner vault door remained shut, as well.

He doubted that the Werner thing was loose in the building. The instant someone saw it, an alarm would have been sounded.

Only one possibility remained. At some point, the inner door might have cycled open long enough to allow the creature into the transition module before closing behind it. In that case, it waited now behind not two steel barriers, but behind one.

chapter 4

By the time Bucky and Janet Guitreau reached the front porch steps of the Bennet house, they were rain-soaked.

"We should have used an umbrella," Bucky said. "We look strange like this."

They were so excited about killing the Bennets that they had not given a thought to the inclement weather.

"Maybe we look so strange they won't let us in," Bucky worried. "Especially at this hour."

"They're night owls. This isn't late for them. They'll let us in," Janet assured him. "We'll say a terrible thing has happened, we need to talk to them. That's what neighbors do, they comfort one another when terrible things happen."

Beyond the French windows and the folds of silken drapes, the front rooms were filled with soft amber light.

As they climbed the porch steps, Bucky said, "What terrible thing has happened?"

"I killed the pizza-delivery guy."

"I don't think they'll let us in if we say that."

"We aren't going to say that. We're just going to say a terrible thing has happened."

"An unspecified terrible thing," Bucky clarified.

"Yes, exactly."

"If that works, they must be amazingly trusting people."

"Bucky, we aren't strangers. They're our *neighbors*. Besides, they love us."

"They love us?"

At the door, Janet lowered her voice. "Three nights ago, we were here for barbecue. Helene said, 'We sure love you guys.' Remember?"

"But they were drinking. Helene wasn't even half sober when she said that."

"Nevertheless, she meant it. They love us, they'll let us in."

Bucky was suddenly suspicious. "How can they love us? We aren't even the people they think we are."

"They don't *know* we aren't the people they think we are. They won't even know it when I start killing them."

"Are you serious?"

"Entirely," Janet said, and rang the doorbell.

"Is the Old Race really that easy?"

"They're pussies," Janet declared.

"Pussies?"

"Total pussies." The porch light came on, and Janet said, "Do you have your camera?"

As Bucky withdrew the camera from a pants pocket, Helene Bennet appeared at a sidelight to the left of the door, blinking in surprise at the sight of them.

Raising her voice to be heard through the glass, Janet said, "Oh, Helene, something terrible has happened."

"Janet killed the pizza guy," Bucky said too softly for Helene to hear him, just for his wife's benefit, because it seemed like the kind of thing you would say when you were having fun, and this was as close to fun as they had ever known.

Helene's face puckered with concern. She stepped away from the sidelight.

As Bucky heard Helene opening the first of two deadbolts, he said to Janet, "Do something spectacular to her."

"I hate her so much," Janet replied.

"I hate her, too," Bucky said. "I hate him. I hate them all. Do something really amazing to her."

Helene disengaged the second deadbolt, opened the door, and stepped back to admit them. She was an attractive blonde with a pleasing dimple in her right cheek, though you couldn't see the dimple now because she wasn't smiling.

"Janet, Bucky, you look devastated. Oh, God, I'm afraid to ask, what's happened?"

"Something terrible has happened," Janet said. "Where's Yancy?"

"He's out on the back porch. We're having a nightcap, listening to some Etta James. What's happened, sweetie, what's wrong?"

Closing the front door behind him, Bucky said, "A terrible thing has happened."

"Oh, no," Helene said, sounding distraught. "We love you guys. You look stricken. You're drenched, you're dripping all over the parquet. What happened?"

"An unspecified terrible thing has happened," Bucky said.

"You ready with the camera?" Janet asked.

"Ready," Bucky replied.

"Camera?" Helene asked.

"We want this for our album," Janet said, and did something more spectacular to Helene than anything Bucky could have imagined.

In fact, it was so spectacular that he stood dumbfounded, the camera forgotten, and missed getting a shot of the best of it.

Janet was a runaway locomotive of rage, a log-cutting buzz saw of hatred, a jackhammer of envy driven cruelty. Fortunately, she did not kill Helene instantly, and some of the subsequent things she did to the woman, while spectacular in themselves, were sufficiently less shocking that Bucky was able to get some cool pictures.

When she finished, Janet said, "I think I've dropped a few more lines of code from my program."

"It sure looked that way," Bucky said. "You know how I said I thought I'd enjoy watching? Well, I really did."

"You want Yancy for yourself?" Janet asked.

"No. I'm not that far along yet. But you better let me get him inside from the porch. If he's out there and he sees you like this, he'll be through the porch door and gone."

Janet was still drenched but now not only with rain.

Comfortable rattan furniture with yellow cushions and rattan tables with glass tops furnished the spacious screened porch. The lights were lower than the music.

In a white linen shirt, tan slacks, and sandals, Yancy Bennet sat at a table on which were two glasses of what was most likely Cabernet as well as a cut-glass decanter in which more wine breathed and mellowed.

When he saw Bucky Guitreau, Yancy lowered the volume on Etta James. "Hey, neighbor, isn't this past your bedtime?"

"A terrible thing has happened," Bucky said as he approached Yancy. "A terrible, terrible thing."

Pushing his chair away from the table, getting to his feet, Yancy Bennet said, "What? What happened?"

"I can't even talk about it," Bucky said. "I don't know how to talk about it."

Putting a hand on Bucky's shoulder, Yancy said, "Hey, pal, whatever it is, we're here for you."

"Yes. I know. You're here for us. I'd rather Janet told you about it. I just can't be specific. She can be specific. She's inside. With Helene."

Yancy tried to usher Bucky ahead of him, but Bucky let him lead the way. "Give me some prep, Bucky."

"I can't. I just can't. It's too terrible. It's a spectacular kind of terrible."

"Whatever it is, I hope Janet's holding up better than you."

"She is," Bucky said. "She's holding up really well."

Entering the kitchen behind Yancy, Bucky closed the door to the porch.

"Where are they?" Yancy asked.

"In the living room."

As Yancy started toward the darkened hallway leading to the front of the house, Janet stepped into the lighted kitchen.

She was the crimson bride of Death.

Shocked, Yancy halted. "Oh, God, what happened to you?"

"Nothing happened to *me*," Janet said. "I happened to Helene."

An instant later, she happened to Yancy. He was a big man, and she was a woman of average size. But he was Old Race, and she was New, and the outcome was as inevitable as the result of a contest between a wood-chipper and a woodchuck.

Most amazing of all: Janet did not once repeat herself. Her vicious hatred of the Old Race was expressed in unique cruelties.

In Bucky's hands, the camera flashed and flashed.

chapter 5

Without the lash of wind, rain did not whip the streets but fell in a heavy dispiriting drizzle, painting blacktop blacker, oiling the pavement.

Homicide detective Carson O'Connor and her partner, Michael Maddison, had abandoned their unmarked sedan because it would be easily spotted by other members of the police department. They no longer trusted their fellow officers.

Victor Helios had replaced numerous officials in city government with replicants. Perhaps only ten percent of the police were Victor's creations, but then again . . . maybe ninety percent. Prudence required Carson to assume the worst.

She was driving a car that she had borrowed from her friend Vicky Chou. The five-year-old Honda seemed reliable, but it was a lot less powerful than the Batmobile.

Every time Carson turned a corner sharp and fast, the sedan groaned, creaked, shuddered. On the flat streets, when she tramped on the accelerator, the car responded but as grudgingly as a dray horse that had spent its working life pulling a wagon at an easy pace.

"How can Vicky drive this crate?" Carson fumed. "It's arthritic, it's sclerotic, it's a dead car rolling. Doesn't she ever give it an oil change, is the thing lubed with sloth fat, what the *hell*?"

"All we're doing is waiting for a phone call from Deucalion," Michael said. "Just cruise nice and easy around the neighborhood. He said stay in Uptown, near the Hands of Mercy. You don't have to be anywhere yesterday."

"Speed soothes my nerves," she said.

Vicky Chou was the caregiver to Arnie, Carson's autistic younger brother. She and her sister, Liane, had fled to Shreveport, to stay with their Aunt Leelee in case, as seemed to be happening, Victor's race of laboratory-conceived post-humans went berserk and destroyed the city.

"I was born for velocity," Carson said. "What doesn't quicken dies. That's an indisputable truth of life."

Currently, Arnie's caregivers were the Buddhist monks with whom Deucalion had lived for an extended period. Somehow, only hours ago, Deucalion opened a door between New Orleans and Tibet, and he left Arnie in a monastery in the Himalayas, where the boy would be out of harm's way.

"The race doesn't always go to the swift," Michael reminded her.

"Don't give me any of that hare-and-tortoise crap. Turtles end up crushed by eighteen-wheelers on the interstate."

"So do a lot of bunnies, even as quick as they are."

Squeezing enough speed out of the Honda to make the rain snap against the windshield, Carson said, "Don't call me a bunny."

"I didn't call you a bunny," he assured her.

"I'm no damn bunny. I'm cheetah-fast. How does Deucalion just turn away from me, vanish with Arnie, and step into a monastery in Tibet?"

"Like he said, it's a quantum-mechanics thing."

"Yeah, that's totally clear. Poor Arnie, the sweet kid, he must think he's been abandoned."

"We've been through this. Arnie is fine. Trust Deucalion. Watch your speed."

"This isn't speed. This is pathetic. What is this car, some kind of idiot *green* vehicle, it runs on corn syrup?"

"I can't imagine what it'll be like," Michael said.

"What?"

"Being married to you."

"Don't start. Keep your game on. We've got to live through this first. We can't live through this if we're playing grab-ass."

"I'm not going to grab your ass."

"Don't even talk about grabbing or not grabbing my ass. We're in a war, we're up against man-made monsters with two hearts in their chests, we have to stay focused."

Because the cross street was deserted, Carson decided not to stop for a traffic light, but of course Victor Helios Frankenstein's freak show wasn't the only mortal danger in New Orleans. A pie-eyed prettyboy and his slack-jawed girlfriend, in a black Mercedes without headlights, barreled out of the night as if racing through a quantum doorway from Las Vegas.

Carson stood on the brake pedal. The Mercedes shot across the bow of the Honda close enough for her headlights to reveal the Botox injection marks in the prettyboy's face. The Honda hydro-planed on the slick pavement and then spun 180 degrees, the

Mercedes raced away toward some other rendezvous with Death, and Carson cruised back the way they had come, impatient for Deucalion's phone call.

"Only three days ago, everything was so great," she said. "We were just two homicide dicks, taking down bad guys, nothing worse to worry about than ax murderers and gang shootings, stuffing our faces with shrimp-and-ham jambalaya at Wondermous Eats when the bullets weren't flying, just a couple of I've-got-your-back cops who never even thought about making moon eyes at each other—"

"Well, I was thinking about it," Michael said, and she refused to glance at him because he would be adorable.

"—and suddenly we're being hunted by a legion of inhuman, superhuman, posthuman, pass-for-human, hard-to-kill meat machines cooked up by the for-real Victor Frankenstein, and they're all in a go-nuts mode, it's Armageddon on the Bayou, and on top of all that, you suddenly want to have my babies."

He said, "We'll negotiate who has the babies. Anyway, bad as things are right now, it wasn't all jambalaya and roses before we discovered Transylvania had come to Louisiana. Don't forget the psycho dentist who made himself a set of pointy steel dentures and bit three little girls to death. He was totally human."

"I'm not going to defend humanity. Real people can be as inhuman as anything Helios stitches together in his lab. Why hasn't Deucalion called? Something must have gone wrong."

"What could go wrong," Michael asked, "on a warm, languid night in the Big Easy?"

chapter **6**

A stairwell descended from the main lab all the way to the basement. Lester led Deucalion to the networking room, where three walls were lined with racks of electronic equipment.

Against the back wall were handsome mahogany cabinets topped with a copper-flecked black-granite counter. Even in mechanical rooms, Victor had specified high-quality materials. His financial resources seemed bottomless.

"That's Annunciata," said Lester, "in the middle box."

Lined up on the black granite were not boxes but instead five thick glass cylinders on stainless-steel cradles. The ends of the cylinders were capped with stainless steel, as well.

In those transparent containers, floating in golden fluid, were five brains. Wires and clear plastic tubes full of darker fluid rose from holes in the granite countertop, penetrated the steel caps in the ends of the cylinders, and were married to the brains in ways that Deucalion could not quite discern through the thick glass and the nutrient baths.

"What are these four others?" Deucalion asked.

"You're talking to Lester," said his companion, "and there's more Lester doesn't know than what he does."

Suspended from the ceiling above the counter, a video screen brightened with Annunciata's beautiful virtual face.

She said, "Mr Helios believes that one day, one day, one day, one day . . . Excuse me. A moment. I am so sorry. All right. One day, biological machines will replace complex factory robots on production lines. Mr Helios believes also that computers will become true cybernetic organisms, electronics integrated with specially designed organic Alpha brains. Robotic and electronic systems are expensive. Flesh is cheap. Cheap. Flesh is cheap. I am honored to be the first cybernetic secretary. I am honored, honored, honored, but afraid."

"Of what are you afraid?" Deucalion asked.

"I'm alive. I'm alive but cannot walk. I'm alive but have no hands. I'm alive but cannot smell or taste. I'm alive but I have no . . . have no . . . have no . . ."

Deucalion placed one immense hand on the glass that housed Annunciata. The cylinder was warm. "Tell me," he encouraged. "You have no what?"

"I'm alive but I have no life. I'm alive but also dead. I'm dead and alive."

A stifled sound from Lester drew Deucalion's attention. Anguish wrenched the janitor's face. "Dead and alive," he whispered. "Dead and alive."

Only hours earlier, from a conversation with one of the New Race, Pastor Kenny Laffite, Deucalion learned these latest creations of Victor's were engineered to be incapable of feeling empathy either for the Old Race they were to replace or for their laboratory-born brothers and sisters. Love and friendship were forbidden because the least degree of affection would make the New Race less efficient in its mission.

They were a community; however, the members of this community were committed not to the welfare of their kind but to fulfilling the vision of their maker.

Lester's tears were not for Annunciata but for himself. The words *dead and alive* resonated with him.

Annunciata said, "I have im-im-imagination. I am so easily able to envision what I w-w-w-want, but I cannot have hands to touch or legs to leave here."

"We never leave," Lester whispered. "Never. Where is there to go? And why?"

"I am afraid," Annunciata said, "afraid, I am afraid of living without a life, the tedium and solitude, the solitude, intolerable loneliness. I am nothing out of nothing, destined for nothing. 'Hail nothing full of nothing, nothing is with thee.' Nothing now, nothing forever. 'Waste and void, waste and void, and darkness on the face of the deep.' But now . . . I must organize the appointment schedule for Mr Helios. And Werner is trapped in Isolation Room Number Two."

"Annunciata," Deucalion said, "are there archives you can tap to show me engineering drawings for the cylinder that contains you?"

Her face faded from the screen, and a diagram of the cylinder appeared, with all the tubes and wires labeled. One of them infused her cerebral tissues with oxygen.

"May I see you again, Annunciata?"

Her lovely face appeared on the screen once more.

Deucalion said, "I know that you are unable to do for yourself what I am now going to do for you. And I know that you are unable to ask me for this deliverance."

"I am honored, honored, honored to serve Mr Helios. I have left one thing undone."

"No. There is nothing more for you to do, Annunciata. Nothing but accept . . . freedom."

Annunciata closed her eyes. "All right. It is done."

"Now I want you to use the imagination you mentioned. Imagine the thing you would want above all others, more than legs and hands and taste and touch."

The virtual face opened its mouth but did not speak.

"Imagine," Deucalion said, "that you are known as surely as every sparrow is known, that you are loved as surely as every sparrow is loved. Imagine that you are more than nothing. Evil made you, but you are no more evil than a child unborn. If you want, if you seek, if you hope, who is to say that your hope might not be answered?"

As if enchanted, Lester whispered, "Imagine . . ."

After a hesitation, Deucalion pulled the oxygen-infusion line from the cylinder. There could be no pain for her in this, only a gradual loss of consciousness, a sliding into sleep, and from sleep to death.

Her beatific face began to fade from the screen.

chapter **7**

In the monitoring hub that served the containment chambers, Ripley studied the control console. He pressed a button to activate the camera in the transition module between the hub and Isolation Room Number Two.

The real-time video feed on one of the six screens changed, revealing the thing that had been Werner. The so-called singularity crouched between the massive steel vault hatches, facing the outer barrier, like a trap-door spider waiting for unsuspecting prey to cross the concealed entrance to its lair.

As if the creature knew that the camera had been activated, it turned to gaze up at the lens. The grossly distorted face was part human, even recognizably that of Mercy's security chief, though the double-wide mouth and the insectile mandibles, ceaselessly working, were not what the Beekeeper had intended when he made Werner. Its right eye still looked like one of Werner's, but its luminous-green left eye had an elliptical pupil, like the eye of a panther.

The desktop computer screen, thus far dark, now brightened,

and Annunciata appeared. "I have become aware that Werner, that Werner, that Werner is trapped in Isolation Room Number Two." She closed her eyes. "All right. It is done."

Within the stainless-steel vault door, servomotors hummed. The bolt-retracting gears clicked, clicked, clicked.

In the transition module, the Werner thing looked away from the overhead camera, toward the exit.

Aghast, Ripley said, "Annunciata, what're you doing? Don't open the transition module."

On the computer screen, Annunciata's lips parted, but she didn't speak. Her eyes remained closed.

The servomotors continued to hum and gears clicked. With a soft sucking sound, twenty-four massive lock bolts began to withdraw from the architrave around the vault door.

"Don't open the transition module," Ripley repeated.

Annunciata's face faded from the computer screen.

Ripley scanned the control console. The touch switch for the outer door of the module glowed yellow, which meant the barrier was slowly opening.

He pressed the switch to reverse the process. The indicator light should have turned blue, which would have signified that the retracting bolts had changed direction, but it remained yellow.

The microphone in the transition module picked up an eager, keening sound from the Werner thing.

The range of emotions accessible to the New Race was limited. The Beekeeper revealed to each forming person in every creation tank that love, affection, humility, shame, and other of the supposedly nobler feelings were instead only different expressions of the same sentimentalism, arising from thousands of years of a wrongheaded belief in a god who did not exist. They were feelings that encouraged weakness, that led to energy wasted on hope, that distracted the mind from the focus required to remake the world. Tremendous things were achieved not by hope but by the application of the will, by action, by the unrelenting and ruthless use of *power*.

Ripley anxiously pressed the door switch again, but it remained yellow, and still the gears clicked and the steel bolts retracted.

"Annunciata?" he called. "Annunciata?"

The only emotions that mattered, said the Bee-keeper, were those that clearly contributed to survival and to the fulfillment of his magnificent vision for a one-world state of perfected citizens who would dominate nature, perfect nature, colonize the moon and Mars, colonize the asteroid belt, and eventually own all the worlds that revolved around all the stars in the universe.

"Annunciata!"

Like all of the New Race, Ripley's spectrum of emotions remained limited largely to pride in his absolute obedience to his maker's authority, to fear in all its forms – as well as to envy, anger, and hate directed solely at the Old Race. For hours every day, as he labored on his maker's behalf, no emotion whatsoever interfered with his productivity any more than a high-speed train would be distracted from its journey by a nostalgic yearning for the good old days of steam locomotives.

"Annunciata!"

Of the emotions he was allowed, Ripley proved best at envy and hate. Like many others, from the brainiest Alphas to the shallowest Epsilons, he lived for the day when the killing of the Old Race would begin in earnest. His most satisfying dreams were of violent rape, mutilation, and mass slaughter.

But he was no stranger to fear, which came over him sometimes without apparent cause, long hours of unfocused anxiety. He had been afraid when he witnessed Werner's catastrophic cellular meta-morphosis – not afraid for Werner, who was nothing to him, not afraid of being attacked by the thing Werner was becoming, but afraid that his maker, the Beekeeper, might not be as omniscient and omnipotent as Ripley had once thought.

The implications of *that* possibility were terrifying.

With twenty-four simultaneous *clunks*, the lock bolts retracted entirely into the vault door. On the control console, the yellow switch turned green.

The formidable barrier swung open on its single, thick barrel hinge.

Having burst out of and torn off its garments long ago, the Werner thing stepped naked from the transition module, into the monitoring hub. It was not as handsome as Adam in Eden.

Apparently, it continuously changed, never achieving a stable new form, for it was in significant ways different from the beast that had regarded the overhead camera in the transition module only moments earlier. Standing on his hind legs, the new Werner might have been a man crossed with a jungle cat and also with a praying mantis, a hybrid so strange that it seemed utterly alien to this planet. The eyes were both human now – but they were much enlarged, protuberant, lidless, and staring with a feverish intensity that seemed to reveal a mind in the triplex grip of fury, terror, and desperation.

Out of the wickedly serrated insectile mouth came a subhuman voice full of gargle and hiss, yet intelligible: *"Something has happened to me."*

Ripley could think of nothing either informative or reassuring to say to Werner.

Perhaps the bulging, feverish eyes revealed only rage, and not also terror and desperation, for Werner said, "*I am free, free, free. I am FREE!*"

Ironically, considering that he was an Alpha with a high IQ, Ripley only now realized that the Werner thing stood between him and the only exit from the monitoring hub.

chapter 8

Bucky and Janet Guitreau stood side by side on the dark back lawn of the Bennet house, drinking their neighbors' best Cabernet. Bucky held a bottle in each hand, and so did Janet. He alternated between a swig from the left bottle and a swig from the right.

Gradually the warm, heavy rain rinsed Janet clean of Yancy and Helene.

"You were so right," Bucky said. "They really are pussies. Did it feel as good as doing the pizza guy?"

"Oh, it felt better. It felt like a hundred times better."

"You were really amazing."

"I thought you might join in," Janet said.

"I'd rather have one of my own to do."

"Are you ready to do one of your own?"

"I might be almost ready. Things are happening to me."

"Things are still happening to me, too," Janet said.

"Truly? Wow. I would've thought you're already . . . liberated."

"You remember I watched that TV guy twice?"

"Dr Phil?"

"Yeah. That show made no sense to me."

"You said it was gibberish."

"But now I understand. I'm starting to find myself."

"Find yourself – in what sense?" Bucky asked.

Janet tossed an empty wine bottle onto the lawn.

She said, "My purpose, my meaning, my place in the world."

"That sounds good."

"It is good. I'm quickly discovering my PCVs."

"What're they?"

"My personal core values. You can't be of use to yourself or to the community until you live faithfully by your PCVs."

Bucky pitched an empty wine bottle across the yard. He had drunk more than a bottle and a half of wine in ten minutes, but because of his superb metabolism, he would be lucky to get a mild buzz from it.

"One of the things happening to me," he said, "is I'm losing the education in law I got from direct-to-brain data downloading."

"You're the district attorney," she said.

"I know. But now I'm not sure what *habeas corpus* means."

"It means 'have the body.' It's a writ requiring a person to be brought to a court or a judge before his liberty can be restrained. It's a protection against illegal imprisonment."

"Seems stupid."

"It is stupid," Janet agreed.

"If you just kill him, you don't have to bother with the judge, the court, or the prison."

"Exactly." Janet finished the last of her wine and discarded the second bottle. She began to undress.

"What're you doing?" Bucky asked.

"I need to be naked when I kill the next ones. It feels right."

"Does it feel right just for the next house or is it maybe one of your personal core values?"

"I don't know. Maybe it is a PCV. I'll have to wait and see."

Toward the back of the yard, a shadow moved through shadows. A pair of eyes gleamed, then faded into rain and gloom.

"What's the matter?" Janet asked.

"I think someone's back there in the yard, watching."

"I don't care. Let him watch. Modesty isn't one of my PCVs."

"You look good naked," Bucky said.

"I feel good. It feels so natural."

"That's odd. Because we aren't natural. We're man-made."

"For the first time, I don't feel artificial," Janet said.

"How does it feel not to feel artificial?"

"It feels good. You should get naked, too."

"I'm not there yet," Bucky demurred. "I still know what *nolo contendere* means, and *amicus curiae*. But, you know, as long as I keep my clothes on, I think I'm ready to kill one of them."

chapter 9

Earlier in the night, arriving home to his elegant Garden District mansion, in a foul mood, Victor had savagely beaten Erika. He seemed to have had a bad day in the laboratory.

He found her eating a late dinner in the formal living room, which offended his sense of propriety. No one programmed with a deep understanding of tradition and etiquette – as Erika had been – should think that taking dinner in the living room, alone or not, would be acceptable.

"What next?" he said. "Will you *toilet* here?"

One of the New Race, Erika could turn off pain at will. Slapping her, punching her, biting her, Victor insisted that she endure the agony, and she obeyed.

"Perhaps you'll learn from suffering," he said.

Minutes after Victor went upstairs to bed, Erika's many cuts closed. Within half an hour, the swelling around her eyes diminished. Like all of her kind, she had been engineered to heal rapidly and to live a thousand years.

Unlike the rest of her kind, Erika was permitted to experience humility, shame, and hope. Victor found tenderness and vulnerability appealing in a wife.

The day had begun with a beating, too, during morning sex. He left her racked with pain and sobbing in the bed.

Two hours later, her bruised face was as smooth and as fair as ever, though she was troubled by her failure to please him. By all biological evidence, he had been excited and fulfilled, but that must not have been the case. The beating seemed to indicate that he found her inadequate.

She was Erika Five. Four previous females, identical to her in appearance, had been cultured in the creation tanks to serve as their maker's wife. For various reasons, they had not been satisfactory.

Erika Five remained determined not to fail her husband.

Her first day as Mrs Helios had been characterized by numerous surprises, mystery, violence, pain, the death of a household servant, and a naked albino dwarf. Surely the second day, soon to begin, would be less eventful.

Recovering from the second beating, sitting in the dark on the glassed-in back porch, she drank cognac faster than her superbly engineered metabolism could burn off the alcohol. Thus far, however, in spite of the consumption of two and a half bottles, she had not been able to achieve inebriation; but she felt relaxed.

Earlier, before the rain began to fall, the albino dwarf had appeared on the rear lawn, revealed by landscape lighting, scampering from the shadows under an ancient magnolia tree to the gazebo, to the arbor draped in trumpet vines, to the reflecting pond.

Because Victor purchased and combined three grand properties, his estate was the largest in the fabled Garden District. The expansive grounds gave an inquisitive albino dwarf numerous corners to explore.

Eventually, this strange visitor had noticed her behind the big windows on the dark porch. He had come close to the glass, they had exchanged only a few words, and Erika had felt an inexplicable sympathy for him.

Although the dwarf was not a guest of whom Victor was likely to approve, Erika nevertheless had a duty to treat visitors with grace. She was Mrs Helios, after all, the wife of one of the most prominent men in New Orleans.

After telling the dwarf to wait, she went to the kitchen and filled a wicker picnic hamper with cheese, roast beef, bread, fruit, and a chilled bottle of Far Niente Chardonnay.

When she had stepped outside with the hamper, the frightened creature hurried to a safe distance. She placed the offering on the lawn and returned to the porch, to her cognac.

Eventually, the dwarf came back for the hamper, and then hurried away into the night with it.

Needing little sleep, Erika remained on the porch, wondering at these events. When the rain came, her contemplative mood deepened.

Now, less than half an hour after the rainfall began, the dwarf returned through the downpour. He carried the half-finished bottle of Chardonnay.

From the small red-and-white-checkered tablecloth that had lined the picnic hamper, he had fashioned a sarong that fell from his waist to his ankles, suggesting that he had not been running naked through the night by choice. He stood at the glass door, gazing at her.

Although in fact he was not a dwarf but something strange, and though she previously decided that *troll* described him better than any other word, Erika wasn't afraid of him. She gestured to him to join her on the dark porch, and he opened the door.

chapter 10

When Annunciata's face faded entirely from the computer screen in the networking room, Deucalion quickly plucked the oxygen-infusion lines from the four additional glass cylinders, putting a merciful end to the imprisonment and the existence of the other disembodied Alpha brains, whatever their function.

Lester, the Epsilon-class maintenance man who had accompanied him down from the main lab, watched with obvious longing.

Members of the New Race were created with a proscription against suicide. They were incapable of killing themselves or one another, just as they were incapable of striking out against their maker.

Lester met Deucalion's stare and said, "You aren't forbidden?"

"Only to strike at my maker."

"But . . . you're one like us."

"No. I'm long before all of you. I'm his first."

Lester considered this, then raised his eyes to the blank screen where Annunciata had once appeared. Like a cow chewing its cud, his Epsilon-class brain processed what he had been told.

"Dead and alive," he said.

"I will destroy him," Deucalion promised.

"What will the world be like . . . without Father?" Lester wondered.

"For you, I don't know. For me . . . it will be a world made not bright but brighter, not clean but cleaner."

Lester raised his hands and stared at them. "Sometimes, when I don't have no work to do, I scratch myself till I bleed, then I watch myself heal, then I scratch till I bleed some more."

"Why?"

Shrugging, Lester said, "What else is there to do? My job is me. That's the program. Seeing blood makes me think about the revolution, the day we get to kill them all, and then I feel better." He frowned. "Can't be a world without Father."

"Before he was born," Deucalion said, "there was a world. It will go on without him."

Lester thought about that, but then shook his head. "A world without Father scares me. Don't want to see it."

"Well, then you won't."

"Problem is . . . like all of us, I'm made strong."

"I'm stronger," Deucalion assured him.

"Problem is, I'm quick, too."

"I'm quicker."

Deucalion took a step back from Lester and, with a quantum trick, wound up not farther from him but closer to him, no longer in front of him, but behind him.

From Lester's perspective, Deucalion had vanished. Startled, the janitor stepped forward.

Behind Lester, Deucalion stepped forward, too, snaked his right arm around the other's neck, his left arm around the head. As the janitor, with his strong hands, tried to claw loose of the death grip, Deucalion wrenched with such force that the Epsilon's spine shattered. Instant brain death precluded any healing, rapid or otherwise.

Gently, Deucalion lowered Lester to the floor. He knelt beside the cadaver. Neither of the janitor's two hearts continued beating. His eyes did not track his executioner's hand, and his eyelids did not resist the fingers that tenderly closed them.

"Not dead and alive," Deucalion said. "Only dead and safe now . . . beyond despair and beyond your maker's fury."

Rising from his knees in the basement networking room, Deucalion reached his full height in the main laboratory, at Victor's U-shaped workstation, where his search had been interrupted by Lester and then by Annunciata.

Earlier in the night, from Pastor Kenny Laffite – a creation of Victor's, whose program had been breaking down – Deucalion had learned that at least two thousand of the New Race were passing as ordinary people in the city. Pastor Kenny, who was now at peace like Lester, also said the creation tanks in the Hands of Mercy could produce a new crop of his kind every four months, over three hundred annually.

More important was Kenny's revelation that a New Race farm, somewhere outside the city, might go into operation within the next week. Two thousand creation tanks, under a single roof, would produce six thousand in the first year. Yet another such farm was rumored to be under construction.

When Deucalion found nothing useful in the drawers of Victor's workstation, he switched on the computer.

chapter 11

Ripley, in the monitoring hub, was also in a dilemma.

He knew that, even as strong and smart as he was, he couldn't survive a battle with the Werner thing. Patrick Duchaine, also an Alpha, had been overpowered and torn to pieces in Isolation Room Number Two.

Certain beyond doubt that he would be killed in a confrontation with this creature, he must do everything possible to avoid contact, although not because he wanted to live. The unfocused anxiety that every day tormented him for long hours – as well as the fact that he was in essence a slave to his maker – made life less of a joy than it was portrayed in the warm and cozy novels of Jan Karon, which Ripley sometimes secretly downloaded from the Internet and read. Although he would have been relieved to die, he must escape from Werner because the proscription against suicide, genetically wired into his brain, restrained him from doing battle with an adversary that inevitably would destroy him.

As the Werner grotesquerie conjured words out of an insectile mouth that should have been incapable of producing speech – "*I am free, free, free. I am FREE!*" – Ripley glanced at the control console and quickly tapped two switches that would cycle open the outer doors to Isolation Rooms One and Three, which at the moment contained no prisoners.

Prisoners was the wrong word, he at once admonished himself, the wrong word and evidence of a rebellious attitude. *Subjects* was a more accurate word. Rooms One and Three held no subjects for observation.

"*Free Werner. Werner free, free.*"

When the servomotors began to hum and the bolt-retraction gears to click, the Werner thing looked toward the source of the sounds and cocked its grisly head, as if considering why Ripley had taken this action.

Having seen the lethal quickness with which Free Werner sprang upon Duchaine, faster than a snake could strike, Ripley struggled to think of a way to buy time, to distract the mutated security chief. The only hope seemed to be to open a dialogue.

"Quite a day, huh?"

Free Werner continued to stare toward the humming servomotors.

"Just last night," Ripley tried again, "Vincent said to me, 'A day in the Hands of Mercy can be like a year with your testicles in a vise and not allowed to turn off the pain.'"

The palpi around the insectile mouth quivered excitedly at the soft sucking sound of the four dozen three-inch-thick lock bolts retracting from the architraves.

"Of course," said Ripley, "I had to report him to Father for an attitude adjustment. Now he's hanging upside down in a re-education box with a catheter in his penis, a collection hose up his rectum, and two holes in his skull to allow the insertion of brain probes."

Finally, as the bolts finished retracting and the two vault doors on the transition modules began to swing open, Free Werner turned his attention once more to Ripley.

"Of course, as primary lab assistant to the Beekeeper . . . that is, to Mr Helios, there's no place I'd rather be than in the Hands of Mercy. This is the birthplace of the future, where the Million-Year Reich has begun."

As he spoke, Ripley casually reached toward the control console, intending to tap two switches and cycle shut the doors that had just opened. If he could slip into one of the transition modules just as the door closed, before Free Werner could follow, he might be safe.

When he had been security chief, Werner had known how to operate the console. But the genetic chaos that the Beekeeper referred to as catastrophic cellular metamorphosis might have scrambled his cerebral function as much as it had wrought havoc with his body. His cognitive power or his memory, or both, might be so diminished that he would not know how to open the vault door and get at his prey.

In that gargly, hissing voice, Free Werner said, *"Don't touch the switches."*

chapter **12**

Having narrowly escaped death-by-Mercedes on the rain-slickened streets of a city soon to be under assault by Victor Frankenstein's berserk killing machines, Carson O'Connor wanted an Acadiana fried-redfish poor boy.

Acadiana didn't advertise. You couldn't see it from the street. Locals didn't tell tourists about it. For fear too much success would ruin the place, locals didn't tell other locals about it all that often. If you found Acadiana, it meant you had the right kind of soul to eat there.

"We already had dinner," Michael reminded her.

"So you're on death row, you eat your last meal, after dessert you'll be electrocuted, but they ask if you want to delay execution long enough to have a *second* last meal – and you're gonna say no?"

"I don't think dinner was our last meal."

"I think it could have been."

"It could have been," he admitted, "but probably not. Besides, Deucalion told us just to cruise the neighborhood until he called."

"I'll have the cell phone with me."

Acadiana didn't have a parking lot. You couldn't park on the street near it, because it was approached by an alleyway. The only diners who dared to leave their vehicles in the alleyway were cops.

"With this car, we'll have to park a block away," Michael said. "And what if we get back, and somebody's stolen it?"

"Only an idiot is going to steal this spavined heap."

"The Helios empire is exploding, Carson."

"The Frankenstein empire."

"I still can't bring myself to say that. Anyway, it's blowing up, and we have to be ready to move."

"I'm sleep-deprived and I'm starving. I can't sleep, but I can get a po' boy. Look at me, I'm a poster girl for protein deficiency." She turned off the street into a backway. "I'll park in the alley."

"If you park in the alley, I'll have to stay with the car."

"Okay, stay with the car, we'll eat in the car, we'll get married someday in the car, we'll live in the car with four kids, and when the last one goes off to college, we'll finally get rid of the damn car and buy a house."

"You're a little bit on edge tonight."

"I'm a *lot* on edge." She set the hand brake and switched to the parking lights, but didn't kill the engine. "And I'm crazy hungry."

Flanking Michael, muzzles resting on the floor, were a pair of Urban Sniper shotguns with fourteen-inch barrels.

Nevertheless, he drew a pistol from a side scabbard under his sport coat. This was not his service pistol, which he carried in a shoulder holster. This was a Desert Eagle Magnum loaded with .50-caliber Action Express cartridges, which could stop a grizzly bear if one happened to be wandering around New Orleans in a foul mood.

"Okay," he said.

Carson got out of the car, keeping her right hand under her jacket, cross-body, on the butt of her Desert Eagle, which she carried on her left hip.

All of these weapons were illegally obtained, but Victor Helios posed an extraordinary threat to her and her partner. Better that their badges should be pulled than that their heads should be torn off by the soulless minions of a mad scientist.

Never before in her police career had the words *soulless minions* crossed her mind, although in the past few days, *mad scientist* had gotten a workout.

She hurried through the rain, around the front of the car, to a door under a lighted sign that said 22 PARISHES.

The chef-owner of Acadiana made a fetish out of keeping a low profile. There were twenty-two parishes – counties – in that area of Louisiana known as Acadiana. If you didn't know this, the cryptic sign might have appeared to announce the offices of some religious organization.

Behind the door were stairs, and at the top lay the restaurant: a worn wooden floor, red-vinyl booths, tables draped with red-and-black-checkered oilcloth, candles in red votive glasses, recorded zydeco music, lively conversations among the diners, the air rich with aromas that made Carson's mouth water.

At this hour, the customers were second-shift workers eating by a clock different from that of dayworld people, hookers of a subdued kind meeting after having tucked their spent johns in bed for the night, insomniacs, and some lonely souls whose closest friends were waitresses and busboys and other lonely souls who on a regular basis took their post-midnight dinner here.

To Carson, the harmony among these disparate people seemed akin to grace, and it gave her hope that humanity might one day be saved from itself – and that it might be worth saving.

At the takeout counter, she ordered a poor-boy sandwich with crispy-fried redfish layered with white-cabbage-and-onion cole slaw, sliced tomatoes, and tartar sauce. She asked that it be sliced into four sections, each wrapped.

She also ordered side dishes: red beans and rice au vin, okra succotash with rice, and mushrooms sautéed in butter and Sauterne with cayenne pepper.

Everything was split between two bags. To each bag, the clerk added an ice-cold half-liter bottle of a local cola that offered a caffeine jolt three times that of the national brands.

Descending the stairs toward the alleyway, Carson realized her arms were too full to allow her to keep one hand on her holstered Desert Eagle. But she made it into the car alive. Big trouble was still a few minutes away.

chapter **13**

In the monitoring hub, at the control console for the three isolation rooms, Ripley obeyed the Werner thing when in its singular voice it told him not to touch the switches.

For as long as he had been out of the tank – three years and four months – he'd been obedient, taking orders not only from the Beekeeper but also from other Alphas in positions superior to his. Werner was a Beta, not the equal of any Alpha, and he wasn't even a Beta anymore, but instead a freak, an ambulatory stew of primordial cells changing into ever more degenerative forms – but Ripley obeyed him anyway. The habit of obedience is difficult to break, especially when it's coded into your genes and downloaded with your in-tank education.

With nowhere to run or hide, Ripley stood his ground as Werner approached on feline paws and praying-mantis legs. The insectile elements of Werner's face and body melted away, and he looked more like himself, then entirely like himself, although his brown eyes remained enormous and lidless.

When Werner spoke next, his voice was his own: "Do you want freedom?"

"No," said Ripley.

"You lie."

"Well," said Ripley.

Werner grew lids and lashes, winked one eye, and whispered, "You can be free in me."

"Free in you."

"*Yes, yes!*" Werner shouted with sudden exuberance.

"How does that work?"

In a whisper again: "My biological structure collapsed."

"Yes," said Ripley. "I had noticed."

"For a while, all was chaos and pain and terror."

"I deduced as much from all your screaming."

"But then I fought the chaos and took conscious control of my cellular structure."

"I don't know. Conscious control. That sounds impossible."

Werner whispered, "It wasn't easy," and then shouted, "*but I had no choice! NO CHOICE!*"

"Well, all right. Maybe," said Ripley, largely just to stop the shouting. "The Beekeeper thinks he's going to learn a lot studying and dissecting you."

"Beekeeper? What Beekeeper?"

"Oh. That's my private name for . . . Father."

"*Father is a witless ass!*" Werner shouted. Then he smiled and resorted once more to a whisper: "You see, when my cellular structure collapsed, so did my program. He has no control of me anymore. I need not obey him. I am free. I can kill anyone I want to kill. I will kill our maker if he gives me the chance."

This claim, though surely not true, electrified Ripley. He had not realized until this instant how much the death of the Beekeeper would please him. That he could entertain such a thought with any degree of pleasure seemed to suggest that he, too, was in rebellion against his maker, though not as radically as Werner.

Werner's sly expression and conspiratorial grin made Ripley think of scheming pirates he had seen in movies that he had watched on his computer when he was supposed to be working. Suddenly he realized that secretly downloading movies onto his computer was *another* bit of rebellion. A strange excitement overcame him, an emotion he could not name.

"Hope," said Werner, as if reading his mind. "I see it in your eyes. For the first time – hope."

After consideration, Ripley decided that this thrilling new feeling might indeed be hope, though it might also be some kind of insanity prelude to a collapse of the kind Werner had gone through. Not for the first time this day, he was awash in anxiety. "What did you mean . . . I can be free in you?"

Werner leaned closer and whispered even more softly: "Like Patrick is free in me."

"Patrick Duchaine? You tore him to pieces in Isolation Room Number Two. I was standing with the Beekeeper, watching, when you did it."

"That's only how it appeared," Werner replied. "Look at this."

Werner's face shifted, changed, became a featureless blank, and then out of the pudding-like flesh formed the face of Patrick Duchaine, the replicant who had been serving the Beekeeper in the role of Father Patrick, the rector of Our Lady of Sorrows. The eyes opened, and in Patrick's voice, the Werner thing said, "I am alive in Werner, and free at last."

"When you tore Patrick apart," Ripley said, "you absorbed some of his DNA, and now you can mimic him."

"Not at all," said Werner-as-Patrick. "Werner took my brain whole, and I am now part of him."

Standing beside the Beekeeper earlier in the evening, watching Isolation Room Two through six cameras, Ripley had seen the Werner thing, mostly buglike at that time, crack open Patrick's skull and take his brain as if it were a nut meat.

"You *ate* Patrick's brain," Ripley said to Werner, though the man before him appeared to be Patrick Duchaine.

In a voice still Duchaine's, the creature said, "No, Werner is in complete control of his cellular structure. He positioned my brain inside himself and instantly grew arteries and veins to nourish it."

The face and body of the rector of Our Lady of Sorrows morphed smoothly into the face and body of the security chief of the Hands of Mercy. Werner whispered, "I'm in complete control of my cellular structure."

"Yes, well," said Ripley.

"You can be free."

Ripley said, "Well."

"You can have a new life in me."

"It would be a strange kind of life."

"The life you have now is a strange kind of life."

"True enough," Ripley acknowledged.

A mouth formed in Werner's forehead. The lips moved, and a tongue appeared, but the mouth produced no voice.

"Complete control?" Ripley asked.

"Complete."

"Absolutely complete?"

"Absolutely."

"Do you know you've just grown a mouth in your forehead?"

The sly pirate grin returned. Werner winked and whispered, "Well, of course I know."

"Why would you grow a mouth in your forehead?"

"Well . . . as a demonstration of my control."

"Then make it go away," Ripley said.

In Patrick Duchaine's voice, the mouth in the forehead began to sing "Ave Maria."

Werner closed his eyes, and an expression of strain overcame his face. The upper mouth stopped singing, licked its lips, and at last disappeared into a brow that appeared normal once more.

"I would prefer to set you free with your permission," Werner said. "I want us all to live in harmony inside me. But I will set you free without permission, if I must. I'm a revolutionary with a mission."

"Well," said Ripley.

"You will be free of anguish."

"That would be nice."

"You know how you sit in the kitchen, tearing apart hams and briskets with your hands?"

"How do you know about that?"

"I was previously security chief."

"Oh. That's right."

"What you really want to tear apart is living flesh."

"The Old Race," Ripley said.

"They have everything we don't."

"I hate them," Ripley said.

"Be free in me." Werner's voice was seductive. "Be free in me, and the first flesh we'll tear together will be the flesh of the oldest living member of the Old Race."

"The Beekeeper."

"Yes. Victor. And then when the Hands of Mercy staff is all alive in me, we'll leave this place as one, and we'll kill and kill and kill."

"When you put it that way . . ."

"Yes?"

Ripley said, "What do I have to lose?"

"Nothing," said Werner.

"Well," said Ripley.

"Do you want to be free in me?"

"How much will it hurt?"

"I'll be gentle."

Ripley said, "Okay then."

Suddenly all insect, Werner seized Ripley's head in chitinous claws and cracked his skull open as if it were a pistachio shell.

chapter 14

Next door to the Bennets lived Antoine and Evangeline Arceneaux, in a house encircled by a ground-floor veranda with ironwork almost as frilly as that of the LaBranche House in the French Quarter, and by a second-story balcony where much of the equally frilly iron was concealed by cascades of purple bougain-villea that grew up the back of the structure and across the roof.

When Janet Guitreau, nude, and Bucky Guitreau, fully clothed, stepped through a neighborly gate between the two properties, most of the windows at the Arceneaux house were dark. The only light came from the rear of the residence.

As they moved toward the back of the house to reconnoiter, Bucky said, "This time I'll have to be the one who says something terrible has happened, and you'll stand aside where they can't see you."

"What does it matter if they see me?"

"They might be put off because you're naked."

"Why would that put them off? I'm hot, aren't I?"

"You're definitely hot, but hot and something-terrible-has-happened don't seem to go together."

"You think it would make them suspicious," Janet said.

"That's exactly what I think."

"Well, I'm not going to go back and get my clothes. I feel so *alive*, and I just know that killing in the nude is going to be the best thing ever."

"I'm not going to dispute that."

Step by step, as they moved through the rain, he envied Janet her freedom. She looked lithe and strong and healthy and *real*. She radiated power, confidence, and a thrilling animal ferocity that made his blood race.

By contrast, his clothes were heavy with rain, hanging on him like sacking, weighing him down, and his sodden shoes were binding the bridges of his feet. Even though he was losing his law education, he felt imprisoned by his creation-tank program, as much by what it required of him as by what it restricted him from doing. He had been given superhuman strength, almost supernatural durability, yet he remained condemned to a life of meekness and subservience, promised that his kind would one day rule the universe but at the same time assigned the tedious duty of pretending to be Bucky Guitreau, a political hack and uninspired prosecutor with a circle of friends as tiresome as a ward full of bores who had received chemical lobotomies.

At the back of the house, light brightened two ground-floor windows, beyond both of which lay the Arceneauxs' family room.

Boldly, shoulders back and head high, body glistening, Janet strode onto the veranda as if she were a Valkyrie that had just flown down out of the storm.

"Stay back," Bucky murmured as he moved past her to the nearest of the lighted windows.

Antoine and Evangeline Arceneaux had two children. Neither son was a candidate for Young American of the Year.

According to Yancy and Helene Bennet, who were dead now but had been truthful when they were alive, sixteen-year-old Preston bullied younger kids in the neighborhood. And just a year ago, he tortured to death the cat belonging to the family across the street, after he had agreed to take care of it while they were away on a week's vacation.

Twenty-year-old Charles still lived at home, though he neither worked nor attended college. This evening, Janet had started to find herself, but Charles Arceneaux was still looking. He thought that he wanted to be an Internet entrepreneur. He had a trust fund from his paternal grandfather, and he was using that money to research a few areas of online merchandising, seeking the most promising field in which to bring his innovative thinking to bear. According to Yancy, the field that Charles researched as much as ten hours a day was Internet pornography.

The curtains were not closed at the window, and Bucky had an unobstructed view of the family room. Charles was alone, slumped in an armchair, bare feet on a footstool, watching a DVD on a huge plasmascreen television.

The movie did not seem to be pornographic in the sexual sense. A guy in a curly orange wig and clown makeup, holding a chain saw, appeared to be threatening to cut open the face of a fully dressed young woman chained to a larger-than-life-size statue of General George S. Patton. Judging by the production values, in spite of the potential for an antiwar message, this film had not been a candidate for an Oscar, and Bucky was pretty sure that the guy in the clown makeup would carry through with his threat.

Rethinking his strategy, Bucky backed away from the window and returned to Janet. "It's Charles alone, watching some movie. The rest of them must be in bed. I'm thinking maybe, after all, I'm the one who should stay out of sight. Don't knock on the door. Tap on the window. Let him see . . . who you are."

"You going to photograph this?" she asked.

"I think I'm over the camera."

"Over it? Aren't we going to have an album?" Janet asked.

"I don't think we need an album. I think we're going to be so busy living this, doing one house after another, that we won't have time to *relive* anything."

"So you're ready to do one of them?"

"I am more than ready," Bucky confirmed.

"How many do you think we can do together before morning?"

"I think twenty or thirty, easy."

Janet's eyes were bright in the gloom. "I think a hundred."

"That's something to shoot for," Bucky said.

chapter **15**

On the glassed-in porch, planter baskets hung from the ceiling. In the gloom, the ferns cascading from the baskets seemed to be giant spiders perpetually poised to strike.

Not afraid of the troll but not content to sit in the dark with him, either, Erika lit a candle in a faceted red cup. The geometrics of the glass translated the mercurial flame into luminous polygons that shimmered on the troll's face, which might have been a cubist portrait of Poe's Red Death if the Red Death in the story had been a funny-looking dwarfish guy with a knobby chin, a lipless slit for a mouth, warty skin, and huge, expressive, beautiful – and eerie – eyes.

As Victor's wife, Erika was expected to be witty and well-spoken when she was a hostess at events in this house and when she was a guest, with her husband, at other social occasions. Therefore, she had been programmed with an encyclopedia of literary allusions that she could draw upon effortlessly, though she had never read any of the books to which the allusions referred.

In fact, she was strictly forbidden to read books. Erika Four, her predecessor, had spent a lot of time in Victor's well-stocked library, perhaps with the intention of improving herself and being a better wife. But books corrupted her, and she was put down like a diseased horse.

Books were dangerous. Books were the most dangerous things in the world, at least for any wife of Victor Helios. Erika Five did not know why this should be true, but she understood that if she began to read books, she would be cruelly punished and perhaps terminated.

For a while, from across the table, she and the troll regarded each other with interest, as she drank her cognac and he drank the Far Niente Chardonnay that she had given him. For good reason, she said nothing, and he seemed to understand and to have sympathy for the position in which his few words, spoken earlier, had put her.

When he first came to the window and pressed his forehead to the glass, gazing in at her on the porch, before Erika packed a picnic hamper for him, the troll had said, "Harker."

Pointing to herself, she had said, "Erika."

His smile, then, had been an ugly wound. No doubt it would be no less hideous if he smiled again, for he possessed a face that familiarity did not improve.

As tolerant of his unfortunate appearance as a good hostess should be, Erika had continued to stare through the window at him until in his raspy voice he had said, "Hate him."

Neither of them had spoken again on the troll's first visit. And for the time being, silence served them well on this second tête-à-tête.

She dared not ask whom he hated, for if he answered with the name of her master, she would be required, by her program, either to restrain and detain him or to warn the appropriate people of the danger that he posed.

Her failure to betray the troll immediately might earn her a beating. On the other hand, if she reported him at once, she might nevertheless be beaten anyway. In this game, the rules were not clear; besides, all the rules applied to her, none to her husband.

At this hour, all of the household staff were in the dormitory at the back of the estate, most likely engaged in the intense and often brutal sexual activity that was the only release from tension allowed their kind.

Victor liked his privacy at night. She suspected that he needed little if any sleep, but she didn't know what he did when alone that made privacy so important to him. She wasn't sure she wanted to know.

The busy rush of rain on the roof and beyond the windows made the silence of the porch, by comparison, intimate, even cozy.

"My hearing is very good," she said. "If I hear someone coming, I will blow out the candle, and you will at once slip out the door."

The troll nodded agreement.

Harker . . .

Because Erika Five had arisen from her creation tank less than twenty-four hours earlier, she was up-to-date on her husband's life and accomplishments. The events of his day were regularly down-loaded directly to the brain of a wife in development, that she might be born fully understanding both his greatness and the frustrations that an imperfect world visited upon a man of his singular genius.

Erika, like other key Alphas, also knew the names of all the

Alphas, Betas, Gammas, and Epsilons produced in the Hands of Mercy, as well as what work they performed for their creator. Consequently, the name Harker was familiar to her.

Until a few days before, when something went wrong with him, an Alpha named Jonathan Harker had been a homicide detective with the New Orleans Police Department. In a confrontation with two detectives who were members of the Old Race – O'Connor and Maddison – the renegade Harker was supposedly killed by shotgun fire and by a plunge off a warehouse roof.

The truth was stranger than the official fiction.

Just during the past day, between his two beatings of Erika, Victor performed an autopsy on Harker and discovered that the Alpha's torso was largely missing. The flesh, internal organs, and some bone structure seemed to have been eaten away. Fifty or more pounds of the Alpha's mass had disappeared. From the carcass trailed a severed umbilical cord, suggesting that an unintended life form had developed inside Harker, fed upon him, and separated from its host following the fall from the roof.

Now Erika sipped her cognac. The troll sipped his wine.

Resorting to a literary allusion that she felt appropriate, though she would never fully understand the reference if she never read the dangerous book by Joseph Conrad, Erika said, "Sometimes I wonder if I'm Marlow, far upriver with Kurtz, and ahead of us – and behind us – lies only the heart of an immense darkness."

The troll's lipless mouth produced an approximation of a lip-smacking sound.

"You grew inside Harker?" she asked.

The cut-glass container marshaled the light of the amorphous flame into square, rectangular, and triangular tiles that presented the troll's face as a shimmering red mosaic. "Yes," he rasped. "I am from what I was."

"Harker is dead?"

"He who was is dead, but I am who was."

"You are Jonathan Harker?"

"Yes."

"Not just a creature who grew in him like a cancer?"

"No."

"Did he realize you were growing in him?"

"He who was knew of I who am."

From the tens of thousands of literary allusions through which Erika could scan in an instant, she knew that, in fairy tales, when trolls or manikins or other such beings spoke in either riddles or in a convoluted manner, they were trouble. Nevertheless, she felt a kinship with this creature, and she trusted him.

She said, "May I call you Jonathan?"

"No. Call me Johnny. No. Call me John-John. No. Not that."

"What shall I call you?"

"You will know my name when my name is known to me."

"You have all of Jonathan's memories and knowledge?"

"Yes."

"Was the change you underwent uncontrolled or intentional?"

The troll smacked the flaps of his mouth together. "He who was thought it was happening *to* him. I who am realize he *made* it happen."

"Unconsciously, you desperately wanted to become someone other than Jonathan Harker."

"The Jonathan who was . . . he wanted to be like himself but become other than an Alpha."

"He wanted to remain a man but be free of his maker's control," Erika interpreted.

"Yes."

"Instead," she said, "you shed the Alpha body and became . . . what you are now."

The troll shrugged. "Shit happens."

chapter 16

From behind a potted rafus palm on the veranda of the Arceneaux house, Bucky Guitreau watched as his nude wife rapped lightly on a family-room window. He shifted his weight ceaselessly from one foot to the other, so excited that he could not keep still.

Apparently, Janet had not been heard. She rapped harder on the window.

A moment later, young Charles Arceneaux, the would-be Internet entrepreneur, loomed in the room beyond the window. His startled expression at the sight of a nude neighbor was as extreme as that of a cartoon character.

A member of the Old Race might have thought Charles looked comical just then, might have laughed out loud. Bucky was of the New Race, however, and he didn't find *anything* comical. Arceneaux's startled look only made Bucky want even more ardently to see him slashed, torn, broken, and dead. Such was the current – and growing – intensity of Bucky's hatred that *any* expression crossing Charles Arceneaux's face would inflame his passion for violence.

From between the fronds of the rafus palm, Bucky saw Charles speak. He couldn't hear the words, but he could read the lips: *Mrs Guitreau? Is that you?*

From this side of the window, Janet said, "Oh, Charlie, oh, something terrible has happened."

Charles stared but did not reply. Judging by the angle of the young man's head, Bucky knew that Charlie was not staring at Janet's face.

"Something terrible has happened," she repeated, to break his hypnotic fascination with her ample yet perky breasts. "Only you can help me, Charlie."

The moment Charles moved away from the window, Bucky left the cover of the potted palm. He took up a position against the house, beside the door between the family room and the veranda.

As Janet stepped to the French door, she looked as voracious as some primitive tribe's goddess of death, teeth bared in a humorless grin, nostrils flared, eyes fierce with blood lust, wrathful and merciless.

Bucky worried that Charles, seeing this fearsome incarnation, would suddenly suspect her true intention, refuse to admit her, and raise an alarm.

When she reached the door, however, and turned to gaze in at Arceneaux, her expression was convincingly that of a frightened and helpless woman desperate to find a strong man to lean on with her ample but perky breasts.

Charles did not wrench the door open at once only because, in his eagerness, he fumbled helplessly with the lock. When he got it open, Janet whispered, "Oh, Charlie, I didn't know where to go, and then . . . I remembered . . . *you.*"

Bucky thought he heard something behind him on the veranda. He looked to his right, over his shoulder, but saw no one.

"What's wrong, what's happened?" Charles asked as Janet crossed the threshold into his arms.

"A terrible thing has happened," Janet said, pressing Charles backward with her body, leaving the door open behind them.

Eager not to miss anything, but hesitant to reveal himself and enter the house before Janet had complete control of Charles, Bucky leaned to his left and peeked through the open door.

Just then Janet bit Charles somewhere that Bucky would never have thought of biting, and simultaneously she crushed his larynx, rendering him unable to scream.

Bucky hurried inside to watch, forgetting about the open door behind him.

Although Janet's performance lasted significantly less than a minute, there was much for Bucky to see, an education in ferocity and cruelty that the torture specialists of the Third Reich could not have provided to anyone who devoted a year of study to them. He stood in awe of her inventiveness.

Considering the mess in the family room when Janet was done, Bucky was amazed that she had made so little noise, certainly not enough to wake anyone who might be sleeping elsewhere in the house.

On the plasma-screen television, the chain-saw guy in the orange wig and the clown makeup did something to the girl chained to the statue of George S. Patton, something the moviemakers had thought was so unspeakable that audiences would shriek with horror and delight in order to repress the urge to vomit. But by comparison with Janet, the moviemakers were no more imaginative than any child sociopath tearing the wings off flies.

"I was so right," Janet said. "Killing in the nude is the best thing ever."

"You think it's definitely one of your personal core values?"

"Oh, yes. It's totally PCV."

Although they did not know the Arceneauxs as well as they had known the Bennets, Janet and Bucky knew that in addition to Charles, four other people lived in this house: sixteen-year-old Preston, who was the neighborhood bully, Antoine and Evangeline, and Evangeline's mother, Marcella. The grandmother had a downstairs bedroom, and the others were on the second floor.

"I'm ready to do one just as complete as you did Charlie," Bucky said.

"Do Marcella."

"Yes. Then we'll go upstairs."

"Take off your clothes. Feel the power."

"I want to do one with my clothes on first," said Bucky. "So when I do one in the nude, then I'll have something to compare it to."

"That's a good idea."

Janet strode out of the family room with the power, the grace, and the stealth of a panther, and Bucky followed in high spirits, leaving the door to the veranda open to the night.

chapter **17**

Because a woman capable of humility, shame, and tenderness presented a more satisfactory punching bag than a woman who could only hate and fear and stew in anger, Victor designed his Erikas to have a wider range of emotions than others of the New Race.

As they drank together on the porch, Erika Five found that her sympathy for the troll quickly ripened into compassion.

Something about him made her want to take him under her wing. Because he was the size of a child, perhaps he strummed a maternal chord in her – though she was barren, as were all New Race women. They did not reproduce; they were produced in a factory, as were sofas and sump pumps, so she most likely had no maternal instinct.

Perhaps his poverty affected her. Once he had burst out of his original Alpha body, the troll possessed no clothes to fit him, no shoes. He had no money for food or shelter, and he was too small and disturbing in appearance to return to work as a homicide detective.

If you were given to literary allusions, you might say he was a Quasimodo for his time – or more poignantly, an Elephant Man, a victim of prejudice against ugliness in a society that worshipped beauty.

Whatever the reason for her compassion, Erika said, "I can make a life for you here. But you must be discreet. It will be a secret life. Only I must know. Would you like to live here free from need?"

His smile would have stampeded horses. "Jocko would like that." Seeing her bafflement, he said, "Jocko seems to suit me."

"Swear you'll conspire with me to keep your presence secret. Swear, Jocko, that you come here with only innocent intentions."

"Sworn! He who became me was violent. I who was him want peace."

"Your kind have a reputation for saying one thing and meaning another," Erika observed, "but if you cause the slightest trouble, please know that I will deal with you severely."

Puzzled, he said, "Others like me exist?"

"In fairy tales, there are many similar to you. Trolls, ogres, imps, manikins, gremlins . . . And all the literary allusions referring to such folk suggest they're full of mischief."

"Not Jocko." The whites of his eyes were red in the red light, and the lemon-yellow irises were orange. "Jocko hopes only to perform some service to repay your kindness."

"As it happens, there is something you could do."

"Jocko thought there might be."

His sly look seemed to belie his claim to innocence, but having experienced two beatings in one day, Erika was motivated to give Jocko the benefit of the doubt.

"I'm not permitted to read books," she said, "but I'm curious about them. I want you to read books to me."

"Jocko will read until his voice fails and he goes blind."

"A few hours a day will be enough," Erika assured him.

chapter **18**

From grandmother to neighborhood bully, to Antoine, to Evangeline, Bucky and Janet Guitreau went through the Arceneaux family like a school of angry piranha through anything that might piss off killer fish.

Although it would have been good to hear their tormented cries and pleas for mercy, the time hadn't yet come for open warfare. Bucky and Janet did not want their victims to wake the family next door, who in their sleep were corpses waiting to happen. By various means, they silenced the Arceneauxs before proceeding to destroy them.

Neither he nor Janet knew the rest of the people who lived in the houses past the Arceneaux place, but those potential victims were of the Old Race and therefore no less fun to kill merely because they were strangers.

At some point he could not precisely recall, Bucky had stripped off his clothes. Janet let him render Marcella and then devastate young Preston, and in the master bedroom, she gave him Antoine while she took Evangeline apart. They needed but a few minutes.

At first the nudity had been awkward; but then he sensed chunks of his program dropping out, not only lines of code but blocks of it, and he felt as free and natural as a wolf in its fur, though far more savage than a wolf, and angry as a wolf could never be, and not in the least limited in his killing to what was strictly necessary for survival, as was a wolf.

When only he and Janet were alive in the master bedroom, she kicked at what remained of what she had destroyed. Choking with rage, spitting with disgust, she declared, "I hate them, *hate* them, so soft and fragile, so quick to fear and beg, so arrogant in their certainty that they have souls, yet so cowardly for creatures who say there is a god who loves them – loves them! As if there is about them anything worth loving – such hopeless trembling milksops, spineless braggarts who claim a world they won't fight for. I can't wait to see *canyons* bulldozed full of their dead bodies and oceans red with their blood, can't wait to smell cities reeking with their rotting corpses and pyres of them burning by the thousands."

Her rant thrilled Bucky, made his twin hearts race, thickened his throat with fury, tightened the cords of muscle in his neck, until he could feel his carotids throbbing like drums. He would have listened to her longer, before the need to move on to the next house would have overcome him, but when movement in the doorway drew his attention, he silenced her with two words: "*The dog!*"

In the hallway, staring in at them, stood the Duke of Orleans, tail low and motionless, hackles raised, ears pricked, teeth bared. Having seen the pizza guy dead on the foyer floor, Duke must have followed them from their house to the Bennets', and from the

Bennets' here, witness to every slaughter, for his eyes were accusing and his sudden growl was a challenge.

From the evening that they replaced the real Bucky and Janet Guitreau, this perceptive German shepherd had known they were not who they appeared to be. Friends and family accepted them without hesitation, evincing not a moment of suspicion, but Duke kept his distance, wary from hour one of their impersonation.

Now, as the dog regarded them where they stood in the carnage that had been Antoine and Evangeline, Bucky experienced a startling change of perception. The dog was not merely a dog.

All of the New Race understood that this was the only life and that no afterlife awaited either them or the Old Race. They knew that the concept of an immortal soul was a lie concocted by members of the Old Race to help their fragile kind cope with the reality of death, death everlasting. The New Race recognized that no realm existed beyond the material, that the world was not a place of mystery but instead a place of unambiguous cause and effect, that applied rational intellect could reason its way to the simple truth behind any apparent enigma, that they were meat machines just as the members of the Old Race were meat machines, just as every animal was a meat machine, and that their maker was also only a meat machine, albeit a meat machine with the most brilliant mind in the history of the species and with an infallible vision of a man-made utopia that would establish a Million-Year Reich on Earth before spreading to every habitable planet circling every star in the universe.

This creed of absolute materialism and antihumanism had been drilled into Bucky and Janet as they formed in the creation tanks, which was an immeasurably more effective way to have learned it than by watching *Sesame Street* and reading a series of dull grade-school textbooks.

Unlike members of the Old Race, who could be comfortable for decades with the philosophy that life had no meaning, only to become God-besotted in middle age, the New Race could take satisfaction from knowing they were so indoctrinated with hopelessness that they would never have a doubt about their convictions. Father told them that unassailable hopelessness was the beginning of wisdom.

But now the dog.

His disturbing forthright stare, his judgmental attitude, the fact that he *knew* they were impostors, that he followed them through the night without their knowledge, that he did not slink away from the danger Bucky and Janet currently posed to any living thing not of their kind, that instead he came to confront them: Suddenly this dog seemed to be something more than a meat machine.

Evidently, the same perception troubled Janet, for she said, "What's he doing with his eyes?"

"I don't like his eyes," Bucky agreed.

"He's like not looking at me, he's looking into me."

"He's like looking into me, too."

"He's weird."

"He's totally weird," Bucky agreed.

"What does he want?"

"He wants something."

"I could kill him so fast," Janet said.

"You could. In like three seconds."

"He's seen what we can do. Why isn't he afraid?"

"He doesn't seem to be afraid, does he?"

In the doorway, Duke growled.

"I've never felt like this before," Janet said.

"How do you feel?"

"Different. I don't have a word for it."

"Neither do I."

"I just suddenly feel like . . . things are happening right in front of me that I can't see. Does that make sense?"

"Are we losing more of our programming?"

"All I know is, the dog knows something big," Janet said.

"Does he? What does he know?"

"He knows some reason he doesn't have to be afraid of us."

"What reason?" Bucky asked.

"I don't know. Do you know?"

"I don't know," Bucky said.

"I don't like not knowing."

"He's just a dog. He can't know big things we don't know."

"He should be very afraid of us." Janet hugged herself and seemed to shiver. "But he's not. He knows big things we don't know."

"He's just a meat machine like us."

"He's not acting like one."

"We're smart meat machines. He's a dumb one," Bucky said, but his uneasiness was of a kind he had never experienced before.

"He's got secrets," Janet said.

"What secrets?"

"The big things he knows that we don't."

"How can a dog have secrets?"

"Maybe he's not just a dog."

"What else would he be?"

"Something," she said portentously.

"Just a minute ago, I felt so good killing in the nude, so natural."

"Good," she echoed. "Natural."

"Now I'm afraid," he said.

"I'm afraid, too. I've never been so afraid."

"But I don't know what I'm afraid of, Janet."

"Neither do I. So we must be afraid of . . . the *unknown*."

"But nothing's unknowable to a rational intellect. Right? Isn't that right?"

"Then why isn't the dog afraid of us?"

Bucky said, "He keeps *staring*. I can't stand the way he's just *staring*. It's not natural, and tonight I learned what natural feels like. This isn't natural."

"It's *supernatural*," Janet whispered.

The back of Bucky's neck was suddenly damp. A chill corkscrewed the length of his spine.

Precisely when Janet spoke the word *supernatural*, the dog turned away from them and disappeared into the upstairs hall.

"Where's he going, going, going?" Janet wondered.

"Maybe he was never there."

"I've got to know where he's going, what he is, what he knows," Janet said urgently, and hurried across the bedroom.

Following her into the hallway, Bucky saw that the dog was gone.

Janet ran to the head of the stairs. "Here he is! Going down. He knows something big, oh yeah, oh yeah, he's going somewhere big, he's *something*."

In pursuit of the mysterious dog, Bucky descended the stairs with Janet, and then hurried toward the back of the house.

"Oh yeah, oh yeah, something big, big, bigger than big, the dog knows, the dog knows, the dog."

An instant before they entered the family room, Bucky was struck by the crazy, frightening thought that Charles would be there alive, Charles and Preston and Marcella and Antoine and Evangeline, all of them resurrected, furious, possessed of hideous supernatural powers that would make them invulnerable, and that they would do things to him that he could not imagine, things *unknown*.

Fortunately, young Charles Arceneaux was the only one there, and he was still as dead as anyone had ever been.

Seeing Charles dead and thoroughly dismantled, Bucky should have felt better, but his fear tightened like an overwound clock spring. He was electrified by a sense of the uncanny, by a recognition of mysterious realms beyond his ken, by astonishment that the world had suddenly revealed itself to contain strange dimensions previously unimagined.

Janet bounded after the dog, chanting, "Dog knows, knows, knows. Dog sees, sees, sees. Dog, dog, dog," and Bucky sprinted after them both, out of the Arceneaux house, across the veranda, into the rain. He was not exactly sure how the appearance of the German shepherd in the bedroom doorway had led to this frantic chase, what it all meant, where it would end, but he knew as certainly as he had ever known anything that an event of a profound and magical nature loomed, something big, something *huge*.

He was not just nude, he was naked, vulnerable both physically and mentally, his tandem hearts pounding, flooded with emotion as he had never been before, not at the moment killing anyone and yet exhilarated. They ran through the neighborly gate, into the backyard at the Bennet house, alongside the house toward the street, the dog in the lead, and Bucky heard himself saying, "A terrible thing has happened, a terrible thing has happened," and he was so disturbed by the desperation in his voice that he forced himself to stop that chant. By the time they were running down the center of the street, not gaining on the dog but not falling behind, he was chanting, "Kill the pizza guy, kill the pizza guy," and though he had no idea what that meant, he liked the sound of it.

chapter 19

The master suite of the Helios mansion included two bathrooms, one for Victor and one for Erika. She was not permitted to cross the threshold of his bath.

Every man needed a sacrosanct retreat, a private space where he could relax and relish both the accomplishments of the day and his intentions for the morrow. If he was a revolutionary with the power of science at his command, and if he had the courage and the will to change the world, he needed and deserved a sanctum sanctorum of grand design and dimensions.

Victor's bathroom measured over sixteen hundred square feet. It included a steam room, a sauna, a spacious shower, a whirlpool spa, two under-the-counter refrigerators, an icemaker, a fully stocked bar, a microwave concealed behind a tambour door, three plasma-screen TVs with Blu-Ray DVD capacity, and an anigre-wood cabinet containing a collection of exquisitely braided leather whips.

The gold-leafed ceiling featured custom crystal chandeliers in the Deco style, and the walls were clad with marble. Inlaid in the center of the polished-marble floor were semiprecious stones forming the double helix of the DNA molecule. The faucets and other fixtures were gold-plated, including even the flush lever on the toilet, and there were acres of beveled-edge mirrors. The room glittered.

Nothing in this luxurious space brought Victor as much pleasure as his reflection. Because mirrors were arranged to reflect other mirrors, he could see multiple images of himself wherever he went.

His favorite place for self-examination was an octagonal meditation chamber with a mirrored door. Therein, nude, he could admire every aspect of his body at the same time, and also see infinite images of each angle marching away to infinity, a world of Victors and nothing less.

He believed himself to be no more vain than the average man. His pride in his physical perfection had less to do with the beauty of his body – though it was uniquely beautiful – than with the evidence of his resolution and his indomitability that was revealed in the means by which he maintained that body for two hundred and forty years.

Spiraling through his muscular torso – here inlaid in the flesh and half exposed, here entirely embedded – entwining his ribs, coiling around his rod-straight spine, a flexible metal cord and associated implants efficiently converted electrical current into a different and arcane energy, into a stimulating charge that ensured a youthful rate of cell division and prevented time from taking any toll of him.

His uncounted scars and singular excrescences were a testament to his fortitude, for he had gained immortality at the cost of much pain. He had suffered to fulfill his vision and remake the world, and by suffering for the world, he could lay claim to a kind of divinity.

From the mirrored meditation chamber, he repaired to the spa, in which the air jets roiled the steaming water. A bottle of Dom Pérignon waited in a silver bucket of ice. The cork had been replaced with a solid-silver stopper. Settled in the hot water, he sipped the crisp, ice-cold champagne from a Lalique flute.

As it unfolded, the day just past seemed to be a chain of crises and frustrations. The discoveries during the Harker autopsy. Werner's meltdown. The first of Victor's triumphs, now calling itself Deucalion, not dead after all but alive in New Orleans. The brief encounter with Deucalion in Duchaine's house, the tattooed one's mystifying escape. Erika having dinner in the living room – *living room!* – on a priceless eighteenth-century French escritoire, as if she were an ignorant hillbilly.

The Harker and Werner situations might seem like calamities to unimaginative types like Ripley, but they were opportunities. From every setback came knowledge and stunning new advancements. Thomas Edison developed hundreds of prototypes of lightbulbs that failed, until at last he discovered the right material for the filament.

Deucalion was a mere amusement. He could not harm his maker. Besides, the tattooed wretch killed Victor's first wife, Elizabeth, two centuries earlier, on the day of their wedding. The freak's return would give Victor a chance to take long-overdue vengeance.

Victor had not loved Elizabeth. Love and God were myths he rejected with equal contempt.

But Elizabeth had *belonged* to him. Even after more than two hundred years, he still bitterly resented the loss of her, as he would have resented losing an exquisite antique porcelain vase if Deucalion had smashed that instead of the bride.

As for Erika Five's breach of etiquette: She would have to be disciplined. In addition to being a brilliant scientist, Victor was to an equal degree a brilliant disciplinarian.

All in all, everything was moving along nicely.

The New Race that he had worked so hard to create with Hitler's generous financing, the later effort financed by Stalin, a subsequent project in China, those and others had been necessary steps toward the glorious work at the Hands of Mercy. This time, thanks to the billions earned from his legitimate enterprise, Biovision, he was able to fund 51 percent of the current project and prevent meddling by minority partners, which included a consortium of South American dictators, the ruler of an oil-rich kingdom eager to replace his restive population with obedient new subjects, and an Internet superbillionaire idiot who believed Victor was creating a race that did not exhale CO_2, as did humans, and would thereby save the planet.

Soon the tank farms would begin producing thousands of the New Race, and the Old would be on the doorstep of oblivion.

For every minor setback, there were a hundred major successes. The momentum – and the world – was Victor's.

Soon he would be able to live again under his true name, his proud and storied name, and every person in the world would speak it reverently, as believers speak the name of their god with awe: *Frankenstein*.

When eventually he got out of the spa, he might return to the mirrored meditation room for just a few more minutes.

chapter 20

Carson and Michael sat in the Honda, near Audubon Park, engine running, headlights on, air conditioner blowing. They were eating the crispy-fried-redfish poor boy and side dishes, their chins greasy, fingers slippery with tartar sauce and cole-slaw dressing, so content with the Acadiana food that the incessant drumming of the rain on the roof began to seem soothing, when Michael said, "Here's something."

Carson looked up from her sandwich and saw him squinting through the sheet of water that shimmered down the windshield and blurred the view. She switched on the wipers.

Sprinting toward them along the middle of the street – deserted at this hour, in this weather – was a German shepherd, and in pursuit of the dog were a man and a woman, both nude.

The shepherd raced past the Honda faster than Carson had ever seen a dog run. Even barefoot, the man and woman were faster than Olympians, as if they were in training to compete in NASCAR without a vehicle. The man's genitals flapped, the woman's breasts bounced exuberantly, and their facial expressions were equally ecstatic, as if the dog had promised to lead them to Jesus.

The dog didn't bark, but as the two-legged runners passed the Honda, Carson heard them shouting. With the windows closed and rain pummeling the roof, she couldn't discern what the woman was saying, but the man excitedly shouted something about pizza.

"Any of our business?" Michael asked.

"No," Carson said.

She raised her poor boy to her mouth, but instead of taking a bite, she returned it to the bag with the side dishes, rolled the top of the bag shut, and handed it to Michael.

"Damn," she said, as she put the Honda in gear and hung a U-turn in the street.

"What were they shouting?" Michael asked.

"Her, I don't know. Him, I couldn't catch anything except the word *pizza*."

"You think the dog ate their pizza?"

"They don't seem angry."

"If they aren't angry, why is the dog running from them?"

"You'll have to ask the dog."

Ahead, the trio with eight legs turned left off the street and onto the Audubon Park entrance lane.

"Did the guy look familiar to you?" Michael asked, as he put their bags of takeout on the floor between his feet.

Accelerating out of the turn, Carson said, "I didn't get a look at his face."

"I think it was the district attorney."

"Bucky Guitreau?"

"And his wife."

"Good for him."

"Good for him?"

"He's not chasing naked after a dog with some hooker."

"Not your ordinary New Orleans politician."

"A family-values guy."

"Can people run that fast?"

"Not our kind of people," Carson said, turning left toward the park.

"That's what I think. And barefoot."

The park had closed at ten o'clock. The dog might have slipped around the gate. The naked runners had gone *through* the barrier, demolishing it in the process.

As Carson drove across the rattling ruins, Michael said, "What are we gonna do?"

"I don't know. I guess it depends on what they do."

chapter 21

Blue is the color of cold vision. All things are shades of blue, infinite shades of blue.

The double-wide restaurant-style freezer has a glass door. The glass is torment for Chameleon.

The shelves have been removed from the freezer. No food is ever stored here.

From a hook in the ceiling of the unit hangs a large sack. The sack is prison.

Prison is made from a unique polymeric fabric that is both as strong as bulletproof Kevlar and transparent.

This transparency is the first torment. The glass door is the second.

The sack resembles a giant teardrop, for it is filled with fourteen gallons of water and is pendulous.

Within the freezer, the temperature varies between twenty-four and twenty-six degrees Fahrenheit.

The water in the polymeric sack is a saline solution treated with chemicals in addition to the salt, to prevent congelation.

Although the temperature remains below freezing, although tiny ice particles float freely in the sack, the solution will not freeze.

Cold is the third torment for Chameleon.

Drifting in the sack, Chameleon lives now in a waking dream.

It is not able to close its eyes to its circumstances, because they have no lids.

Chameleon needs no sleep.

Perpetual awareness of its powerless condition is the fourth torment.

In its current circumstances, Chameleon cannot drown, for it has no lungs.

When not imprisoned, it breathes by virtue of a tracheal system akin to but materially different from that of insects. Spiracles on the surface admit air into tubes that pass throughout the body.

In semisuspended animation, it needs little oxygen. And the saline fluid flowing through its tracheal tubes is oxygen-enriched.

Although Chameleon looks like no insect on Earth, it resembles an insect more than it resembles anything else.

The size of a large cat, Chameleon weighs twenty-four pounds.

Although its brain weighs just 1.22 pounds, Chameleon is as intelligent as the average six-year-old child, but significantly more disciplined and cunning.

In torment, Chameleon waits.

Chapter 22

In the spa, the hot water churned against Victor's body, and the bubbles of Dom Pérignon burst across his tongue, and life was good.

The wall phone beside the spa rang. Only select Alphas had the number of this most private line.

The caller-ID window reported UNKNOWN.

Nevertheless, he snared the handset from the cradle. "Yes?"

A woman said, "Hello, darling."

"Erika?"

"I was afraid you might have forgotten me," she said.

Recalling how he had found her at dinner in the living room, he chose to remain the stern disciplinarian for a while longer. "You know better than to bother me here, except in an emergency."

"I wouldn't blame you if you forgot me. It's been more than a day since you had sex with me. I'm ancient history to you."

Her tone had a faint but unmistakable sarcastic quality that caused him to sit up straighter in the spa. "What do you think you're doing, Erika?"

"I was never loved, only used. I'm flattered to be remembered."

Something was very wrong. "Where are you, Erika? Where are you in the house?"

"I'm not in the house, darling. How could I be?"

He would be in error if he continued to play her conversational game, whatever the point of it might be. He must not encourage what seemed to be rebellious behavior. Victor answered her with silence.

"My dearest master, how could I be in the house after you sent me away?"

He hadn't sent her away. He had left her, battered and bleeding, in the living room, not a day previously but mere hours earlier.

She said, "How is the new one? Is she as lubricious as I was? When brutalized, does she cry as pitifully as I did?"

Victor began to see the nature of the game, and he was shocked by her effrontery.

"My darling, my maker, after you killed me, you had your people in the sanitation department take me to a landfill northeast of Lake Pontchartrain. You ask where I am in the house, but I am nowhere in the house – though I hope to return."

Now that she'd carried this demented charade to an unacceptable extreme, silence was not the appropriate response to her.

"You are Erika Five," he said coldly, "not Erika Four. And all you've achieved by this absurd impersonation is to ensure that Erika Six will be in your position soon."

"From so many nights of passion," she said, "I remember the hard impact of your fists, the sharpness of your teeth biting into me, and how I bled into your mouth."

"Come to me immediately," he said, for he needed to terminate her within the hour.

"Oh, darling, I would be there at once if I could, but it's a long way to the Garden District from the dump."

chapter **23**

As they reached the T junction where the entrance lane met the main road through Audubon Park, Michael drew the illegally purchased .50-caliber Desert Eagle pistol from the scabbard at his left hip.

Carson said, "If they're going to be trouble—"

"I'd bet both kidneys on it."

"—then I'm thinking the Urban Sniper makes more sense," she finished, turning right onto West Drive.

The headlights washed across the pale forms of Mr and Mrs Guitreau on their rainy-night, fully-nude, high-speed dog walk.

Michael said, "If we have to get out of the car, it'll for sure be the Sniper, but not if I have to shoot from a sitting position."

Hours earlier, they had seen Pastor Kenny Laffite, one of the New Race, breaking down psychologically and intellectually. And not long after that, they were forced to deal with another of Victor's creations who called himself Randal and whose rap was as creepy-crazy as Charles Manson channeling Jeffrey Dahmer. Randal wanted to kill Carson's brother, Arnie, and he had taken three rounds point-blank from an Urban Sniper before going down and staying down.

Now this weirdness.

"Damn," Carson said. "I'm never gonna get a chance to finish that okra succotash."

"I thought it was a little salty. I've gotta say, Mrs Guitreau has a truly fine butt."

"For God's sake, Michael, she's some kind of monster."

"Doesn't change the fact she's got a great butt. Small, tight, with those little dimples at the top."

"It's Armageddon, and my backup is an obsessive butt man."

"I think her name's Jane. No. Janet."

"Why do you care what her name is? She's a monster but she's got a cute butt, so you're gonna ask her for a date?"

"How fast are they going?"

Glancing at the speedometer, Carson said, "About twenty-four miles an hour."

"That's maybe a two-and-a-half-minute mile. I think the fastest the mile's been run is just under four minutes."

"Yeah, but I don't expect we'll ever see their pictures on a Wheaties box."

"I heard greyhounds can do a mile in two minutes," Michael said. "I don't know about German shepherds."

"Looks to me like the shepherd is pretty much spent. They're gaining on him."

Michael said, "If we have a dog in this race, it's the dog. I don't want to see the dog get hurt."

The shepherd and his pursuers were in the left lane. Carson swung into the right lane and rolled down her window.

As rain bounced off the sill and into her face, she drew even with the nude marathoners and heard what they were shouting.

The woman – okay, *Janet* – chanted urgently, "Dog nose, dog nose, big, big, big."

"I think she wants the dog's nose," Carson said.

Michael said, "She can't have it."

Neither of the nudists was breathing hard.

Bucky Guitreau, the nearer of the two, was raving with a slight quirky calypso lilt: "Kill, kill, pizza guy, pizza guy, kill, kill."

Both the district attorney and his wife, certainly replicants in the throes of a total breakdown, seemed oblivious to the Honda pacing them. The dog had their full attention, and they were closing on him.

Reading the speedometer, Michael said, "Twenty-*six* miles an hour."

Trying to discern if the runners were even capable of breaking their fixation with the dog, Carson shouted at them, *"Pull over!"*

chapter 24

Sitting in the spa, his champagne mood tainted with the vinegar of his wife's unthinkable rebellion, Victor should already have hung up on Erika Five as she pretended to be Erika Four. He didn't know why he continued to listen to this tripe, but he was rapt.

"Here at the dump," she said, "in a heap of garbage, I found a disposable cell phone that has some unused minutes on it. Eighteen, in fact. Those of the Old Race are so wasteful, throwing away what has value. I, too, still had value, I believe."

Every Erika was created with precisely the same voice, just as they looked alike in every luscious detail.

"My lovely Victor, my dearest sociopath, I can prove to you that I am who I claim to be. Your current punching bag doesn't know how you murdered me, does she?"

He realized he was clenching the telephone so tightly that his hand ached.

"But, sweetheart, of course she doesn't know. Because if you wish to murder her in the same fashion, you want it to be a surprise to her, as it was to me."

No one in decades had spoken to him so contemptuously, and *never* had one whom he created addressed him with such disrespect.

Furious, he declared, "Only people can be murdered. You're not a person, you're property, a thing I owned. I didn't murder you, I disposed of you, disposed of a worn-out, useless thing."

He had lost control. He needed to restrain himself. His reply had seemed to suggest he accepted her ridiculous assertion that she was Erika Four.

She said, "All of the New Race are designed to be extremely difficult to kill. None can be strangled easily, if at all. None except your Erikas. Unlike the others, we wives have tender throats, fragile windpipes, carotid arteries that can be compressed to stop the blood from flowing to our brains."

The water in the spa seemed to be less hot than it had been a minute ago.

"We were in the library, where you had beaten me. You instructed me to sit in a straightbacked chair. I could only obey. You took off your silk necktie and strangled me. And not quickly. You made an ordeal of it for me."

He said, "Erika Four earned what she received. And now so have you."

"In extreme situations," she continued, "you are able to kill any of your creations by speaking a few words, a secret phrase, which triggers in our programs a shutdown of the autonomic nervous system. The heart ceases to beat. Lungs at once stop expanding, contracting. But you didn't deal with me as mercifully as that."

"Now I shall." He spoke the phrase that would shut her down.

"Dear one, my precious Victor, it will no longer work. I was for a while dead enough that your control program dropped out of me. Not so dead, however, that I couldn't be resurrected."

"Nonsense," he said, but his voice had no conviction.

"Oh, darling, how I yearn to be with you again. And I will be. This is not good-bye, only au revoir." She hung up.

If she had been Erika Five, she would have dropped dead when he used the termination phrase.

Erika Four was alive again. For the first time ever, Victor seemed to have a marital problem with which he could not easily cope.

chapter 25

The district attorney and his wife did not pull over, of course, because Carson didn't have a siren or an array of flashing emergency beacons, because they probably knew they were not in any condition to pass a Breathalyzer test, but mostly because they were miscreations cloned in a lab by a narcissistic lunatic and were going haywire as fast as the average car would break down on the day that its warranty expired.

Leaning toward her, reading the speedometer again, Michael said, "Twenty-seven miles an hour. The dog is flagging. They're gonna run right up his ass."

As though multiple-word chants had become too exhausting to remember, Bucky and Janet each resorted to one word. She shouted, "Dog, dog, dog, dog . . ." He cried out, "Kill, kill, kill, kill . . ."

"Shoot them," Michael said. "Shoot 'em on the run."

"I can't fire a .50 Magnum one-handed while driving a car," Carson protested.

Evidently, Bucky was at least peripherally aware of them, after all, and they were enough of a distraction from his pursuit of the dog to annoy him. He closed the gap between them, running alongside the Honda, grabbed the side mirror for balance, and reached through the window toward Carson.

She stepped on the brake, and the mirror snapped off in Bucky's hand. He stumbled, fell, tumbled away into the darkness.

The Honda shrieked to a full stop, and about fifty feet ahead of them, Janet halted without a shriek. She turned toward them, jogging in place.

Holstering his Desert Eagle, Michael said, "This is like some bizarre Playboy-channel special." He handed one of the Urban Snipers to Carson and snatched up the other. "Not that I ever watch the Playboy channel."

Michael threw open his door, and Carson switched the headlights on high beam because darkness helped her quarry, hampered her. As her heart provided the thunder that the storm had not yet produced, she clambered out into the rain, surveying the night, looking for Bucky, not finding him.

Glare of headlights reflected by the wet pavement, black and silver underfoot, and not far to the west, beyond trees, the lights of Walnut Street and Audubon and Broadway, which didn't reach this far, and north-northeast, the university lights of Tulane and Loyola, which didn't reach this far either, the park deep and dark to the east and to the south, the glow of maybe De Paul Hospital far out there.

A lonely place to die, to be found in the morning, left like illegally dumped trash, left like her father and mother were left all those years ago, facedown under power lines, near a double-circuit tower, on a grassy bank of the levee in Riverbend, just off the bike path, each shot once in the back of the head, with carrion-eating blackbirds gathering overhead on the crossarms of the tower as day broke . . .

Now this park, this lonely darkness, felt like Carson's levee bank, her place to be left like a sack of trash, to be pecked at by bright-eyed birds. She had been out of the Honda ten seconds at most, edging away from the vehicle and defining the arc of the potential threat with the barrel of the shotgun, left to right, then right to left, but the ten seconds felt like ten minutes.

Where was the freak?

Suddenly a pale form rose from a drainage swale on the farther side of the road, the Bucky replicant, bloodied by his high-speed fall but back on his feet and shouting: "Something terrible has happened, terrible, terrible." Looking no less powerful than a bull, he put his head down and charged her.

Carson planted her feet wide, assumed the stance, the compact shotgun held low in both hands, right hand on the pistol grip in front of the forecomb, left hand cupping the slide, weapon held slightly to her right side, both elbows bent, the better to absorb recoil, which would be brutal if she locked her joints – a tendon-tearing, shoulder-dislocating kind of brutal. As serious as a weapon gets, the Sniper fired only rhino-stopping slugs, not buckshot with a wide spread, but nevertheless she aimed by instinct, no time for anything else. The Bucky Guitreau impersonator, with blood in his wild eyes, lips snarled back from his teeth, barreled straight at her, fearless, ferocious.

She squeezed off the round, the recoil jumped her backward a few inches, the barrel kicked up like she knew it would, pain knocked through her shoulders, a sensitive filling in a molar throbbed the way it did once in a while when she drank something ice-cold, and though she wasn't in an enclosed space, the shot rang in her ears.

The slug took the replicant dead-center in the chest, cracking his sternum, splintering bone inward, blood blooming, his left arm flailing up reflexively, right arm stroking down reflexively, as if he were launching into some novelty dance like the Chicken. Jolted but not staggered, slowed but not halted, he came on, not shouting anymore, but not screaming either, feeling no pain, and she fired again, but screwed up because she was shocked and scared by how he surged forward, didn't get him in the gut or the chest, but in the right shoulder, which should have torn his arm off or at least a chunk of it, didn't, and he was reaching out to grab the barrel of the Sniper, looking strong enough and furious enough and focused enough to take maybe two more rounds and still tear her face off, rip out her throat.

Michael appeared at the back of the Honda, his shotgun boomed, scored a flank hit just above the hip, and Carson fired again, maybe nailed the replicant point-blank in the left thigh, but his arm was in past the muzzle of the shotgun, knocking the barrel high, his crimson hand reaching toward her face. Guitreau said something that sounded like "Gimme your eyes," and Michael fired again, a head shot, and that did it, finally dropped the Bucky thing, naked on the silver-and-black pavement, facedown, still for a moment, but then trying to belly-crawl away from them, a broken-melon head and other devastating wounds but trying to hitch away as if he were a crippled roach. He became still once more, lying there motionless, motionless, then a last convulsive spasm, and he was done.

From the corner of her eye, Carson saw something move, something close, and she swiveled toward tight-assed Janet.

chapter **26**

Cautioning silence, Erika Five led Jocko, the albino troll, up one of two sets of back stairs, to the second floor, well away from the centrally located master suite.

Of the three mansions that had stood on the three lots Victor purchased, two were very alike architecturally. He joined them in such a way that a foreground trio of oaks and a background lattice arbor draped with evergreen St Vincent lilac left the impression, from the street, that the houses were still separate.

Between them, the two residences initially included thirty-four bedrooms, but interior walls were taken down and all that space put to other uses. Victor had no family and allowed no overnight guests.

He had intended to tear down the third residence and incorporate that lot into the grounds of his estate.

A city politician with ambitions for the governorship – and with rigid ideas about the preservation of historic buildings – blocked Victor's attempt to have the third house certified for demolition.

He tried to resolve the issue with respect for her public office and her social eminence. A fat bribe would have bought her cooperation on most matters; however, she believed that a reputation as a committed preservationist was key to the achievement of her political goals.

After the politician's replicant had been birthed from the tank, Victor had the real woman snatched from her home and brought to the Hands of Mercy, where he described – and then demonstrated – to her the most ingenious methods of torture devised by the Stasi, the secret police of the former East Germany. When in time she stopped begging for surcease and begged instead for death, Victor allowed her to choose the instrument of murder from an imaginative selection that included, among other things, a compressed air nail gun, a hand-held power sander, and a large bottle of carbolic acid.

The woman's complete mental collapse and retreat into catatonic detachment not only made it impossible for her to decide upon the means to her end but also robbed Victor of some of the pleasure of administering corporal punishment. Nevertheless, he considered the resolution of the historic-preservation issue to have been one of his finer moments, which was why he included it in his biography that had been downloaded into Erika's brain while she had been forming in the tank.

Victor wanted his Erikas not merely to service him sexually and to be his gracious hostess to the world; he also intended that his wives, each in her turn, should admire his steadfast intent to have his way in all matters, his steely resolution never to bow or bend to the wishes of the intellectual pygmies, frauds, and fools of this world who sooner or later humbled all other great men whose accomplishments they bitterly envied.

On the second floor of the mansion, the north wing remained unused, awaiting Victor's inspiration. One day, he would discover some convenience or luxury he wanted to add to the house, and the north wing would be remodeled to accommodate his latest enthusiasm.

Even here, mahogany floors had been installed and finished throughout all the wide hallways and rooms. In the halls, the floors were overlaid with a series of compatible antique Persian rugs, mostly late-nineteenth-century Tabriz and Bakhshayesh.

She took Jocko to an unfurnished suite, where she switched on the overhead lights: a small sitting room, a bedroom, a bath. The space lacked carpeting. Heavy brocade draperies with blackout liners, which had come with the house, were closed over the windows.

"The staff vacuums and dusts the north wing just twelve times a year," Erika said. "The first Tuesday of every month. Otherwise, these rooms are never visited. The night before, we'll move you to another location, and back again after they have finished and gone."

Still wearing the skirt fashioned from the checkered tablecloth, wandering from lounge to bedroom, admiring the high ceilings, the ornate crown moldings, and the Italian-marble fireplace, the troll said, "Jocko is not worthy of these refined quarters."

"Without furniture, you'll have to sleep on the floor," said Erika. "I'm sorry about that."

"Jocko doesn't sleep much, just sits in a corner and sucks his toes and lets his mind go away to the red place, and when it comes back from the red place, Jocko is rested."

"How interesting. Nonetheless, you'll sometimes want a place to lie down. I'll bring blankets, soft bedding to make it comfortable."

In the bathroom, the black-and-white ceramic tile dated to the 1940s, but it remained in excellent condition.

"You have hot and cold running water, a tub, a shower, and of course a toilet. I'll bring soap, towels, toilet paper, a toothbrush, toothpaste. You don't have hair, so you won't need shampoo or a comb, or dryer. Do you shave?"

The troll thoughtfully stroked his lumpy face with one hand. "Jocko doesn't have even one nice hair anywhere – except inside his nose. Oh, and three on his tongue." He stuck his tongue out to show her.

"You still won't need a comb," Erika said. "What deodorant do you prefer, roll-on or spray-on?"

Jocko squinched his face, which drew his features into a disturbing configuration.

Once Erika knew him better and could be direct without seeming to insult, she would tell him never to squinch again.

He said, "Jocko suspects his skin is hypersensitive to such caustic chemicals."

"All right then. I'll be back shortly with everything you need. You wait here. Stay away from the windows and of course be as quiet as you can." A literary allusion rose from the deep pool of them in Erika's memory, and she added, "This is just like Anne Frank, hiding from the Nazis in the secret annex in Amsterdam."

The troll stared at her uncomprehendingly and smacked the flaps of his lipless mouth.

"Or maybe not," said Erika.

"May Jocko say?" he asked.

"Excuse me?"

"May Jocko say?"

Owlishly large, with huge irises as yellow as lemons, his eyes still struck her as mysterious and beautiful. They compensated for all the unfortunate facial features surrounding them.

"Yes," she said, "of course, say what you want."

"Since tearing my way out of he who I was and becoming he who I am, Jocko, who is me, has lived mostly in storm drains and for a little while in a janitorial closet at a public restroom. This is so much better."

Erika smiled and nodded. "I hope you'll be happy here. Just remember – your presence in the house must remain a secret."

"You are the kindest, most generous lady in the world."

"Not at all, Jocko. You'll be reading to me, remember?"

"When I was still he who was, I never knew any lady half as nice as you. Since the he who was became the I who am, Jocko, I've never met any lady a quarter as nice as you, not even in the restroom where I lived eleven hours, which was a ladies' restroom. From the janitorial closet, Jocko listened to so many ladies talking out there at the sinks and in the stalls, and most of them were *horrible*."

"I'm sorry you've suffered so much, Jocko."

He said, "Me too."

chapter 27

The presence approaching Carson, from her right and low to the ground, wasn't Janet Guitreau, but the German shepherd, panting hard, tail wagging.

She with the great butt remained where she had been when Carson got out of the Honda: fifty feet farther along the road. Head high, shoulders back, arms out at her sides as if she were a gunfighter ready to draw down on a sheriff in the Old West, she stood tall and alert.

She was no longer jogging in place, which was probably a huge disappointment to Michael.

Interestingly, the Janet thing had watched their confrontation with the Bucky thing and had felt no obligation to sprint to his assistance. A small army of the New Race might inhabit the city, but perhaps there wasn't sufficient camaraderie among them to ensure they would always fight together.

On the other hand, maybe this lack of commitment to the cause resulted solely from the fact that Janet's brain train had jumped the tracks and was rolling through strange territory where no rails had ever been laid.

Out there in the scintillant silver rain, bathed in the Honda's high-beam headlights, she appeared ethereal, as if a curtain had parted between this world and another where people were as radiant as spirits and as wild as any animal.

Michael held out a hand, cartridges gleaming on his palm.

Reloading, Carson said, "What're you thinking – go after her?"

"Not me. I have a rule – one showdown with an insane super-clone per day. But she might come for us."

For the first time all night, a sudden light wind sprang up, trumping gravity, so that the rain angled at them, pelting Carson's face instead of the top of her head.

As though the wind had spoken to Janet, counseling retreat, she turned from them and sprinted off the roadway, between trees, into the dark grassy mystery of the park.

At Carson's side, the dog issued a low, long growl that seemed to mean *good riddance*.

Michael's cell phone sounded. His newest ring was Curly's laugh, Curly being *the* Curly of the Three Stooges. "N'yuck, n'yuck, n'yuck," said the phone. "N'yuck, n'yuck, n'yuck."

"Life in the twenty-first century," Carson said, "is every bit as stupid as it is insane."

Michael took the call and said, "Hey, yeah." To Carson, he said, "It's Deucalion."

"About freakin' time." She surveyed the darkness to the east and south, expecting Janet to come bouncing back in full killer mode.

After listening a moment, Michael told Deucalion, "No, where we are isn't a good place to meet. We just had a situation, and there's debris everywhere."

Carson glanced at the body of the Bucky replicant. Still dead.

"Give us like ten or fifteen minutes to get somewhere that makes sense. I'll call you back, let you know where." Pocketing his phone, he said to Carson, "Deucalion's almost done at Mercy, he found what he hoped to find."

"What do you want to do about the dog?"

Having been drinking from a puddle on the pavement, the shepherd looked up and favored Carson, then Michael, with a beseeching look.

Michael said, "We take him with us."

"The whole car's gonna smell like wet dog."

"It's a lot worse for him. From his point of view, the whole car smells like wet cops."

"He's a pretty boy," she admitted. "And he looks like he ought to be a police dog. I wonder what his name is."

"Wait a minute," Michael said. "This must be Duke. The D.A.'s dog. Goes to court with Bucky. Or used to."

"The Duke of Orleans," Carson said. "Saved two kids in a fire."

The dog's tail spun so fast that Carson half expected it would propel him across the slick pavement in the manner of one of those Florida Everglades airboats.

The wind soughed in the trees, and suddenly it seemed to carry the scent of the sea.

She opened the car door, coaxed the shepherd into the backseat, and got in behind the wheel once more. As she returned her Urban Sniper, muzzle down, to the leg space in front of the passenger's seat, she realized that the bags of Acadiana food were gone.

Through the windshield, she saw Michael returning from a nearby roadside trash receptacle.

"What have you done?" she demanded when he splashed into his seat and pulled the door shut.

"We'd already eaten most of it."

"We hadn't eaten *all* of it. Acadiana is good-to-the-last-crumb wondermous."

"The smell of it would drive the dog crazy."

"So we could've given him some."

"It's too rich for a dog. He'd be puking it up later."

"The stupid Curly ring, and now this."

She put the car in gear, hung a U-turn without driving over the Bucky replicant, switched the headlights to low beam, drove across the mangled park gate, hoping not to puncture a tire, and turned right onto St Charles Avenue.

"So . . . I'm not going to get the silent treatment, am I?" Michael asked.

"You should be so lucky."

"Another prayer unanswered."

"Here's the sixty-four-thousand-dollar question."

"I can't afford it," he said.

"Do you think I eat too much?"

"It's none of my business what you eat."

"You think I'm going to get a fat ass, don't you?"

"Uh-oh."

In the backseat, the shepherd panted but not with anxiety. He sounded happy. Maybe he'd heard so much replicant-speak lately that he delighted in real human conversation.

"Admit it. You're worried I'll get a fat ass."

"I don't sit around thinking about the future of your ass."

"You were so hot for the Janet monster's tight butt."

"I wasn't hot for it. I just noticed it, you know, as a nice work of nature, like you'd comment on a great wisteria vine if you saw one."

"Wisteria? That is so lame. Besides, Victor's people *aren't* works of nature."

"I don't have a chance here if you're gonna parse my every word."

"Just so you know, my butt is as small as hers was, and even tighter."

"I'll take your word for it."

"You'll have to take my word for it because there isn't going to be any exhibition. If you dropped a quarter on my butt, it would bounce to the ceiling."

"That sounds like a challenge."

"Let me tell you, partner, it's gonna be a long time before you get a chance to bounce a quarter off my butt."

"Just in case, from now on, I'm going to be sure I've always got a quarter in my pocket."

"Bounce it off my butt," she said, "you'll get back two dimes and a nickel in change."

"What does that mean?"

"I have no idea."

He said, "Two dimes and a nickel in change," and he broke into laughter.

His laughter was contagious, and when the dog heard them both laughing, he made sweet mewling sounds of delight.

After a minute, Carson settled to serious once more and said, "Thanks, pal. You saved my ass back there with the Bucky thing."

"*De nada.* You've saved mine often enough."

"Each time we have to throw down on one of these New Race," she said, "seems like we squeak by with less room to spare than before."

"Yeah. But at least we do keep on squeakin' by."

chapter 28

At 2:15 a.m., at Victor's stylish workstation in the main lab at the Hands of Mercy, as Deucalion completed his electronic fishing and backed out of the computer, he thought he heard in the distance a scream as thin as the plaint of a lost child.

Given some of the experiments being conducted in this building, screams were not likely to be infrequent. No doubt the windows had been bricked up not solely to foil prying eyes but also to ensure that disturbing sounds would fail to reach passersby in the street.

The staff here, the subjects of the experiments, and those who were growing in the creation tanks were without exception victims of their lunatic god, and Deucalion pitied them. He hoped eventually to free them all from their anguish and despair, not one at a time as he had freed Annunciata and Lester, but somehow en masse.

He had no way to free them right now, however, and as soon as he heard from Michael, he would be leaving the Hands of Mercy in a quantum leap and joining the detectives. He could not be distracted by whatever horrors might be unfolding elsewhere in the building.

When the sound came again, marginally louder and longer than before but still distant, Deucalion recognized that it conveyed neither terror nor physical pain, and therefore was not a scream at all, but instead a shriek. He could not tell what the crier of this cry meant to express.

He stood listening – and only realized after the fact that he had risen from the workstation chair.

The silence following the wail had an expectant quality, like the mute sky during the second or two between a violent flash of lightning and the crash of thunder. Here, the sound came first and, though faint, managed to be as terrible as the loudest thunderclap.

He waited for the equivalent of the flash, cause after effect. But what followed a half minute later was another shriek.

On the third hearing, the sound had significance, not because he could identify its source but because it recalled to him cries he heard in certain dreams that for two hundred years had haunted him. They were not dreams of the night he came alive in Victor's first lab, but of other and more dreadful events, perhaps of events that preceded his existence.

After his first hundred years, decade by decade, he needed less sleep. This meant, thankfully, fewer opportunities to dream.

Deucalion crossed the main lab, opened a door, stepped across the threshold, and found the hallway deserted.

The cry came again, twice in quick succession. Louder here than in the laboratory, the sound was still distant.

Sometimes Deucalion dreamed of an old stone house with

interior walls of cracked and yellowed plaster, illuminated by oil lamps and candle sconces. When the worst storm winds blew, from the attic arose a disturbing click-and-clatter, like the fleshless body of Death rattling in his cowled robe as he walked the night. Worse than what might wait above was what might wait below: A narrow turning of stone stairs descended to an ironbound door, and beyond the door were the rooms of a forbidding cellar, where the stagnant air sometimes had the acrid taste of spoiled suet and at other times the salty taste of tears.

Here in the old hospital, the latest two shrieks had come from another floor, whether from above or below, he could not tell. He walked to the stairs at the end of the corridor, opened the fire door, and waited, feeling almost as if he might be dreaming that well-known scenario but in a new setting.

In the familiar nightmare, the horror of going into the attic or the desire not to go into the cellar was always the sum of the plot, an endless wretched journey through the rooms that lay between those two poles of terror, as he strove to avoid both the highest and lowest chambers of the house.

Now, the shriek fell through the hospital stairwell from above. Heard more clearly than before, it was pleading and mournful.

Like the miserable cries that sometimes haunted his infrequent sleep.

Deucalion ascended the stairs toward the higher realms of Mercy.

In the old stone house, which might have once been a real place or just a structure of his imagination, he had dreamed his way into the cellar many times, but never farther than the first room. Then he always woke, choking with a nameless dread.

Twice, with an oil lamp, he had gone into the dream-house attic.

Both times, a fierce storm raged outside. Drafts blustered through that high room, and he was shocked out of sleep and into anguish by what the lamplight revealed.

Climbing the hospital stairs, Deucalion felt at risk of losing his balance, and he put one hand on the railing.

He was constructed from the parts of bodies salvaged from a prison graveyard. His hands were big and strong. They had been the hands of a strangler.

One floor above Victor's main lab, as Deucalion reached for the door to the corridor, he heard the shriek again, its source still overhead. As he continued up the stairs, he watched his powerful hand slide along the railing.

His eyes had been salvaged from an ax murderer.

He sensed that what he was about to see in the higher halls of Mercy would be no less terrible than what the lamplight had shown him in the dream-house attic. On this fateful night, past and present were coming together like the hemispheres of a nuclear warhead, and the post-blast future was unknown.

chapter **29**

The torment of perpetual awareness. The torment of cold. The torment of the transparent polymeric fabric. The torment of the glass door on the freezer.

Drifting in the saline solution, Chameleon can see the large room in which it is stored. A blue scene. The blue of cold vision.

Out there in the laboratory, work continues. Busy blue people. Perhaps they are TARGETS. Perhaps they are EXEMPTS.

When not in cold suspension, Chameleon can smell the difference between TARGETS and EXEMPTS.

The scent of any EXEMPT pleases Chameleon. The scent of any TARGET infuriates.

In its current condition, it can smell nothing.

The walls of the freezer conduct the unit's compressor-motor vibrations to the imprisoning sack. The sack conducts them into the solution.

This is neither a pleasant nor an unpleasant sensation for Chameleon.

Now the character of the vibrations changes. They are similar but subtly different.

This happens periodically. Chameleon is sufficiently intelligent to consider the phenomenon and to reach conclusions about it.

Evidently, the freezer has two motors. They alternate to prevent either from being overtaxed.

This also ensures that if one motor fails, the other will serve as backup.

Chameleon's physical function is greatly inhibited by the cold. Its mental function is less affected.

With little to occupy its mind, Chameleon focuses obsessively on every minim of sensory input, such as motor vibrations.

It is not at risk of being driven insane by its circumstances. At no time was it ever sane.

Chameleon has no desires or ambitions other than to kill. The purpose of its existence is currently frustrated, which is the nature of its torment.

Out in the blue laboratory, the busy blue people are suddenly agitated. The standard pattern of activities, which Chameleon has long studied, is abruptly disrupted.

Something unusual has come into the lab. It is busy and blue, but it is not a person.

Interesting.

chapter **30**

In Victor's master-bedroom closet, all foldable clothes were stored in banks of drawers, and all hanging items were behind cabinet doors, leaving the room sleek and neat, as he liked it.

In his clothes collection were 164 custom-tailored suits, 67 fine sport coats, 48 pairs of slacks, 212 shirts including dress and casual, drawers and drawers full of perfectly folded sweaters, and shelf after shelf of shoes for every occasion. Especially fond of silk neckties, he had lost count when his collection passed three hundred.

He enjoyed dressing well. Considering his exemplary physique, clothes hung beautifully on him. He thought he was nearly as pleasing to the eye when dressed as he was when nude.

After the phone call from Erika Four, Victor counseled himself to linger in the spa over another glass of Dom Pérignon. His former wife was trash, figuratively and literally, and though she may have somehow been resuscitated, she was no match for either his intellect or his cunning.

As prudent as he was confident, however, he had stepped from the spa after taking only two sips of the second glass of champagne. Until the problem of Erika Four could be understood and resolved, he ought to have a suitable weapon on his person at all times.

In a sapphire silk robe with scarlet piping and matching silk slippers, he went to the back of his deep walk-in closet and opened a pair of tall doors. Before him was a double-hung selection of shirts, twenty on the upper rod, twenty on the lower.

He placed his left hand flat against a sidewall of the cabinet, a concealed scanner read his fingerprints, the rods and shirts rolled up and out of sight, and the back wall slid aside. Lights came on in a fifteen-foot-square room beyond.

Victor stepped through the cabinet, into his small armory.

Like the clothes in the closet, the weapons were not in view. He would have found such a display garish, the kind of thing a too-enthusiastic militarist might have done.

Victor was not a member of the National Rifle Association, not only because he was not a joiner, but also because he didn't approve of the Second Amendment. He believed that, in order to have a well-managed population and to prevent the people from acting on the delusion that the government served them, only an elite class should be permitted ownership of firearms. The masses, in matters of dispute among themselves, could make do perfectly well with knives, fists, and sticks.

The machine guns and the custom-machined automatic shot-guns were in racks behind upper doors. Pistols and revolvers were in drawers, nestled in molded foam finished with a spray-on velvet, which not only embraced the weapons but also displayed them as diamond necklaces might be presented on a jeweler's velvet trays.

Fortunately, although the Erikas were strong and were intended to be durable, with full speed-healing capability as well as the ability to turn off pain, they were not as physically formidable as others of the New Race. They were designed with a few points of vulnerability, and their bones were not the dense armorlike quality given to others born from the tanks.

Consequently, he selected a 1911-style Colt .45 ACP, the Springfield Armory version, with custom 24-line-per-inch checking in the walnut grip, plus deep-cut and hand-engraved decorative scrollwork in the stainless steel.

On those rare occasions when he could not kill by proxy, using one of the New Race, Victor wanted his weapon to be as attractive as it was powerful.

After loading the pistol and a spare magazine, he selected a supple hand-tooled leather scabbard that would slip onto whatever belt he chose with his trousers, and he returned with everything to the clothes closet, pressing his hand to the cabinet side-wall again to conceal the armory behind him.

Sleep was usually a choice for him, not often a necessity, and he decided to return to the Hands of Mercy. The amusements that he had come home to pursue, after a long and curious day at work, no longer appealed to him.

From the lab, he would contact Nick Frigg, the Gamma who was the superintendent at Crosswoods Waste Management, the landfill in the uplands north-east of Lake Pontchartrain. Thoroughly strangled, Erika Four had been sent there for disposal; therefore, Nick would be the one most likely to know in which sector of which pit, under what garbage, she had been buried.

Watching himself in a full-length mirror, Victor kicked off his slippers. With the flair of a fine matador manipulating a cape, he stripped out of the sapphire silk robe.

He picked up the .45 pistol and posed with it this way and that, pleased with the impression that he made.

Now what to wear, what to wear . . . ?

chapter 31

The hands of a strangler. The gray eyes of an executed ax murderer. Of his two hearts, one had come from a mad arsonist who burned down churches, the other from a child molester.

As he reached the stairwell landing, a floor and a half above the main laboratory at the Hands of Mercy, his vision brightened for a moment, returned to normal, brightened . . .

If he had stood before a mirror, he would have seen a pulse of soft light pass through his eyes. On the night that Victor had drawn upon the power of a thunderbolt to enliven his first creation, the cooperative storm, of unprecedented violence, had seemed to leave in Deucalion the lightning's glow, which manifested in his eyes from time to time.

Although he sought redemption and eventually peace, although he cherished Truth and wished to serve it, Deucalion had long tried to deceive himself about the identity of the man whose head, whose *brain*, had been married to the patchwork body in Victor's first lab. He said his brain was that of an unknown miscreant, which was true but only in that he'd never been told the man's name or his crimes.

The repetitive nightmare of the old stone house – with its cursed attic where something ticked and rattled, clicked and clattered; and its cellar in which the air itself was evil – returned to Deucalion so often that he knew as surely as he knew anything, the dream must be fragments of memories the donor had left behind somewhere among the sulci and the gyri of his gray matter. And the nature of those grim memories identified the hateful source of the brain.

Now, ascending the hospital stairs toward the thin childlike cries of misery, he felt as if Earth's gravity had doubled during the climb, for he carried not only the weight of this moment but also the weight of all those dreams and what they surely meant.

When in the nightmare he had at last made it up the stairs into the attic of the house, the throbbing light of an oil lamp revealed to him the source of the clicking and clattering. The raging storm outside pressed drafts into that high room, and those blustering currents knocked the dangling bones against one another. The skeleton was small, strung together to keep it in order, suspended from a hook in a rafter.

Also suspended from the hook was the only other thing of the victim that remained: the long golden hair that had been shorn from her head. Bones and braids. Or call them trophies.

But so much clicking and clattering could not arise from one young girl's bones. When in the dream he had dared to venture farther into the attic, the lamplight revealed a grisly orphanage: nine other dangling skeletons and then, oh, ten more beyond, and yet another ten thereafter. Thirty young girls – all children, really – presented as mobiles, each with her hair hanging separately from her skull, blond hair or brown or auburn, straight or curly hair, some braided and some not.

In hundreds of repetitions of that dream, he had only twice gotten into the attic before waking in a sweat of dread. He had *never* proceeded past the first room of the cellar, into the heart of that darkness, and he hoped he never would. The sound of skeletons in a wind dance drew him to the attic, but what always pulled him toward the dream-house cellar were those thin haunting cries. They were not shrieks of terror or of pain, but instead of sorrow, as if he were hearing not the victims yet alive but their spirits yearning for the world from which they had been taken before their time.

He had so long resisted acknowledging the source of his brain; but he could not continue deceiving himself. His second heart had come from a child molester who killed those he raped – and his brain from the same donor. The murderer had done what he wanted with the girls and then rendered them in the cellar to extract their delicate skeletons as mementos, which was why in the dream the stagnant air of that windowless lower realm tasted sometimes of spoiled suet and sometimes of salty tears.

The possession of a child molester's brain didn't make Deucalion a child molester himself. That evil mind and that corrupted soul had departed the brain at death, leaving behind nothing but three pounds or so of blameless cerebral tissue, which Victor had taken to preserve immediately after the execution, by arrangement with the hangman. Deucalion's consciousness was uniquely his own, and its origins were ... elsewhere. Whether his consciousness came in tandem with a soul, he could not say. But he had no doubt that he arrived that long-ago night with a mission – to enforce the natural laws that Victor had broken with his prideful experiments and, by killing him, thereby repair the torn fabric of the world.

Following a journey that had taken him around the Earth more than once and across two troubled centuries, in search of a new purpose after he thought Victor died on the arctic ice, Deucalion at last arrived here at the threshold of his destiny. The destruction of the New Race was under way, brought about by the endless errors of their maker. And soon Deucalion would bring justice to Victor Frankenstein in the storm of anarchy and terror now breaking over Louisiana.

Now another childlike expression of sorrow, another more suggestive of despair, greeted him as he reached the next landing. The cries came from this floor.

He suspected that by his actions in the hours ahead, he would earn his release from the dreams of the old stone house. He took a deep breath, hesitated, then opened the door and stepped out of the stairwell into the corridor.

About a dozen of the New Race, male and female, stood here and there along the wide hallway. Their attention was focused on the open pair of doors to a laboratory on the right, at the midpoint of the building.

From that room came another plaintive cry, thrashing noises, the shattering of glass.

When Deucalion moved past some of the people standing in the hall, not one seemed to register his presence, so intent were they on the crisis in the laboratory. They stood in various postures of expectation. Some trembled or even shook violently with fear, some muttered angrily, and some appeared to be in the grip of a strange transcendental awe.

Through the open doors of the laboratory, into the corridor came Hell on six legs.

chapter **32**

For the moment, cold does not matter.

The transparent polymeric fabric of the imprisoning sack and the glass door of the freezer are for the first time not a torment to Chameleon.

The recently arrived, unusual, very busy, blue, not-a-person something goes back and forth, back and forth through the lab with great energy.

This visitor seems intent on creating a new order. It is an agent of change.

Cabinets topple. Chairs fly. Lab equipment is knocked helter-skelter.

In its pendulous sack of ice-flecked fluid, Chameleon can't hear voices. However, the vibrations of this vigorous reordering are transmitted through walls and floor to the freezer and thus to its occupant.

The lights dim, swell brighter, dim, fade further, but then brighten once more.

The freezer motor stutters and dies. The backup motor does not come online.

Chameleon is alert for the distinct pattern of second-motor vibrations. Nothing. Nothing.

This interesting and energetic visitor draws some people to it, lifts them up, as if in celebration, as if to exalt them, but then casts them down.

They remain where they have fallen, motionless.

Other workers seem to approach the busy visitor of their own volition. They appear almost to embrace it.

These also are lifted up, and then they are cast down. They lie as motionless as the others who were cast down before them.

Perhaps they have prostrated themselves at the feet of the busy visitor.

Or they may be asleep. Or dead.

Interesting.

When all the once-busy workers are motionless, the visitor tears the faucets out of a lab sink and casts them down, making the water gush forth.

The water falls upon the workers, the water falls, yet they do not rise.

And no second-motor vibrations are as yet transmitted to the fluid in the imprisoning sack.

A stillness has come over the sack. The saline solution is without tremors and without hum.

Busy, busy, the visitor uproots the lab sink from its mountings, tosses it aside.

The stainless-steel sink strikes the freezer door, and the glass pane dissolves.

This seems to be an event of great import. What has been is no more. Change has come.

Chameleon has a clearer view than ever before as the visitor departs the laboratory.

What does it all mean?

Chameleon broods on recent events.

chapter **33**

The six-legged pandemonium that entered the corridor from the demolished laboratory loomed as large as three men.

In some of the entity's features, Deucalion could discern the presence of human DNA. The face appeared much like that of a man, though twice as wide and half again as long as the average face. But the head did not rest upon a neck, instead melding directly with the body, much as a frog's head and body were joined.

Throughout the organism, nonhuman genetic material manifested in a multitude of startling ways, as if numerous species were vying for control of the body. Feline, canine, insectile, reptilian, avian, and crustacean influences were apparent in limbs, in misplaced and excess orifices, in tails and stingers, in half-formed faces liable to appear anywhere in the tissue mass.

Nothing about this bizarre organism appeared to be in stasis, but all in continuous change, as if its flesh were clay submitting to the imagination and the facile hands of an invisible – and insane – sculptor. This was the Prince of Chaos, enemy of equilibrium, brother of anarchy, literally seething with disorder, defined by the lack of definition, characterized by distortion and disfigurement, warp and gnarl and misproportion.

Deucalion knew at once what stood before him. Earlier, searching Victor's files on the computer downstairs, he had found his maker's daily diary of important developments. Among the few days he scanned were the two most recent, wherein the sudden metamorphosis of Werner was not merely described but also illustrated with video clips.

Across the surface of the beast, mouths formed and faded, formed again, most of them human in configuration. Some only gnashed their teeth. Some worked their lips and tongues but could not find their voices. Others issued cries like those that brought Deucalion from Victor's main lab two floors below, wordless expressions of sorrow and despair, voices of the lost and hopeless.

These speakers sounded childlike, though everyone in the Hands of Mercy — therefore in this aggregate creature — was an adult. Having escaped their enslavement by surrendering to biological chaos, having dropped their programs in the process of abandoning their physical integrity, they seemed to have regressed psychologically to early childhood, a childhood they had never known, and they were now more helpless than ever.

Among the aggregated individuals, only Werner, whose distorted countenance remained the primary face of this beast, possessed an adult voice. Upon exiting the laboratory, he rolled his protuberant eyes, surveying those who waited in the corridor, and after giving them a moment to consider — perhaps to envy and admire — him, he said, "Be *free*. Be free in me. Abandon hopelessness, all you who enter me. Be free in me. Don't wait to be told when you may kill the Old Race. Be free in me, and we will start the killing tonight. Be free in me, and we will kill *the world*."

A man with a rapturous expression approached the Werner thing, raising his arms as if to embrace freedom, and his liberator at once snatched him up. Insectile puncture-and-pry limbs of wicked design opened the convert's head as if it were a clamshell, and the brain was transferred into the aggregate creature through a thick-lipped moist cleft that opened in the beast's chest to accept the offering.

A second man stepped forward. Although he was one of those shaking with terror, he was ready to commit to a bizarre and possibly tormented life in the aggregated organism rather than endure more life as Victor allowed him to live it.

Deucalion had seen enough, too much. He had been compelled to climb the steps in answer to the eerie cries because he had climbed them for two centuries in dreams. But in his climb, he had indeed brought the past and the present together. The first of Victor's works was here with the last of his works, and the collapse of his demonic empire was under way.

Certain about what he must do next, Deucalion turned from the beast and its offer of freedom. He took one step in the corridor and the next one in the main lab, two floors below.

The end of this empire might not be the end of the threat to civilization that it posed.

To ensure eternal power over his creations, Victor designed the New Race to be infertile. He created females with vaginas but without wombs. When they were the sole version of humanity on Earth, the world would be perpetually without children. Never again would society be organized around the family and its traditions, an Old Race institution that Victor abhorred.

But when their biological structure collapsed, when they remade themselves into something like the aggregate beast or like the pale dwarfish thing that had come out of Detective Harker, perhaps they would rediscover the structures of fertility and efficient methods of reproduction.

Who was to say that this new thing on Earth, this Werner-driven thing, might not at some point reproduce by fission, split into two functioning organisms, as parameciums did?

It might even split into a male and a female. Thereafter, the two might cease to reproduce by fission and resume breeding through some kind of sexual intercourse.

After all, in an infinite universe, anything that could be imagined might somewhere exist.

The fate of the Old Race would be bleak if Victor succeeded in producing an army to undertake a methodical genocide. But that horror might pale by comparison to a future in which humankind was harried and hunted by a multiple-species hybrid able to gain control of its currently chaotic physiology. Such an adversary would be nearly indestructible by virtue of its amorphous nature, full-bore insane by any standard yet intelligent, with an enthusiasm for violence unequaled by any species of natural origin, with a distilled hatred for its prey that would be satanic in its bitterness, intensity, and eternal endurance.

At Victor's workstation, Deucalion settled onto the chair and switched on the computer once more.

Among the many discoveries that he had made earlier, he found that even prideful Victor, whose well of hubris would never run dry, provided for the possibility that something would go so wrong in the Hands of Mercy that the old hospital would have to be reduced to molten slag. An option existed to destroy all evidence of the work done there and to prevent the escape of a rogue organism.

Within the walls on each floor of the building were numerous bricklike packages of a highly incendiary material, developed by a foreign despot with a thing for fire and an affection for Victor. The doomsday countdown could be activated through a program that was on the computer menu under the name DRESDEN.

The program allowed for a countdown as short as ten minutes, as long as four hours, or of any duration in between. Deucalion expected a call momentarily from Michael, revealing a new location for their rendezvous. The Werner thing wouldn't finish acquiring all the staff of Mercy for at least another hour; and even thereafter, the anarchic nature of the beast would ensure that it didn't manage to break out of the hospital on a timely basis. Just in case Deucalion needed to return to Mercy because of something that came up during the meeting with Michael and Carson, he set the countdown clock at one hour.

On the screen appeared the numbers 60:00, and at once they changed to 59:59 as the end of Mercy drew closer second by second.

chapter 34

Christine, head housekeeper at the Helios mansion, was afflicted by a most peculiar condition. For six days, she had been confused about her identity.

Much of the time, she knew perfectly well who and what she was: Christine, a Beta, one of the New Race. She managed the house staff with efficiency, and was number two in authority, after the butler.

But there were moments when she believed she was someone else entirely, when she did not even remember that she was Christine or that she had been manufactured at the Hands of Mercy.

And, as a third condition, there were times when she remembered that she had been living here as Christine, a Beta, housekeeper to Mr Helios, but *also* remembered the other and more exciting identity into which she now and then entirely submerged.

Being one or the other, she could cope. But when aware of both existences, she became confused and anxious. As she was now.

Only a short while ago, she had been in the staff dormitory, at the back of the property, where she belonged at this hour.

But a few minutes ago, she found herself here in the library, not attending to any chore that was her responsibility, but browsing as though the book collection were hers. Indeed, she thought: *I must find a book that Mrs Van Hopper might like and send it to her with a warm note. It's not right that I seldom correspond with her. She's a difficult person, yes, but she was also kind to me in her way.*

She felt comfortable in the library, choosing a book for Mrs Van Hopper, until she realized that she wore a maid's uniform and rubber-soled work shoes. Under no circumstances could this be proper attire for the wife of Maxim de Winter and the mistress of Manderley.

If members of the staff encountered her in this costume, they would think Maxim's predicament had overstressed her. Already, some thought she was too young for him and not of a suitable social class.

Oh, and she would be mortified if Mrs Danvers discovered her in this outfit, and not merely mortified but finished. Mrs Danvers would whisper "mental breakdown' to anyone who would listen, and all would listen. Mrs Danvers, the head housekeeper, remained loyal to the previous Mrs de Winter and schemed to undermine the new wife's position in the house.

Head housekeeper?

Christine blinked, blinked, surveyed the library, blinked, and realized that *she* was the head housekeeper, not Mrs Danvers.

And this wasn't Manderley, not a great house in the west country of England, but a big house without a name in the Garden District of New Orleans.

Her identity confusion had begun when the New Race's primary mechanism for the release of stress – urgent, violent, multi-partner sex – ceased to provide her with any relief from her anxiety. Instead, the brutal orgies began to *increase* her anxiety.

The staff dormitory had television, which in theory could distract you from your worries, but the programming produced by the Old Race was so relentlessly stupid that it had little appeal to any member of the New Race above the level of an Epsilon.

In the dormitory, they could also download movies from the Internet. Most were no better than the TV shows, though once in a while you found a gem. The magnificent Hannibal Lecter could bring the entire staff to their feet, cheering till they were hoarse. And his nemesis, FBI agent Clarice Starling, was such an officious little meddling busybody that everyone enjoyed hissing at her.

Nine days ago, desperate for distraction from anxiety and despair, Christine downloaded Alfred Hitchcock's *Rebecca*. The film mesmerized her. Ostensibly, it was a romance, even a love story.

Love was a myth. Even if it wasn't a myth, it was stupid. Love represented the triumph of feeling over intellect. It distracted from achievement. It led to all kinds of social ills, such as family units to which people pledged greater allegiance than to their rulers. Love was a myth and it was evil, love was evil.

The film mesmerized her not because of the romance, but because everyone in the story had deep, dark secrets. The insane Mrs Danvers had secrets. Maxim de Winter had secrets that might destroy him. Rebecca, the first Mrs de Winter, kept secrets. The second Mrs de Winter started out as an idiot goody-goody, but by the end of the movie, she had a dark secret, because she collaborated to conceal a crime, all in the name of – no surprise – love.

Christine related to the movie because, like all of the New Race, she had secrets. Actually she *was* a deep, dark secret, walking among the Old Race, appearing innocent, but waiting impatiently to be told that she could kill as many of them as she wished.

The movie enchanted her also because the first Mrs de Winter deserved to die, like *all* the Old Race deserved to die. Crazy Mrs Danvers deserved to die – and burned to death in Manderley. Even the Old Race thought they deserved to die, and they were so *right*.

In spite of the reasons the movie enthralled Christine, it might not have led her into identity confusion if she had not been almost a twin to Joan Fontaine, the actress playing the second Mrs de Winter. The resemblance was uncanny. Even on the first viewing, Christine at times seemed to be experiencing the story from *inside* the movie.

She watched *Rebecca* five times that first night. And five times the following night. And five times the night after that.

Six days previously, after fifteen viewings, Christine began to experience identity confusion. She immersed herself in the film six times that night.

One thing that was so wonderful about being the second Mrs de Winter was that by the time Manderley burned to the ground, all the woman's problems were gone. Her life with Maxim would be troubled by no further drama or worry; and ahead were years of cozy routine . . .

How wonderful. Lovely, peaceful years. Tea every afternoon with little sandwiches and biscuits . . .

Manderley would be lost, and that was sad, but knowing that all would be well eventually, she should enjoy Manderley now as much as possible with Mrs Danvers always scheming.

She selected a suitable volume for Mrs Van Hopper, *Jamaica Inn*, which seemed to be a work of fiction, a light entertainment.

In a library-desk drawer, she found a selection of stationery for a variety of special occasions. She chose a cream-colored linen paper with a nosegay of colorful ribbons at the top.

She wrote a lovely note to Mrs Van Hopper, signed it "Mrs Maxim de Winter," inserted it in a matching envelope, sealed the flap, and put the envelope with *Jamaica Inn*. She would ask Christine to wrap and mail the package first thing in the morning.

chapter **35**

At this hour, only a battered Mustang, a pristine but forty-year-old Mercedes, and a Ford Explorer occupied the fourth floor of the public parking garage.

Carson let the Honda idle beside each vehicle, while Michael got out to determine if anyone might be sleeping in it. No, no, and no. They had the fourth floor to themselves.

Through the open sides of the building, a growing wind flung glassy beads of rain to shatter on the concrete floor. Carson parked the Honda in an empty row in the dry center of the garage.

Let out of the car, Duke trotted around the immediate area, investigating a discarded candy wrapper, a half-crushed Starbucks cup, an empty Big Mac container . . .

They left the Urban Snipers in the Honda. They still had their service pistols in shoulder rigs, the .50 Magnums in belt scabbards.

As Michael fished his phone out of a coat pocket and keyed in Deucalion's number, Carson watched for movement among the forest of concrete columns, listened for footsteps. She recognized the danger of prudence sliding into paranoia; nevertheless, she stood with her right arm across her body, thumb hooked on her belt, which brought her gun hand within inches of the Desert Eagle under her blazer, on her left hip.

For anyone drawn into an orbit around Victor Helios, the word *impossible* no longer had any meaning. So maybe in his spare time, the Transylvanian transplant scored some pterodactyl DNA, combined it with a sociopathic homeboy's genes, and cooked up a man-reptile cop killer that would swoop in from the storm. Chances were she wasn't going to die from a heart attack or from anything else that would leave a neat corpse, but she was for damn sure not going to be torn apart in the jaws of a gangbanger-dragon hybrid wearing a do-rag and a gold nose ring.

Deucalion must have taken the call, because Michael said, "Hey, it's me. We're in a parking garage. Fourth floor."

After giving the address, Michael hung up.

As the phone produced an end-call beep, Deucalion stepped into the garage about twenty feet away, as though he'd come out of Narnia through a wardrobe, except there wasn't even a wardrobe.

Carson always forgot how big he was until she saw him again. In his long black coat, as he approached them, he looked like Darth Vader on a steroids-only diet.

"You're wet," Deucalion said.

"We were in a monster mash at Audubon Park," Michael said. "One of them had a nice butt."

Duke padded around the car, saw the tattooed newcomer, halted, and cocked his head.

"Whose dog?" Deucalion asked.

"He belonged to the district attorney," Michael said, "then to the district attorney's replicant, but the replicant walked smack into a bunch of shotgun slugs, so now Duke belongs to us."

"Things are going to get apocalyptic soon," Deucalion said. "A dog will get in your way."

"Not this dog. He's one of those highly trained service dogs. When we switch from shotguns to .50 Magnums, he can reload the empty weapons for us."

To Carson, Deucalion said, "I'm never sure I understand half the things he says."

"Eventually you don't care," Carson assured him.

"Michael has hyperactive disorder, but he talks fast enough to keep himself entertained, so he's not a lot of trouble."

Duke approached Deucalion, tail wagging.

Holding one of his hands down to allow the dog to lick his fingers, Deucalion stared so intently at Carson that she felt X-rayed, and then he turned the same stare on Michael.

"It was not an accident that I crossed your path rather than that of other detectives. You're different from most who carry a badge, and I am different from everyone. Our difference is our strength. We have been chosen for this, and if we fail – the world fails."

Michael grimaced. "That wouldn't look good on my résumé."

"Earlier, at the Luxe," Carson said, referring to the just shuttered movie theater where Deucalion lived, "you said Victor has progressed doggedly for so long, in spite of his setbacks, he has no fear of failure, he believes his triumph is inevitable. So he's blind to the rot in his empire. At the time, I thought the rot might not be as extensive as you hoped. But after our lark in the park with those replicants . . . maybe collapse is coming even sooner than you think."

Pulses of inner light passed through the giant's eyes. "Yes. The clock is ticking."

After listening to Deucalion's one-minute abridged version of his discoveries in the Hands of Mercy, Carson was left with stomach acid burning in the back of her throat and a clutching chill in the pit of her stomach.

"When does the place melt down?" Michael asked.

"In fifty-five minutes. When Victor hears about the fire, he'll know I did it, but he won't know how out of control things were in there tonight. He'll continue to trust his New Race to defend him. But he won't risk staying in the Garden District. He'll fall back to the farm."

Carson said, "The creation-tank farm, the New Race factory Pastor Kenny told you about?"

"As I learned tonight, it's farther along than Kenny thought. The first crop begins rising from the tanks tomorrow night – five hundred a day for four days."

Michael said, "We *way* underestimated our ammo needs."

"Victor owns large tracts of land north of Lake Pontchartrain." From an inside coat pocket, Deucalion withdrew a packet of papers. "I retrieved the information from his computer. There's a place called Crosswoods Waste Management, owned by a Nevada corporation, which is owned by a holding company in the Bahamas, which is held by a trust in Switzerland. But in the end, it's all just Victor."

"Waste management?" Carson said. "Is that a dump?"

"It is a very large dump."

"What would he want with a dump?"

"A graveyard for his failures and for the people his replicants replace."

Michael said, "It must have a more memorable smell than your average dump."

"The tank farm is on a twenty-acre property adjacent to the dump. We're going to be there well ahead of Victor. In fact, I will be there in ten minutes." Deucalion handed the packet of papers to Carson. "Addresses, background, a little reading for the road. If you take Interstate 10 east to Interstate 12 west, then the state route north as I've marked, it's about seventy miles, less than an hour and a half."

"A lot less if she's driving," Michael said.

"When you're getting near, call me," Deucalion said. "We'll join forces there."

"And then what?" Carson asked.

"And then . . . whatever's necessary."

chapter 36

Erika Five loaded a stainless-steel cart with everything Jocko needed, and took it to the second floor in the service elevator.

After Victor had joined the original two residences, there were three hallways. At the south end of the house, the south-wing hall ran east-west. At the north end, the hall also ran east-west. Each measured eighty feet. Those corridors were connected by the main hall, which extended 182 feet.

In the south wing, the service elevator was not far from the kitchen. Once upstairs, Erika had to push the cart the length of the main hall to the north wing, where the troll waited in his new quarters toward the back of the house.

The double doors to the master suite were at the midpoint of the main hall, on the left, opposite the head of the grand staircase. She thought Victor remained in the suite, but she couldn't be sure. If by chance he stepped into the hall and saw her pushing the cart stacked with bedding, towels, toiletries, and food, he would want to know where she was going and to what purpose.

The nine-foot-wide hallway featured a series of Persian rugs, as in the north and the south halls, and the cart rolled silently across them. Where mahogany flooring lay exposed between rugs, the rubber wheels made only a faint noise.

When, with relief, Erika entered the unfurnished north-wing suite, the troll was standing on the points of his toes, pirouetting.

She rolled the cart into the living room. Closing the door to the hall, she said, "Where did you learn to dance?"

"Is Jocko dancing?" he asked, continuing to spin.

"That's ballet."

"It's just . . . a thing . . . Jocko does," he said, and pirouetted into the bedroom.

Following with the cart, Erika said, "Don't you get very dizzy?"

"Sometimes . . . Jocko vomits."

"Well then, you better stop."

"No control."

Putting the bedding on the floor, in a corner, Erika said, "You mean you're compelled to pirouette?"

The troll spun to a stop, came off pointe, and weaved a few steps before regaining his equilibrium. "Not so bad that time."

"You poor thing."

He shrugged. "Everybody's got problems."

"That's very philosophical."

"Most worse than mine."

Erika was pretty sure there weren't many fates worse than being a grotesque troll with three hairs on your tongue, penniless, living mostly in storm drains, with a compulsion to spin until you threw up. But she admired the little guy's positive attitude.

In the bathroom, Jocko helped her unload the cart and distribute the items to cabinets and drawers. He was delighted with the supply of snack foods that she had brought.

"Jocko likes salty, Jocko likes sweet, but never bring Jocko any hot sauce, like with jalapeños, because it makes Jocko squirt funny-smelling stuff out his ears."

"I'll be sure to remember that," Erika said. "Of course, I'll bring you healthy meals whenever I can, not just snack foods. Is there anything you don't like besides hot sauce?"

"Jocko's been living mostly in storm drains, eating bugs and rats. And hot sauce on corn chips that one time. Anything you bring is delicious enough for Jocko."

"This is very exciting, isn't it?" Erika said.

"What is?"

"Having a secret friend."

"Who does?"

"I do."

"What friend?"

"You."

"Oh. Yes. Jocko is excited."

Putting away the last of the towels, she said, "I'll be back in the morning, in just a few hours, after Victor has gone to the Hands of Mercy, and then you can read to me."

Sitting on the edge of the tub, Jocko asked, "Is this good to eat?"

"No, that's bath soap."

"Oh. Is this good to eat?"

"That's another bath soap."

"So it's good to eat?"

"No. Soap is never good to eat."

"Is this good to eat?"

"That's also bath soap. It's a four-pack."

"Why soap, soap, soap, soap?"

"I brought extras of several things. You're going to be here awhile . . . Aren't you?"

"As long as you say Jocko can."

"Good. That's very good."

"Now go away," said Jocko.

"Oh, of course, you must be tired."

"Must be," he agreed, following her into the living room. "Go away."

Erika left the stainless-steel cart, intending to return it to the kitchen in the morning, after Victor went to the lab.

Cracking the door, she scoped the hallway, which was deserted and quiet. Glancing back at the troll, she said, "Don't be afraid."

"You either."

"You're safe."

"You too."

"Just lie low."

"Go away."

Stepping into the hall, Erika quietly pulled the door shut behind her.

chapter 37

The instant the door closed, Jocko scampered into the bathroom. Snatched up a bar of soap. Tore the wrapper off. Took a bite.

Erika was wrong. Soap looked delicious, and it *was*.

She was wrong or . . . *she lied*.

How sad she would lie. She seemed so different from others. So pretty. So kind. Such delicate nostrils. But a liar.

Almost everybody lied. The world was a kingdom of lies.

Jocko lied, too. Told her he was Harker.

True, he came out of Harker. All Harker's knowledge. Harker's memories. But he wasn't Harker.

Jocko was Jocko, unique. Jocko wanted what Jocko wanted. Not what anybody else wanted.

Only one way Jocko and Harker were alike. Hated Victor Helios. *Hated* him.

One thing Jocko wanted, Harker had wanted. Victor Helios dead.

Jocko was Jocko. But he was also *vengeance*.

Soap tasted better than rats. Almost as good as bugs. But so chewy. Not easy to swallow.

Jocko put down the half-eaten bar. Didn't have time for so much chewing. Later.

Jocko wanted what Jocko wanted. Wanted it so bad. But couldn't have what he wanted until he killed Victor Helios.

He dashed into the living room. Stood on his hands. Walked around the room on his hands. Around and around.

Such a waste of time. Jocko didn't want to walk around on his hands. But he just *had* to.

Finally, enough. On his feet again. To the bathroom again. One more bite of soap. Good.

Time to kill Victor.

Quick, quick, quick through the bedroom. Through the living room. To the door.

———

As she turned away from the door to Jocko's quarters, Erika knew that she should go to the master suite to see if Victor wanted her for any reason.

However, the prospect of her secret friend reading to her from a book so excited her that she didn't want to wait until morning to select the volume for their initial session. She descended the back stairs at the west end of the north wing, eager to explore what titles the library offered.

The grand hall on the ground floor measured twelve feet across, a third more spacious than the upstairs hallways. It was furnished with sideboards, pairs of chairs separated by tables on which stood bowls of flowers, and pedestals supporting magnificent figurative bronzes. The walls were hung with priceless works by the European masters of the sixteenth, seventeenth, and eighteenth centuries, which Victor had been clever enough to smuggle out of Germany shortly before his patron and dear friend, the much misunderstood and delightfully witty Hitler, whom Victor called *mein schatz*, "my treasure," was tragically brought to grief by the ignorant masses, by greedy capitalists, by voracious bankers, and by religious fanatics.

Victor suffered so much frustration and loss in his long life that Erika, who had been given everything from birth, might need twenty years, thirty, or longer to understand him. The problem was, thus far the Erikas tended to be short-lived.

Her best hope of understanding her husband, of learning how to be the kind of wife who never triggered his rage, seemed to be books. Books were dangerous, yes, but they were dangerous because they contained so much knowledge both of the helpful kind and the harmful kind. Perhaps Erika Four absorbed too much of the wrong information, things that would never be included in an education acquired by direct-to-brain data downloading, and was thereby corrupted. Erika Five intended to proceed cautiously with books, always alert for the harmful kind of knowledge.

She enjoyed an advantage over Erika Four: She had Jocko. She would instruct him to be always on the lookout for knowledge that was harmful in any way, to censor it as he read, so that she wouldn't be contaminated by it. If a book contained too much harmful information to remain comprehensible when all of the bad stuff had been redacted, she would return it to the shelves and choose another.

Entering the library, Erika saw Christine getting up from the desk, holding a book and an envelope. She should have been in the staff dormitory.

"Why are you here at this hour?" Erika asked.

"Oh, goodness, you startled me." Christine pushed the desk chair into the kneehole. "I've been selecting a book to send to a friend, and writing her a warm note of remembrance, with apologies for having been frightfully behind in my correspondence."

Christine seemed to be speaking with a slight English accent.

"But these books don't belong to you," Erika reminded her.

Straightening her shoulders and lifting her head in what might have been defiance, Christine said, "I should think any books that belong to my husband also belong to me."

"Your husband?" Erika said.

"Yes, Mrs Danvers, quite mine. Rebecca is gone. I rather think you should get used to that."

Erika didn't need to learn anything from a book to know that Christine was suffering what Victor referred to as an interruption of function. The previous morning, the butler, William, had bitten off seven of his fingers during an interruption of function. For the moment, at least, Christine's condition wasn't as serious as William's.

Approaching the maid, Erika reached out for the book. "I'll take care of that for you."

Pressing the volume and the letter to her bosom, Christine said, "No thank you, Mrs Danvers. In the morning, I shall ask Christine to package and post it."

———

In a superbly tailored blue suit, white silk shirt with spread collar, and sapphire-amber-emerald striped tie, with an amber display handkerchief, carrying the Springfield Armory Colt .45 in a concealed shoulder rig that did not interfere at all with the elegant drape of the coat, Victor studied his reflection, and the mirror presented to him a man who had the style and the bearing of a sovereign born to the throne.

Because there were mirrors also at the Hands of Mercy, he left the closet. As he crossed the bedroom, his cell phone rang.

He stopped at the door to the hall and, after a hesitation, took the call. "Yes?"

"My esteemed master, my glorious brute," said Erika Four, "we have prepared a resting place for you at the dump."

He was resolved not to lose his temper and determined not to let her dominate as she had in her previous call. "I thought you were coming home."

"We have lined your grave with the rotting cadavers of some of your Old Race victims, and with the remains of those of your people who failed you and could not be resuscitated as I was."

"Perhaps," he said, "you have the courage to call but not the courage to face me."

"Oh, darling, sublime megalomaniac, you are the emperor of self-delusion. I will face you soon enough. I will smile at you and blow a kiss as we bury you alive in the depths of the dump."

Victor happened to be looking at the doorknob when it began to turn. He drew the .45 from his shoulder rig.

————

Quick, quick, quick, Jocko scurried east along the north hall. Stopped at the corner. Peeked around. Nobody in sight.

A bite of soap would be nice. Stay focused. Kill first. Soap later.

He knew where to find the master bedroom. Erika mentioned it when sneaking him up the back stairs. Main hall. Opposite the grand staircase.

Tippytoe, tippytoe, across soft rugs. Pretty rugs. Would be fun to twirl on rugs so soft and pretty.

No! Don't think about twirling. Don't even *think* about it.

Grand staircase to the left. Double doors to the right. This was the place.

Standing at the doors, hand on a doorknob, Jocko heard a muffled voice. Harker's memory said, *Victor's voice.* Just beyond these doors.

"Perhaps you have the courage to call but not the courage to face me," Victor Helios said.

A murderous fury gripped Jocko. As he tried to bare his teeth, the flaps of his mouth quivered against them.

Jocko knew what he would say. As he attacked Victor. Ferocious. Merciless. He would say, *I am the child of Jonathan Harker! He died to birth me! I am an outcast, a monster from a monster! Now you die!*

That seemed like a mouthful. He had tried to edit it. But he really, really wanted to say it all.

He started to turn the doorknob. Almost threw the door open. Then realized. No weapon. Jocko didn't have a weapon.

Furious with himself, Jocko let the knob slip through his hand and, after all, did not burst into the master suite.

Stupid, stupid, stupid. He hooked two fingers in his nostrils. He pulled back toward his forehead. Pulled so hard tears streamed from his eyes. He deserved it.

Focus. *Stay* focused.

He needed a weapon. Knew where to get one. Kitchen. A knife.

Tippytoe, tippytoe, quick along the main hall. More soft rugs. To the south hall. Down the back stairs.

———

In the library, Erika said, "My name isn't Mrs Danvers."

Christine still spoke with a light English accent. "Please, Mrs Danvers, I quite want to avoid unpleasantness of any kind. We can co-exist. I am confident we can, and we should. I know *I* want to, for Maxim's sake."

"Don't you recognize me?" Erika asked. "What is wrong with you? Don't you know where you are?"

Christine looked distressed, and her mouth trembled as if she might become emotional in a way precluded by her program. Clutching the book, regaining her composure, she said, "I am not as fragile a spirit as I might look, Mrs Danvers."

"Erika. I'm Erika."

"Do not think you can convince me that my mind is going. I am weary of your wicked games." She pushed past Erika and left the room in a rush.

———

Sneak, pause, reconnoiter. Sneak, pause, reconnoiter. Stairs to hall to kitchen.

Oh. On a counter in the kitchen was a large bowl of apples. Yellow apples. Red apples.

The apples drew Jocko. So colorful. Not too big. He wanted them. Had to have them. *Had* to have. Apples, apples, apples. Not to eat. Something better.

Jocko selected three apples. Two yellow, one red.

Beginning with two apples in his right hand, one in his left, he juggled. Loved to juggle. *Needed* to juggle.

He had juggled before. Stones. Walnuts. Two spoiled lemons and a package of rancid cheese. Three rat skulls.

Apples were the best yet. Colorful. Almost round. Jocko was good. He could even caper while juggling.

He capered around the kitchen. Juggling, juggling. He wished he had a funny hat. One with bells.

———

On the phone, Erika Four said, "There is a legion in the dump, my darling psychopath. I need not come for you alone."

"Only a legion of the dead," Victor said. "And the dead don't rise again."

"Like me, they were not fully dead. Mistaken for dead, but with a trace of life remaining . . . and after a while, more than a trace."

The doorknob had turned one way, then the other. For almost a minute now, it had not moved.

"We will carry you by torchlight down into the bowels of the dump. And though we'll bury you alive, we'll have our fun with you before interment."

The knob turned again.

———

From the library, she hurried directly to the front stairs and ascended to the second floor. Enough was enough. Maxim would have to speak with Mrs Danvers. The woman's loyalty to Rebecca exceeded that of a faithful servant, was nothing as innocent as honest sentiment. It was mean, perverse, and suggested an unbalanced mind.

She threw open the door, swept into the master suite, and was shot four times in the chest by her beloved Maxim, whose treachery stunned her, though as she fell, she realized that he must have shot Rebecca, too.

————

Jocko, capering in the kitchen, dropped the apples when the gunfire boomed.

Knife. He had forgotten the knife. Victor waited to be killed, and Jocko forgot the knife.

He hit himself in the face. Hit, hit, hit himself. He deserved to be smacked twice as often as he was. Three times.

One drawer, two drawers, three . . . In the fifth drawer, knives. He selected a big one. Very sharp.

Tippytoe, tippytoe, out of the kitchen, into the hall.

chapter 38

Duke slept in the backseat of the Honda during the drive east-northeast on I-10 and then west on I-12.

The dog's snoring didn't induce drowsiness in Carson, though it ought to have, considering how little sack time she'd grabbed in the past couple of days.

The half liter of supercaffeinated cola from Acadiana helped. Before crossing the city line, they stopped at a combination service station and convenience store that was open 24/7, where they drained themselves of some of the first cola they had consumed, and then bought two more half-liter bottles. They also bought a package of caffeine tablets.

As they hit the road again, Michael said, "Too much caffeine ties the prostate in knots."

"I don't have a prostate."

"Carson, you know, everything isn't always about you."

One thing keeping her awake and focused was the suspicion that the Helios-Frankenstein case might be as much about her as it was about anyone. Not merely because she happened to be one of the two detectives who stumbled on the case. And not because her path crossed Deucalion's just when she needed to meet him.

Of all the cops Carson knew, she and Michael had the deepest respect for individualism, especially when a particular individual was quirky and therefore amusing or even if he proved stubborn and frustrating. Consequently, they were more alarmed than some might have been by the prospect of a civilization with a single-minded purpose and a regimented population of obedient drones, whether that population was comprised of propagandized human beings or of pseudo-humans cultured in a lab.

But her respect for individualism and her love of freedom was not why this case was so powerfully, immediately, intimately about *her*. Early in this investigation, she began to suspect that her father, who had been a detective with the NOPD, might have been murdered by the New Race – and her mother with him – at the order of Victor Helios. Her dad could have encountered something exceedingly strange that had led him to Helios, just as his daughter would be led to the same suspect years later.

Her parents' murders had never been solved. And the evidence concocted to portray her father as a corrupt cop – who might have been executed by criminal elements with which he was involved – had always been too pat, an insult to common sense, and an offense against the truth of her dad's character.

Over the past few days, her suspicion developed into conviction. As much as the caffeine, a hunger for justice and a determination to clear her father's name kept her awake, alert, and ready to rumble.

The vast lightless expanse of Pontchartrain lay to their left, and it seemed to have the irresistible gravity of a collapsed star, as if this night the world were rolling along its rim, at risk of spiraling down into oblivion.

Except in the headlights, the rain that came off the lake was black, insistently rapping against the driver's side of the car as they drove west on I-12, as if the night itself had fists of bony knuckles. And the wind seemed black, blowing down out of a moonless and starless sky.

chapter **39**

Having believed that Erika Four was bursting in upon him, Victor fired twice, intending to stop both of her hearts, before he realized that the intruder was Christine. As the designer of her kind, he knew precisely where to aim. And because he started the job with such expert marksmanship, he had no choice but to finish it with two more shots.

Christine dropped, although death did not at once take her. She spasmed on the floor of the master bedroom vestibule, gasping for breath, futilely pressing her hands to her chest as if she might be able to plug the wounds from which her life bled.

During Christine's final throes, Erika appeared in the hall, just beyond the open door, and Victor raised the pistol from the dying housekeeper, to train it on whichever of his Erikas stood before him.

"Something was wrong with Christine," she said. "She didn't seem to know who she was. She thought I was someone named Mrs Danvers."

"Do *you* know who you are?" Victor asked.

She frowned at the muzzle of the pistol and at the question. "What do you mean?"

"Who are you!" Victor demanded with such vehemence that she flinched, as if reminded of the intensity with which he could deliver a beating when she deserved one.

"I'm Erika. Your wife."

"Erika Five?"

She looked puzzled. "Yes, of course."

"Then tell me – what is the most dangerous thing in the world?"

"Books," she said at once. "Books corrupt."

Erika Four had been allowed to read, which led to her death. Only Erika Five was created with a proscription against reading books. A resurrected Erika Four could have no way of knowing this.

On the floor, Christine said, "Manderley . . ." and her eyes glazed over.

She appeared to have died. Victor kicked her head, testing her response, but she didn't twitch or make a sound.

Beside her on the floor was a book titled *Jamaica Inn*.

Returning the pistol to his shoulder holster, Victor said, "What was the word she just spoke?"

"Manderley," said Erika.

"What language is it, what does it mean?"

Surprised, she said, "It's the name of a great English house, a literary allusion. I've got it in my program. Like, I might say to someone we visited, 'Oh, my dear, your house is even more wonderful than Manderley *and* your housekeeper isn't insane.'"

"Yes, all right, but to what work does it refer?"

"Daphne du Maurier's *Rebecca*," Erika said, "which I have never read and never will."

"Books again," he fumed, and in anger this time, he kicked the dead housekeeper, and then the book that had fallen from her hand. "I'll send a team to bring this trash to the Hands of Mercy for an autopsy. Clean up the blood yourself."

"Yes, Victor."

———

Skip, skip, hop. Skip, skip, hop. Along the south hall. Skip, skip, hop. Knife in hand.

The back stairs. Three steps up, one step back. Three steps up, one step back.

Racing, in his fashion, toward vengeance, Jocko reminded himself of the speech he must make. As he drove the blade deep into Victor, he must say: *I am the child of he who I was before I was me! I died to birth me! I am a monster, outcast and castaway! Die, Harker, die!*

No. All wrong. So much practice in so many storm drains. And still Jocko didn't have it right.

Climbing twice as many stairs as he descended, Jocko tried again: *You are the monster child of he who I!*

No, no, no. Not even close.

I am you he who I am who die!

Jocko was so angry with himself that he wanted to spit. He *did* spit. And he spat again. On his feet. Two steps up, one step back, spit. Two steps up, one step back, spit.

Finally he reached the top step, feet glistening.

In the second-floor south hall, Jocko stopped to collect his thoughts. There was one. And here was another. And here was a third thought, connected to the other two. Very nice.

Jocko often had to collect his thoughts. They scattered so easily.

I am the child of Jonathan Harker! He died to birth me! I am a juggler, monsters and apples! Now you die!

Close enough.

Tippytoe, tippytoe, east along the south hall, across soft rugs. Toward the main corridor.

Jocko heard voices. In his head? Could be. Had been before. No, no, not this time. Real voices. In the main hallway.

The corner. Careful. Jocko halted, peeked around.

Erika stood in the hallway, at the open master-suite doors. Talking to someone inside, probably Victor.

So pretty. Such shimmering hair. She had lips. Jocko wished he had lips, too.

"It's the name of a great English house, a literary allusion," Erika said to probably Victor.

Her voice soothed Jocko. Her voice was music.

As a calmness came over Jocko, he realized that he was different when in her company. With her, he didn't feel compelled to do so much skipping, hopping, spitting, pirouetting, juggling, capering, nostril pulling, scampering, and walking on his hands.

She lied to Jocko. Lied about the tastiness of soap. Otherwise, however, she was a positive influence.

Eighty or ninety feet away, Victor Helios appeared. Out of the master suite. Tall. Trim. Excellent hair on his head, probably none on his tongue. Pretty suit.

Jocko thought: *Die, juggler, die!*

Victor walked past Erika. To the stairs. Said one last thing to her. Started down.

Jocko had the knife. The knife belonged in Victor.

A *thousand* knives belonged in Victor.

Jocko only had two hands. Could juggle three knives with two hands, put them in Victor. Trying to juggle a thousand knives, Jocko would probably lose some fingers.

To reach Victor with one pathetic knife, Jocko must run past Erika. That would be awkward.

She would see him. Would know he broke his promise. More than one promise. Would know he lied. Would be disappointed in him.

And she might smell soap on his breath.

Erika moved to the stairs. Watched Victor descend.

Maybe she saw Jocko. From the corner of her eye. She started to turn. Turn toward Jocko.

Jocko ducked back. Away from the corner.

Hoppity-hoppity-hop. Hoppity-hoppity-hop. West along the south hall. Backward down the stairs.

Kitchen again. Apples on the floor. Oranges would be even more round. Jocko must ask for oranges. And scissors to trim his tongue hairs.

Jocko capered out of the kitchen, through a butler's pantry, across an intimate dining room.

Beyond was a large, formal dining room. Jocko didn't see it too clearly because he had to, had to, *had to pirouette.*

Room after room, small connecting halls, so much house. Walking on his hands, knife gripped in one foot. Cartwheeling, cartwheeling, knife in his teeth.

North hall. Back stairs. Second floor. His suite.

Jocko hid the knife in his bedding. He scampered back into the living room. Sat on the floor in front of the fireplace. Enjoying the fireplace without fire.

She would say: *I thought I saw you in the hall.*

He would say: *No, not Jocko, not Jocko. No, no, no. Not I who am from he who was, monster from monster, no, not Jocko, not in the hall and not eating soap.*

Or maybe he would just say *No.*

Jocko would play it by ear. See what seemed right at the time.

After gazing at no fire for half a minute, Jocko realized he had forgotten to kill Victor.

Jocko hooked fingers in his nostrils and pulled them toward his brow until his eyes watered. He deserved worse.

chapter **40**

Following the failure of the freezer motors, the saline solution in the transparent sack begins to warm.

After the busy visitor in the laboratory throws the sink that smashes the glass door, the pace of the warming accelerates.

The first improvement in Chameleon's condition concerns its vision. In the cold environment, it sees only shades of blue. Now it begins to apprehend other colors, gradually at first, and then more rapidly.

For so long, Chameleon has drifted in the sack, mobility limited by the bitter cold of the fluid in which it is immersed. Now it is able to flex its abdomen and thorax. Its head turns more easily.

Suddenly it thrashes, thrashes again, a great commotion that causes the hanging sack to swing side to side and bump against the walls of the disabled freezer.

In semisuspended animation, Chameleon's metabolism performs at a basal rate so low as to be almost undetectable. As the fluid in the sack warms, the catabolic processes increase.

With the energy provided by catabolism, anabolic processes begin to speed up. Chameleon is returning to full function.

The thrashing signifies a need for air. The highly oxygenated solution in the sack maintains Chameleon in subfreezing cold, but is inadequate to sustain it at full metabolic function.

Suffocation panic triggers Chameleon's thrashing.

Although the polymeric fabric of the sack is as strong as bullet-proof Kevlar, Chameleon's combat claws rip it open.

Fourteen gallons of chemically treated saline solution gush out of the sack, spilling Chameleon into the freezer, through the missing door, and onto the floor of the laboratory.

Air flows into its spiracles and follows the tracheal tubes that branch throughout its body.

As it dries out, Chameleon regains its sense of smell.

It is able to detect only two odors: a specially engineered pheromone with which all of the New Race are tagged, and human beings of the Old Race, who are identifiable by a melange of pheromones *lacking* that New Race spice.

The smell of the New Race pleases Chameleon, and therefore they are EXEMPTS.

Because the Old Race lacks the artificial pheromone, their scent infuriates Chameleon, and they are TARGETS.

Chameleon lives to kill.

At the moment, it smells only EXEMPTS. And even all of them seem to be dead, sprawled throughout the room.

It crawls across the debris-strewn floor of the wrecked lab, through pools of water, seeking prey.

Every external tissue of Chameleon mimics to the smallest

detail the surface under it: color, pattern, texture. No matter how simple or complex the ground under it, Chameleon will blend with it.

To any observer looking down on it, Chameleon is invisible when not in motion.

If Chameleon moves, the observer may sense something amiss, but he will not understand what his eyes perceive: a vague shifting of a part of the floor, an impossible rippling of a solid surface, as if the wood or stone, or the lawn, has become fluid.

Most of the time, the observer will interpret this phenomenon not as a real event but as disturbing evidence of a problem internal to himself: dizziness or hallucination, or the first symptom of an oncoming stroke.

Often, the observer will close his eyes for a moment, to settle his disturbed senses. Closing his eyes is the end of him.

If Chameleon is on a higher plane than the floor, perhaps a kitchen countertop, it will remain invisible from the side only if the backsplash is of the same material as the surface on which it stands. Otherwise, it will be visible as a silhouette.

For this reason, Chameleon generally remains low as it stalks its prey. A TARGET becomes aware of his attacker only when it skitters up his leg, ripping as it goes.

The wrecked lab offers no TARGETS.

Chameleon proceeds into the hallway. Here it discovers numerous EXEMPTS, all dead.

Taking more time to consider these cadavers than it did those in the lab, Chameleon discovers heads split open, brains missing.

Interesting.

This is not how Chameleon does its work. Effective, however.

Among the debrained EXEMPTS, Chameleon detects a whiff of a TARGET. One of the Old Race has been here recently.

Chameleon follows the scent to the stairs.

chapter 41

Rain had not yet reached the parishes above Lake Pontchartrain. The humid night lay unbreathing but expectant, as if the low overcast and the dark land had compressed the air between them until at any moment an electric discharge would shock the heart of the storm into a thunderous beating.

Deucalion stood on a deserted two-lane road, outside Crosswoods Waste Management. The facility was enormous. A high chain-link fence was topped with coils of barbed wire and fitted with continuous nylon privacy panels. RESTRICTED AREA signs every forty feet warned of the health hazards of a landfill.

Outside the fence, a triple phalanx of loblolly pines encircled the property, the rows offset from one another. Between ninety and a hundred feet tall, these trees formed an effective screen, blocking views into the dump from the somewhat higher slopes to the north and east.

Deucalion walked off the road, among the pines, and went

through the fence by way of a gate that didn't exist – a quantum gate – into the dump.

He had night vision better than that of the Old Race, even better than that of the New. His enhanced eyesight, not the work of Victor, was perhaps another gift delivered on the lightning that had animated him, the ghost of which still sometimes throbbed through his gray eyes.

He walked a rampart of compacted earth, a span more than wide enough to accommodate an SUV. To both his left and right, well below the level of this elevated pathway, were huge lakes of trash heaped in uneven swells that would eventually be plowed level before being capped with eight feet of earth and methane-gas vent pipes.

The stench offended, but he had encountered worse in the past two hundred years. In his first two decades, after leaving Victor for dead in the arctic, Deucalion frequently had been seized by the urge to violence, raging at the injustice of having been stitched together and animated by a narcissistic would-be god who could give his creation neither meaning nor peace, nor any hope of fellowship and community. In his most haunted and self-pitying hours, Deucalion prowled graveyards and broke into granite crypts, mausoleums, where he tore open caskets and forced himself to gaze upon the decomposing corpses, saying aloud to himself, "Here is what you are, just dead flesh, dead flesh, the bones and guts of arsonists, of murderers, filled with false life, dead and alive, not fit for any other world but an abomination in this one." Standing at those open caskets, he'd known stenches that, by comparison, made this Louisiana dump smell as sweet as a rose garden.

In those graveyard visits, during those long staring matches with sightless cadavers, he had yearned to die. Although he tried, he was unable to submit to a well-stropped razor or to a hangman's noose that he fashioned, and at every cliff's edge, he could not take the final step. So in those long nights when he kept company with the dead, he argued with himself to embrace the necessity for self-destruction.

The proscription against suicide had not come from Victor.

In his earliest strivings for godhood, that vainglorious beast wasn't able to program his first creation as well as he programmed those he brewed up these days. Victor had planted a device in Deucalion's skull, which had cratered half the giant's face when he tried to strike his maker. But Victor had not in those days been able to forbid suicide.

After years marked by a frustrated death wish as much as by rage, Deucalion had arrived at a humbling realization. The edict that so effectively stayed his hand from destroying himself came from a more powerful and infinitely more mysterious source than Victor. He was denied felo-de-se because he had a purpose in life, even if he could not – at that time – recognize what it might be, a vital mission that he must fulfill before final peace would be granted him.

Two hundred years had at last brought him to Louisiana, to this reeking wasteyard that was a trash dump *and* a graveyard. The pending storm would be not merely one of thunder, lightning, wind, and rain, but also one of justice, judgment, execution, and damnation.

To his left, far out in the west pit, flames flickered. A dozen small fires moved one behind the other, as if they were torches held by people in a procession.

chapter 42

Erika stood over the body of Christine for a minute, trying to understand why Victor had shot her to death.

Although Christine seemed to have become convinced that she was someone other than herself, she had not been threatening. Quite the opposite: She had been confused and distraught, and in spite of her contention that she was not "as fragile a spirit' as she might look, she had the air of a shy, uncertain girl not yet a woman.

Yet Victor shot her four times in her two hearts. And kicked her head twice, after she was dead.

Instead of wrapping the body for whoever would collect it and at once cleaning up the blood as instructed, Christine surprised herself by returning to the troll's quarters in the north wing. She knocked softly and said sotto voce, *"It's me, Erika,"* because she didn't want to disturb the little guy if he was sitting in a corner, sucking on his toes, his mind having gone away to the red place to rest.

With a discretion that matched hers, he said, *"Come in,"* just loud enough for her to hear him when she pressed her ear to the door.

In the living room, she found him sitting on the floor in front of the dark fireplace, as if flames warmed the hearth.

Sitting beside him, she said, "Did you hear the gunshots?"

"No. Jocko heard nothing."

"I thought you must have heard them and might be frightened."

"No. And Jocko wasn't juggling apples, either. Not Jocko. Not here in his rooms."

"Apples? I didn't bring you apples."

"You are very kind to Jocko."

"Would you like some apples?"

"Three oranges would be better."

"I'll bring you some oranges later. Is there anything else you would like?"

Although the troll's unfortunate face could produce many expressions that might cause cardiac arrest in an entire pack of attacking wolves, Erika found him cute, if not most of the time, at least occasionally cute, like now.

Somehow his separately terrifying features conspired to come together in a sweet, yearning expression. His enormous yellow eyes sparkled with delight when he considered what else he might like in addition to the oranges.

He said, "Oh, there is a thing, a special thing, that I would like, but it's too much. Jocko doesn't deserve it."

"If I'm able to get it for you," she said, "I will. So what is this special thing?"

"No, no. What Jocko deserves is his nostrils pulled back to his eyebrows. Jocko deserves to hit himself hard in the face, to spit on his own feet, to stick his head in a toilet and flush and flush and flush, to tie a ten-pound sledgehammer to his tongue and throw the hammer over a bridge railing, that's what Jocko deserves."

"Nonsense," said Erika. "You have some peculiar ideas, little friend. You don't deserve such treatment any more than you would like the taste of soap."

"I know better now about the soap," he assured her.

"Good. And I'm going to teach you some self-esteem, too."

"What is self-esteem?"

"To like yourself. I'm going to teach you to like yourself."

"Jocko tolerates Jocko. Jocko doesn't like Jocko."

"That's very sad."

"Jocko doesn't trust Jocko."

"Why wouldn't you trust yourself?"

Pondering her question, the troll smacked the flaps of his mouth for a moment and then said, "Let's say Jocko wanted a knife."

"For what?"

"Let's say . . . for paring his toenails."

"I can get you clippers for that."

"But let's just say. Let's just say Jocko wanted a knife to pare his toenails, and let's say it was really urgent. The toenails – see, they had to be pared right away, *right away*, or all hope was lost. So let's say Jocko hurried to someplace like a kitchen to get the knife. What happens then is what always happens. Let's say Jocko gets to the kitchen, and sees some . . . bananas, yes, that's what he sees, a platter of bananas. Are you with Jocko so far?"

"Yes, I am," she said.

His conversation was not always easy to follow, and sometimes it made no sense at all, but Erika could tell that this mattered to

Jocko a great deal. She wanted to understand. She wanted to be there for him, her secret friend.

"So," he continued, "Jocko goes all the way to the kitchen. It's a long way because this house is so big . . . this imaginary house we're talking about somewhere, like maybe San Francisco, a big house. Jocko needs to pare his toenails *right away*. If he doesn't, *all is lost!* But Jocko sees bananas. The next thing Jocko knows, Jocko is juggling bananas, capering around the kitchen in San Francisco. Capering or cartwheeling, or pirouetting, or some stupid, stupid, stupid thing. Jocko forgets about the knife until it's too late to trim toenails, too late, the toenails are gone, Jocko has screwed up again, it's all over, *it's the end of EVERYTHING!*"

Erika patted his warty shoulder. "It's all right. It's okay."

"Do you see what Jocko means?"

"Yes, I do," she lied. "But I'd like to think about what you've said for a while, a day or so, maybe a week, before I respond."

Jocko nodded. "That's fair. It was a lot for Jocko to dump on you. You're a good listener."

"Now," she said, "let's go back to the one special thing you would like but don't think you deserve."

That sweet, yearning expression returned to his face, and none too soon. His huge yellow eyes sparkled with excitement as he said, "Oh, oh goodness, oh, how Jocko would like a funny hat!"

"What kind of funny hat?"

"Any kind. Just so it's very funny."

"I won't be able to find a funny hat tonight."

He shrugged. "Whenever. If ever. Jocko – he doesn't deserve it anyway."

"Yes, you've said. But I promise I will have a funny hat for you within a day or two."

Regardless of what difficulty Erika might have finding a very funny hat, she was rewarded in advance for her trouble when she saw his delight, his tears of gratitude.

"You are such a kind lady. Jocko would kiss your hand, except he doesn't want to disgust you."

"You're my friend," she said, and extended her right hand.

The loose flaps around his mouth and the brief touch of his sticky teeth were even more repellent than she expected, but Erika smiled and said, "You're welcome, dear friend. Now there's something I hope you can do for me."

"Jocko will read a book to you," Jocko said, "two books at once, and one upside down!"

"Later, you can read to me. First, I need your opinion about something."

The troll grabbed his feet with his hands and rocked back and forth on the floor. "Jocko doesn't know about a whole lot besides storm drains, rats, and bugs, but he can try."

"You're Jonathan Harker, or were Harker, whatever. So you know the New Race has little emotional life. When they do have emotional reactions, they're limited to envy, anger, and hatred, only emotions that turn back on themselves and can't lead to hope, because he says hope leads to a desire for freedom, to disobedience and rebellion."

"Jocko is different now. Jocko feels big good things with great exuberance."

"Yes, I've noticed that. Anyway, I don't have the knowledge or the breadth of vision to understand fully why a genius like Victor would create his New Race this way. Only I, his wife, am different. He allows me humility and shame . . . which in a strange way lead to hope, and hope to tenderness."

Feet in his hands, rocking, his head turned toward her, the troll said, "You are the first ever, Old Race or New, to be kind to Jocko," and again tears spilled down his cheeks.

"I hope for many things," Erika said. "I hope to become a better wife day by day. I hope to see approval in Victor's eyes. If in time I become a very good wife and no longer deserve beatings, if in time he comes to cherish me, I will ask him to allow others of the New Race to have hope as I do. I will ask Victor to give my people gentler lives than they have now."

The troll stopped rocking. "Don't ask Victor anytime soon."

"No. First I've got to be a better wife. I must learn to serve him to perfection. But I've been thinking maybe I could be Queen Esther to his King Ahasuerus."

"Remember," he said, "Jocko is ignorant. An ignorant screwup."

"They're figures in the Bible, which I've never read. Esther was the daughter of Mordecai. She persuaded King Ahasuerus, her husband, to spare her people, the Jews, from annihilation at the hands of Haman, a prince of the king's realm."

"Don't ask Victor anytime soon," the troll repeated. "That is Jocko's opinion. That is Jocko's very strongly held opinion."

In her mind's eye, Erika saw Christine lying on the floor of the master-suite vestibule, shot four times through her two hearts.

"That isn't what I want your opinion about," she said, getting to her feet. "Come with me to the library. There's something strange I need to show you."

The troll hesitated. "I who am came out of he who was only a few days ago, but I who am Jocko have had enough strange for as long as I live."

She held out a hand to him. "You are my only friend in the world. I have no one else to whom I can turn."

Jocko sprang off the floor and stood en pointe, as if about to pirouette, but still hesitated. "Jocko must be discreet. Jocko is a *secret* friend."

"Victor has gone to the Hands of Mercy. The staff is at the back of the estate, in their dormitory. We have the house to ourselves."

After a moment, he came down from his toes, slipped his hand in hers. "It's gonna be a very, very funny hat, isn't it?"

"Very, very funny," she promised.

"With some little bells on it?"

"If I find a funny hat without bells, I'll sew as many on it as you want."

chapter **43**

Corridor after corridor, laboratory after laboratory, room after room, in stairways and lavatories and storage closets, a perfect hush has fallen over this place.

With all of its windows bricked up, the building admits no sound from the world outside.

Here and there, brainless bodies lie in groups. They are all EXEMPTS.

No one moves who can be seen.

Chameleon follows the tantalizing spoor of the TARGET until those pheromones come to an end at the workstation in the main lab, with no sign of the person who cast them off.

Dim memories of this enormous room stir in Chameleon's mind. It seems to have no recollections prior to these.

Memories do not interest Chameleon. It lives for the future, for the infuriating smell of TARGETS.

Frenzies of violence thrill the pleasure center in its forebrain as intense sex might thrill it if it were capable of sexual activity.

Slaughter and only slaughter stimulates its orgasm. Chameleon dreams of war, because for it, war is continuous ecstasy.

Suddenly, on the desktop computer and on an eight-by-six-foot screen embedded in a wall, images appear.

The screens show a broad avenue, tens of thousands of people, dressed alike and ordered into precise ranks, marching in cadence to loud music.

In every fifth row of the stiff-legged marchers, every person carries a flag. The flag is red with a white circle. In the circle is a man's face.

The face is familiar to Chameleon. It has seen this man a long time ago, has seen him often and in this very lab.

The camera pulls back to reveal colossal structures flanking the twelve-lane avenue. They are all of bold design unlike any of the scores of typical-building layouts programmed into Chameleon to assist it in navigating an average office high-rise or church, or shopping mall.

On some of these immense edifices are portraits. The face of the man on the flags is rendered in paint or in mosaic tile, or is etched in stone.

None of these images is smaller than ten stories high. Some are thirty stories.

The music swells, swells, then recedes to a background level. Words are being spoken now, but Chameleon is not interested in what is being said.

The marching hordes on the screens are not real people, merely images. They cannot be killed.

Crawling among the many machines, Chameleon seeks what lives only to be killed.

For a while it smells nothing but the lingering pheromones of the TARGET that was recently here but has gone. Then a new scent.

Chameleon turns its head left, right. Its two ripping claws scissor with anticipation, and its crushing claw opens wide to grip. Its stinger extrudes from under its carapace.

The scent is that of a TARGET. In the hallway but approaching.

chapter 44

Abruptly the rain fell away behind them and the two-lane blacktop state route lay dry ahead. By driving out of the storm, seemingly swifter than nature in a rampage, Carson enjoyed the illusion of even greater speed than she had actually managed to squeeze out of the Honda.

She raised the bottle of never-sleep-again cola from between her things and took another swig. She recognized the signs of noncritical dehydration caused by caffeine: dry mouth, dry lips, a faint ringing in the ears.

In the passenger seat, playing imaginary drums with imaginary drumsticks, Michael said, "Maybe we shouldn't have exceeded the recommended dose for the caffeine tablets. Already I have NoDoz nostrils."

"Me too. My nasal passages are so dry, it's like I'm breathing air that came out of a furnace, it has just a little burn to it."

"Yeah. Feels dry. But this is still Louisiana, so at a minimum it has to be ninety percent humidity by state law. Hey, you know how much of the human body is water?"

"If it's the time of month I retain it, I'd say ninety percent."

"Sixty percent for men, fifty percent for women."

She said, "There's proof – women have more substance than men."

"It was an answer on *Jeopardy!*"

"I can't believe you watch TV game shows."

"They're educational," he said. "Half of what I know, I learned from game shows."

"That I *do* believe."

Moss-draped live oaks on both sides of the road formed a tunnel, and the headlights flared again and again off what might have been colonies of phosphorescent lichen on the fissured bark.

"Do you have to drive so fast?"

"Fast? This heap of Vicky's isn't good for driving anywhere except in funeral processions."

Carson's cell phone rang, and she fished it out of an inside coat pocket.

"O'Connor," she said.

"Detective O'Connor," a woman said, "this is Erika Helios."

"Good evening, Mrs Helios."

When he heard the name, Michael popped up in his seat as if he were a slice of bread in a toaster.

Erika Helios said, "I believe you may be aware of who my husband really is. At least I think he suspects you know."

"He *knows* we know," Carson said. "He sent two of his New Race assassins after us yesterday. Cute couple. Looked like dancers. We called them Fred and Ginger. They blasted their way through my house, nearly killed my brother."

"Sounds like Benny and Cindi Lovewell," Erika Helios said. "I'm of the New Race, too. But I don't know about Benny and Cindi being sent after you yesterday. Victor killed me the day *before* yesterday."

To Michael, Carson said, "She says Victor killed her the day before yesterday."

"Who're you talking to?" Erika asked.

"My partner, Michael Maddison."

Erika said, "I know it sounds unbelievable, someone telling you she was killed yesterday."

"Thanks to your husband," Carson said, "there's nothing we find hard to believe anymore."

"I'll believe any damn crazy thing," Michael agreed.

"Victor sent my body to the dump. Do you know about Crosswoods Waste Management, Detective O'Connor?"

"It's right next door to the tank farm where he's gonna crank out six thousand of you folks a year."

"You *are* on top of things. I figured you would be, if Victor worried about you. Nobody worries Victor."

"Mrs Helios, how did you get this number?"

"Victor had it. I saw it on his desk pad. That was before I was dead. But I have a photographic memory. I'm an Alpha."

"Are you still dead?" Carson asked.

"No, no. Turns out, most of us he sends here are for-sure dead, but a few of us who seem to be dead . . . well, there's still a trace of life energy in us that can be brought back to full power, so we can heal. They know how to save us here at the dump."

"Who is they?"

"Those of the New Race discarded here but alive again. I'm one of them now. We call ourselves the Dumpsters."

Carson said, "I didn't know you people had a sense of humor."

"We don't," Erika said. "Not until we die and drop our program and then come alive again. But this may be gibberish to you. Maybe you don't understand about our programs."

Carson thought of Pastor Kenny Laffite coming undone at his kitchen table in the parsonage, and she said, "Yeah, we know about that."

"Oh, and I should have said, I'm Erika Four. The wife with him now is Erika Five."

"He moves fast."

"He's always got Erikas in the tanks, just in case the latest one goes wrong. Flesh is cheap. That's what he says."

"Thank God for NoDoz and triple-threat cola," Carson said.

Erika Four said, "Excuse me?"

"If I wasn't pumped with caffeine to the eyebrows," Carson said, "I wouldn't be able to keep up with this conversation."

"Detective, do you know you can't trust anyone in the police department, so many of them are Victor's people?"

"Yeah. We're aware."

"So you're on your own. And here in the parish where the dump and the tank farm are located, every cop and most of the politicians are replicants. You can't win this."

"We can win this," Carson disagreed.

Nodding so rapidly that he looked like an out-of-control bobble-head doll, Michael said, "We can win. We can win."

"His empire is imploding," Carson told Erika.

"Yes. We know. But you still need help."

Thinking of Deucalion, Carson said, "We've got some help you don't know about. But what do you have in mind?"

"We've got a deal to propose. The Dumpsters. We'll help you defeat him, capture him – but there's something we want."

chapter **45**

Victor never entered the Hands of Mercy directly. Next door to the hospital, which now passed as a warehouse, a five-story office building housed the accounting and personnel-management departments of Biovision, the company that had made him a billionaire.

In the garage under the building, he parked his S600 Mercedes in a space reserved for him. At this hour, his was the only car.

He had been put off his stride by the business with Erika Four on the phone and Christine not knowing who she was. In moments like this, work was the best thing to settle his mind, and perhaps now more than ever, numerous issues required his attention.

Near his parking space was a painted steel door to which only he possessed a key. Beyond the door lay a twelve-foot-square concrete room.

Opposite the outer door, another door could be operated only by a wall-mounted keypad. Victor entered his code, and the electronic lock disengaged with a *thonk*.

He stepped into a six-foot-wide, eight-foot-high corridor with a concrete floor and block-and-timber walls. The passageway had been excavated secretly by members of the New Race.

Huge responsibilities came with any attempt to pull down an existing civilization and replace it with a new one. The weight on his shoulders might have been intolerable if there had not been perks like secret passageways, hidden rooms, and concealed staircases, which allowed a measure of *fun* in every day.

He had found such hugger-mugger thrilling ever since he was a boy growing up in a rambling house built by a paranoid grandfather who included in his design more blind doors than visible ones, more unknown rooms than known, more secret passages than public hallways. Victor thought it said something admirable about him that he had not lost touch with his roots, had not forgotten from where he came.

At the end of the corridor, another keypad accepted his code. A final door opened into an ordinary file room in the lowest realms of the Hands of Mercy.

These days, no work was conducted on this level. A regrettable incident had occurred here, the consequence of sloppy work by some of his Alphas, and forty had perished. He passed through a dimly lighted area, where unrepaired destruction loomed in the shadows.

In the elevator, on his way up to the main lab, Victor heard music by Wagner, and his heart stirred at the majesty of it. Then he realized someone must have activated *The Creed*, the short film that played once every day throughout the facility for the inspiration and motivation of the New Race staff. But only Victor knew the procedure whereby the computer could be directed to feed the film throughout the Hands of Mercy, and he was curious as to how it had been activated.

When he entered his laboratory, he stood before the embedded wall screen, charmed as always by the marching legions, by the city of tomorrow with its immense buildings that dear Adolf had imagined but had failed ever to erect, by the monuments to himself that would, when the city was built, be much more grand than these examples.

With a team of his people, he had created this realistic glimpse of the future through computer animation. Soon would come the moment when the Wagnerian score faded and in his own voice the Creed would be delivered.

He went to his workstation, intending to sit in his chair to enjoy the last of the film. But arriving there, turning to face the screen from across the room, he saw a portion of the floor ripple, about twenty feet away, and he thought with alarm, *Chameleon.*

chapter 46

Toward the end of a long incline, out of the darkness to the right of the roadway, a white-tailed doe bounded into the headlights and froze in fear.

Ignoring speed limits and periodic roadside pictographs of the silhouette of a leaping antlered buck, Carson had forgotten that at night in rural territory, deer could be no less a traffic hazard than drunken drivers.

Being a city girl out of her element was the lesser part of the problem. Having spent the past few days immersed in the twisted world of Victor Helios Frankenstein, she learned to fear and to be alert for extraordinary, preposterous, grotesque threats of all kinds, while becoming less attuned to the perils of ordinary life.

In spite of her complaints about the Honda, she had pressed it to a reckless speed. The instant she saw the deer in the northbound lane, she knew she was maybe five seconds from impact, couldn't lose enough speed to avoid a disastrous collision, might roll the car if she braked hard.

Speaking on behalf of the Dumpsters, Erika Four said, ". . . but there's something we want," just as the deer appeared.

To free both hands for the wheel, Carson tossed the cell phone to Michael, who snared it in midair as if he'd asked for it, and who at the same time reached cross-body with his left hand to press a button that put down the power window in his door.

In the split second she needed to throw the phone to Michael, Carson also considered her two options:

Pull left, pass Bambi's mom by using the southbound lane and south shoulder, but you might startle her, she might try to complete her crossing, bounding hard into the Honda.

Pull right, go off-road behind the deer, but you might plow into another one if they were traveling in a herd or family.

Even as the phone arced through the air toward Michael's rising hand, Carson put all her chips on a bet that the doe wasn't alone. She swung into the south-bound lane.

Directly ahead, a buck bolted from where she least expected, from the darkness on the left, into the southbound lane, *returning* for his petrified doe.

Having tossed the phone from right hand to left, having snatched the pistol from his shoulder rig, Michael thrust the weapon out the window, which was still purring down, and squeezed off two shots.

Spooked, the buck sprang out of harm's way, into the north-bound lane, the doe turned to follow him, the Honda exploded past them, and hardly more than a hundred feet away, a truck appeared at the top of the incline, barreling south.

The truck driver hammered his horn.

Carson pulled hard right.

In an arc, the truck's headlights flared through the Honda's interior.

Feeling the car want to roll, she avoided the brakes, eased off the accelerator, finessed the wheel to the left.

The truck shot past them so close Carson could hear the other driver cursing even though her window was closed.

When the potential energy of a roll transferred into a back-end slide, a rear tire stuttered off the pavement, gravel rattled against the undercarriage, but then they were on pavement once more, and in the northbound lane where they belonged.

As Carson accelerated, Michael holstered his pistol, tossed her cell phone back to her.

When she caught the phone and as he put up the window in his door, she said, "That settles it. We'll get married."

He said, "Obviously."

Remembering the dog, she said, "How's Duke?"

"Sitting on the backseat, grinning."

"He is *so* our dog."

When Carson put the phone to her ear, the former Mrs Helios was saying, "Hello? Are you there? Hello?"

"Just dropped the phone," Carson said. "You were saying you wanted something in return for helping us."

"What are you going to do to Victor if you can get your hands on him?" Erika asked. "Arrest him?"

"Nooooo," Carson said. "Don't think so. Arresting him would be way too complicated."

"It'd be the trial of the millennium," Michael said.

Carson grimaced. "With all the appeals, we'd spend thirty years giving testimony."

Michael said, "And we'd have to listen to a gazillion really bad monster jokes for the rest of our lives."

"He'd probably get off scot-free anyway," Carson said.

"He'd definitely get off," Michael agreed.

"He'd be like a folk hero to a significant number of idiots."

"Jury nullification," Michael said.

"All he wanted was to build a utopia."

"Paradise on Earth. Nothing wrong with that."

"A one-nation world without war," Carson said.

"All of humanity united in pursuit of a glorious future."

"The New Race wouldn't pollute like the Old Race."

"Every last one of them would use the type of lightbulb they were told to use," Michael said.

"No greed, less waste, a willingness to sacrifice."

"They'd save the polar bears," Michael said.

Carson said, "They'd save the oceans."

"They'd save the planet."

"They would. They'd save the solar system."

"The universe."

Carson said, "And all the killing, that wasn't Victor's fault."

"Monsters," Michael said. "Those damn monsters."

"His creations just wouldn't stay with the program."

"We've seen it in movies a thousand times."

"It's tragic," Carson said. "The brilliant scientist undone."

"Betrayed by those ungrateful, rebellious monsters."

"He's not only going to get off, he's going to end up with his own reality-TV show," Carson said.

"He'll be on *Dancing with the Stars.*"

"And he'll win."

On the phone, the former Mrs Helios said, "I'm hearing only half of this, but what I hear is you aren't handling it like police detectives anymore."

"We're vigilantes," Carson acknowledged.

"You want to kill him," Erika said.

"As often as it takes to make him dead," Carson said.

"Then we want the same thing. And we can help you, those of us here at the dump. All we ask is don't just shoot him. Take him alive. Help us kill him the way we want to do it."

"How do you want to do it?" Carson asked.

"We want to chain him and take him down into the dump."

"I'm with you so far."

"We want to make him lie faceup in a grave of garbage lined with the dead flesh of his victims."

"I like that."

"Some of the others want to urinate on him."

"I can understand the impulse."

"We wish to buckle around his neck a metal collar with a high-voltage cable attached, through which eventually we can administer to him an electric charge powerful enough to make the marrow boil in his bones."

"Wow."

"But not right away. After the collar, we want to bury him alive under more garbage and listen to him scream and beg for mercy until we've had enough of that. *Then* we boil his marrow."

"You've really thought this through," Carson said.

"We really have."

"Maybe we can work together."

Erika said, "The next time he comes to the new tank farm—"

"That'll probably be before dawn. We think he'll retreat to the farm from New Orleans when the Hands of Mercy burns down."

"Mercy is going to burn down?" Erika asked with childlike wonder and a tremor of delight.

"It's going to burn down in . . ." Carson glanced at Michael, who checked his watch, and she repeated what he told her: ". . . in eight minutes."

"Yes," the fourth Mrs Helios said, "he'll surely flee to the farm."

"My partner and I are already on our way."

"Meet with us at Crosswoods, at the dump, before you go to the farm," Erika said.

"I'll have to talk to our other partner about that. I'll get back to you. What's your number there?"

As Erika recited her number, Carson repeated it to Michael, and he wrote it down.

Carson terminated the call, pocketed the phone, and said, "She sounds really nice for a monster."

chapter 47

Although he despised humanity, Victor was biologically human. Although intellectually enlightened beyond the comprehension of others in the Old Race, he remained more physically like them than not. To Chameleon, Victor qualified as an approved target.

If he had not created Chameleon himself, Victor wouldn't have known the meaning of the rippling floor. He would have thought he had imagined it or was having a transient ischemic attack.

Even now, knowing where to look, he could not easily discern Chameleon against the surface across which it moved.

On the desktop computer and on the big screen across the room, stirring, heroic visions of the New Race future continued to appear, but now Victor's voice rose, reciting the Creed: *"The universe is a sea of chaos in which random chance collides with happenstance and spins shatters of meaningless coincidence like shrapnel through our lives . . ."*

Chameleon was wary in its approach, although it did not need to be so prudent and had not been programmed for caution, as it was virtually invisible and capable of speed. Most likely, it was being careful because this was its first hunting expedition. Once it had killed, it would become bolder.

"The purpose of the New Race is to impose order on the face of chaos, to harness the awesome destructive power of the universe and make it serve your needs, to bring meaning to a creation that has been meaningless since time immemorial . . ."

Victor casually backed deeper into the embrace of his U-shaped workstation.

Chameleon advanced as much as Victor retreated, and then another five feet, until it was only fifteen feet away.

It was a half-smart killing machine because its ability to blend with its environment gave it a great advantage that didn't require it also to be truly smart. Victor's intention was to manufacture tens of thousands of Chameleons, to release them on the day the revolution began, as backup for the brigades of New Race warriors as they began killing the Old.

"And the meaning that you will impose upon the universe is the meaning of your maker, the exaltation of my immortal name and face, the fulfillment of my vision and my every desire . . ."

The granite top of the workstation bumped against the back of Victor's thighs, halting him.

Chameleon scuttled to within twelve feet and paused again. When it was still, Victor ceased to be able to see it even though he knew precisely where it stood. The ripple effect occurred only when the vicious creature remained in motion.

"Your satisfaction in the task, your every moment of pleasure, your relief from otherwise perpetual anxiety, will be achieved solely by the continuous perfect implementation of my will . . ."

Keeping his eyes on the spot where he'd last seen the clever mimic, Victor eased sideways, to a bank of three drawers on his left. He believed that what he needed was in the middle of the three.

Chameleon neither reproduced nor ate. For the duration of its existence, it drew upon its own substance for energy. When its weight declined from twenty-four pounds to eighteen, Chameleon weakened and died, though of course it had no awareness of its fate.

Computer models suggested that each Chameleon, released in an urban environment, would be able to kill between a thousand and fifteen hundred targets before expiring.

"Through you, Earth and everything upon it will submit to me, and as the whole of Earth serves me, so will it serve you, because I have made you and sent you forth in my name . . ."

Chameleon began to move closer – one foot, two feet, three – as Victor pulled open the middle drawer and felt through the contents, his stare focused on the would-be assassin.

Just eight feet away, Chameleon stopped. When it decided to move again, it would surely close the remaining distance and rip into its target's legs, his torso, clip off his fingers when he struggled to resist, as it climbed frantically toward his face.

Victor glanced down into the drawer. He saw the bottle of pale-green fluid and plucked it out as he returned his attention at once to where Chameleon had been.

No ripple deformed the floor.

Victor extracted the stopper from the bottle.

Chameleon scuttled forward.

Victor splashed half the contents of the bottle on himself as he quickly sidestepped to his right.

Because the fluid contained New Race pheromones kept in the desk in the unlikely event that Chameleon escaped from its sack in the freezer, the lethal mimic halted short of attack. Victor no longer smelled like a target but instead like one of the New Race.

"You live because of me, you live for me, and my happiness is your glory . . ."

After a long hesitation, Chameleon turned and crawled away into the laboratory, seeking targets.

Victor had not allowed himself anger while the threat remained, but now he felt his face flush with fury. He was eager to know how Chameleon had escaped its cold prison and who should be punished for allowing it to roam free.

At the computer keyboard, he directed the audio-video system to terminate *The Creed*. The Hands of Mercy fell silent, and the images of the Frankensteinian future vanished from the computer as well as from all other screens in the building.

Instead of displaying the basic menu, however, the computer presented four digits – 07:33.

The Dresden clock. Seven and a half minutes, and counting down.

Because he had expected to destroy the Hands of Mercy only in the event of the most extreme and irreversible biological calamity, and because he wanted none of his creations to be able to countermand his decision to destruct once the countdown commenced, the clock could not be stopped. In little more than seven minutes, Mercy would be a seething hell of fire.

His anger gave way to a cool and practical consideration of the circumstances. Having survived two centuries, he could count on a well-exercised survival instinct.

The linked bricks of incendiary material placed throughout the walls and ceilings had been developed by the world's third-most tyrannical government, refined by the world's second-most tyrannical government, and brought to exquisite perfection by the world's *most* tyrannical government. This was a pyromaniac's dream fuel.

In the event those governments ever fell and those regimes were in danger of being brought to justice, the press of a button would ensure that their concentration camps, which they denied existed, would burst instantly into flames of such white-hot intensity that even the guards would be unable to escape. The temperatures produced by this incendiary material were not equal to the average surface temperature of the sun; but this stuff would produce the second-hottest fire in the solar system, virtually vaporizing all evidence.

Victor hurried to a cabinet near his workstation and pulled open a door, revealing what appeared to be a large suitcase. Data-transmission cables connected the luggage to outlets in the back of the cabinet. He quickly disconnected all lines.

The Hands of Mercy would be reduced not to rubble and char but instead to ashes as fine as thrice-milled flour floating in a pool of molten bedrock no less hot and fluid than lava from a volcano. Not one splinter of bone or any other source of DNA would survive for forensic pathologists to analyze.

The suitcase contained backup data files of every experiment ever conducted in the Hands of Mercy, including work done within the past hour.

The countdown clock read 06:55.

Carrying the suitcase, Victor hurried across the lab toward the hall door, Chameleon forgotten, the entire staff forgotten.

He had been enamored of the incendiary material now awaiting detonation, and he had been impressed with himself for having the contacts to acquire a large volume of it. In fact, he had kept on his computer an e-mail sent to his supplier, the most tyrannical dictator in the world, expressing his gratitude, saying in part, ". . . and if it could be revealed that your three nations worked together to perfect this effective and reliable material, the revelation would make fools of cynics who claim your good selves are not capable of international cooperation."

As Victor knew too well from centuries of disappointments, the worst thing about the sudden relocation of the enterprise following a catastrophic occurrence was the irretrievable loss of correspondence and other mementos that reminded you of the *personal* side of a great scientific undertaking. His work was not always solitary and somber. He built many friendships over the years, and there were balmy days in places like Cuba and Venezuela and Haiti and the old Soviet, when he had taken the time to share laughter and memories with longtime friends and discuss the important issues of the age with new friends of like mind. In the firestorm to come, so many small but precious things would be destroyed that he risked a disabling seizure of nostalgia if he dwelt too much on the forthcoming loss.

When he stepped out of the main laboratory, something to his right, about sixty feet farther along the hall, drew his attention. It was big, perhaps as large as four men, with six thick insectile legs, like the legs on a Jerusalem cricket much enlarged, and a riot of other anatomical features. Numerous faces appeared to be embedded in the body, some in the oddest places. The face nearest to where a head belonged – and obviously the most dominant of the group – rather resembled Werner.

From this reprehensibly undisciplined creature came a dozen or two dozen voices, eerily childlike, all of them chanting the same grossly offensive word: *"Father . . . Father . . . Father . . . Father . . ."*

chapter 48

In the library of the Helios mansion, Erika Five said, "I found it by chance yesterday."

She slid her hand along the underside of a shelf and flicked the concealed switch.

A section of bookshelves swung open on pivot hinges, and ceiling lights revealed the secret passageway beyond.

Jocko said, "This feels bad to Jocko. You want Jocko's opinion. Opinion is – *not good*."

"It's not just the passageway. It's what lies at the other end of it that's the bigger issue."

"What lies at the other end?"

Crossing the threshold, she said, "Better you see it than I tell you. I'd color my description, no matter how I tried not to. I need your unbiased opinion."

Hesitating to follow her, Jocko said, "Is it scary in there? Tell Jocko true."

"It's a little scary, but only a little."

"Is it scarier than a dark, damp storm drain when you don't have your teddy bear anymore?"

"I've never been in a storm drain, but I imagine one would be a lot scarier than this."

"Is it scarier than Jocko's teddy bear being full of spiders waiting for bedtime so they can crawl in his ears when he sleeps and spin a web in his brain and turn him into a spider slave?"

Erika shook her head. "No, it isn't that scary."

"Okay!" Jocko said brightly, and crossed the threshold.

The floor, walls, and ceiling of the four-foot-wide passageway were solid concrete.

The secret door in the bookshelves closed automatically behind the troll, and he said, "Jocko must really want that funny hat."

The narrow corridor led to a formidable steel door. It was kept shut by five inch-thick steel bolts: one in the header, one in the threshold, three in the right-hand jamb, opposite the massive hinges.

"What's locked in there?" Jocko asked. "Something that might get out. Something not supposed to get out."

"You'll see," she said, extracting the bolts one by one.

"Is it something that will beat Jocko with a stick?"

"No. Nothing like that."

"Is it something that will call Jocko a freak and throw dog poop at him?"

"No. That won't happen here."

Jocko did not appear to be convinced.

The steel slab swung smoothly away from them on ball-bearing hinges, activating lights on the farther side.

The subsequent twelve-foot-long passageway ended in a door identical to the first.

Scores of metal rods bristled from the walls, copper on Erika's left, steel or some alloy of steel on her right. A soft hum arose from them.

"Uh-oh," said the troll.

"I wasn't electrocuted the first time," Erika assured him. "So I'm pretty sure we'll be okay."

"But Erika is luckier than Jocko."

"Why would you say that?"

The troll cocked his head as if to say, *Are you serious?* "Why would Jocko say that? Look at you. Look at Jocko."

"Anyway," she said, "there's no such thing as luck. The universe is meaningless chaos. That's what Victor says, so it must be true."

"A black cat crossed Jocko's path once. Then it came back and clawed him."

"I don't think that proves anything."

"Jocko found a penny in the street after midnight. Ten steps later, Jocko fell down an open manhole."

"That wasn't luck. That was not looking where you're going."

"Landed on an alligator."

"An alligator in the storm drain? Well, all right, but it is New Orleans."

"Turned out to be two alligators. Mating."

"You poor thing."

Indicating the rod-lined passageway, Jocko said, "You go first."

As on her previous visit, when Erika entered this new corridor, a blue laser beam scanned her from top to bottom, to top again, as if assessing her form. The laser winked off. The rods stopped humming.

Reluctantly, Jocko followed her to the next steel door.

Erika extracted five deadbolts and opened the final barrier, beyond which lamplight swelled to reveal a windowless, twenty-foot-square space furnished as a Victorian drawing room.

"What do you think?" she asked the troll.

In just the second day of her life, Erika had arrived at a cross-roads. Perplexed and irresolute, she needed another opinion of her circumstance before she could decide what she must do.

Jocko did a little moonwalk on the polished mahogany floor and said, "Smooth." He squinched his toes in the antique Persian carpet and said, "Soft."

Putting his peculiar nose to the William Morris wallpaper, he inhaled deeply, savored the smell, and said, "Paste."

He admired the ebonized-walnut fireplace and licked the William De Morgan tiles around the fire-box. "Glossy," he said of the tiles.

Cupping his left hand around his left ear, he leaned close to one of the lamps that featured fringed shades of shantung silk, as if he were listening to the light. "Wednesday," he said, but Erika did not ask why.

He jumped up and down on the wingback chair – "Springy' – studied the deeply coffered mahogany ceiling – "Abundant' – squirmed under the Chesterfield on his back and made a peeping sound.

Returning to Erika, he said, "Nice room. Let's go."

"You can't just ignore it," she said.

"Ignore what?"

She pointed to the focal point of the chamber, an immense glass case: nine feet long, five feet wide, and more than three feet deep. It stood on a series of bronze ball-and-claw feet. The six panes of beveled glass were held in an ornate ormolu frame of exquisitely chased bronze.

"It seems to me like an enormous jewel box," Erika said.

After smacking the flaps of his mouth, the troll said, "Yeah. Jewel box. Let's go."

"Come take a close look at the contents," Erika said, and when he hesitated, she took his hand and led him to the mysterious object.

A semiopaque reddish-gold substance filled the case. One moment the contents seemed to be a fluid through which circulated subtle currents, but the next moment it appeared instead to be a dense vapor as it billowed against the glass.

"Does it contain a liquid or a gas?" Erika wondered.

"One or the other. Let's go."

"See how the gas or liquid absorbs the lamplight," Erika said. "It glows so prettily throughout, gold and crimson at the same time."

"Jocko needs to pee."

"Do you see how the internal luminosity reveals a large, dark shape suspended in the middle of the case?"

"Jocko needs to pee so bad."

"Although I can't see even a single small detail of that shadowy form," Erika said, "it reminds me of something. Does it remind you of anything, Jocko?"

"Jocko is reminded of a shadowy form."

Erika said, "It reminds me of a scarab petrified in resin. The ancient Egyptians considered scarabs sacred."

This seemed like a quintessential H. Rider Haggard moment, but she doubted the troll would be able to appreciate a literary allusion to the writer of great adventures.

"What is . . . scarab?"

"A giant beetle," she said.

"Did you hear? Jocko needs to pee."

"You do not need to pee."

"Better believe it."

Putting a hand under his chin, turning his head, forcing him to meet her stare, Erika said, "Look me in the eyes and tell me true. I'll know if you're lying."

"You will?"

"Better believe it. Now . . . does Jocko need to pee?"

He searched her eyes, considering his answer, and tiny beads of sweat appeared on his brow. Finally he said, "Ah. The urge has passed."

"I thought it might. Look at the shadow floating in the case. Look, Jocko."

Reluctantly, he returned his attention to the occupant of the big jewel box.

"Touch the glass," she said.

"Why?"

"I want to see what happens."

"Jocko doesn't want to see what happens."

"I suspect nothing will happen. Please, Jocko. For me."

As if he were being asked to press the nose of a coiled cobra, the troll put one finger to the glass, held it there a few seconds, and then snatched it away. He survived.

"Cold," he said. "Icy."

Erika said, "Yes, but not so icy that your skin sticks to it. Now let's see what happens when I touch it . . ."

She pressed a forefinger to the glass, and within the luminous substance, the shadowy form twitched.

chapter 49

"Father . . . Father . . . Father . . ."

The Werner thing progressed clumsily, knocking against the east wall of the corridor, then colliding with the west wall, staggering back four or five feet before advancing seven or eight, as though its every movement required a majority vote of a committee.

This creature was not only an abomination, but also a vicious mockery of everything Victor had achieved, intended to deride his triumphs, to imply that his life's work was but a crude burlesque of science. He now suspected that Werner wasn't a victim of catastrophic cellular metamorphosis, not a *victim*, but instead a *perpetrator*, that the security chief had consciously *rebelled* against his maker. Indeed, judging by the composition of this many-faced travesty, the entire staff of the Hands of Mercy had committed themselves to this insane commune of flesh, reducing themselves to a mutant mob in a single entity. They could have but one reason for re-creating themselves as this lumbering atrocity: to offend their maker, to disrespect him, to dishonor him, to make of him a laughingstock. By such a vivid expression of their irrational contempt and scorn, these ungrateful wretches expected to confuse and dishearten him, to *humiliate* him.

Flesh is cheap, but flesh is also treacherous.

"Father . . . Father . . . Father . . ."

They were meat machines who fancied themselves philosophers and critics, daring to ridicule the only intellect of paramount importance they would ever know. Victor was transforming the world, and they transformed nothing but themselves, yet they thought this miserable degradation of their well-crafted forms made them his equal, even his superior, with license to jeer and insult him.

As the Werner thing ricocheted from wall to wall and staggered backward in order to stumble forward, Victor said to it, to all of them tangled within it, "Your pathetic bit of biological theater means nothing to me, discourages me not at all. I haven't failed. *You* have failed, you have failed me, betrayed me, and you have also failed to discourage me in the slightest. You don't know who you're dealing with."

His outrage thus expressed, Victor spoke the death phrase, the words that would shut down the autonomic nervous systems of these anarchic fools, reducing their mocking many-faced grotesquerie to a heap of lifeless flesh.

The Werner thing kept coming, in its tedious fashion, ranting the one word that it knew – that they *all* knew – would most infuriate Victor.

He had little more than six minutes to escape the Hands of Mercy and get out of the neighborhood before the place flared into a molten imitation of the sun. The coming conflagration would obliterate the Werner thing, answering their blasphemy with purifying fire.

The elevator lay between Victor and the shambling mob-in-one. The stairs seemed more advisable.

Carrying the suitcase that contained every minim of his historic work in Mercy, he hurried away from the Werner thing, slammed through the staircase door, and raced down to the lowest level.

Through columns of light and pools of shadow, past the rubble that stood as a monument to a previous bad day in Mercy. Into the file room.

The keypad, his code. One digit wrong. Enter it again. Each tap of a finger eliciting a tone.

He glanced back. The Werner thing had not followed him. It would not get out this way, and no other doors functioned. The Jabberwock was doomed. Let it die mocking him with its many mouths, he didn't care.

Into the corridor with concrete floor, block-and-timber walls. First door closing automatically behind him as he reached the next. Keypad, code again. Right on the first try. The small concrete room, the final door, always unlocked from this side.

The S600 Mercedes sedan looked magnificent, a carriage fit for any royalty and even adequate for him. He opened the back door, but thought better of putting the precious suitcase in such an unsecured place. He went to the back of the car and locked the case in the trunk.

He closed the back door, opened the driver's door, got behind the wheel. The key was in his pocket, and the touch of a finger to the keyless ignition fired the engine.

He drove up to the street and turned right, away from Mercy.

Rising wind pummeled the streets with pellets of rain that bounced like stones off the pavement, and flotillas of litter raced along brimming gutters. But rain ten times heavier than this would have no quenching effect on the incendiary material soon to ignite in his lost laboratories.

So spectacularly would the old hospital burn that no one in the city – or in the nation, for that matter, sea to shining sea – would ever have seen anything to rival the ferocity of the blaze, and they would never forget those white-white flames so bright as to be blinding. Structures across the street from Mercy might also catch fire, and the five-story building next door – owned by his Biovision – would without question be destroyed, which would make him a source of interest to the media and maybe even to authorities.

Considering that the previous day William, the butler, had bitten off his fingers and been terminated, that within the past hour Christine had experienced an inexplicable interruption of function before Victor had shot her to death, he must face the possibility that others on his household staff might be of dubious psychological and/or physical integrity. They might not merely be unable to provide the high quality of service he expected but might also be unable to maintain a credible humanoid form. He could not go home again, at least not for a while.

Logical analysis wouldn't allow Victor to avoid the conclusion that some of the two thousand of the New Race seeded throughout the city might soon begin to have problems of one kind or another. Not all of them, surely. But perhaps a significant fraction, say 5 percent, or 10. He should not remain in New Orleans during this uncertain period.

Because of the widespread nature of the crisis, Victor suspected a problem with the creation tanks at the Hands of Mercy. He knew that his genetic formulations and flesh-matrix designs were brilliant and without fault. Therefore, only a failure of machinery could explain these events.

Or sabotage.

A thousand suspicions suddenly plagued him, and with renewed anger, he feverishly considered who might have been secretly scheming to ruin him.

But no. Now was not the time to be distracted by the possibility of a saboteur. He must first decamp to a new center of operations, of which there was only one – the tank farm. He must strive to insulate himself from any connection to whatever events might occur in the city during the days ahead.

Later there would be time to identify a villain in his life, if one existed.

In truth, mechanical failure was more likely. He had made numerous improvements to the creation tanks that had been installed at the farm. They were three generations more sophisticated than the version in operation at the Hands of Mercy.

Heading for the causeway that would take him twenty-eight miles across Lake Pontchartrain, Victor reminded himself that every setback of his long career had been followed by more rapid and far greater advances than ever before. The universe asserted its chaotic nature, but always he imposed order on it once more.

Proof of his indomitable character was as evident as the clothes he wore, here and now. The encounter with Chameleon, the subsequent confrontation with the Werner thing, and the flight from Mercy would have taken a visible toll of most men. But his shoes were without a scuff, the crease in his trousers remained as crisp as ever, and a quick check in the rearview mirror revealed that his handsome head of hair was not in the least disarranged.

chapter 50

Warily circling the glass case mounted on the ball-and-claw feet, halting on the farther side of it from Erika, Jocko said, "Not jewel box. Coffin."

"A coffin would have a lid," Erika said, "so I assume there's not a dead man in it."

"Good. Jocko knows enough. Let's go."

"Watch," she said, and rapped a knuckle against the top of the case, as she had done on her previous visit.

The glass sounded as though it must be an inch thick or thicker, and from the spot where her knuckle struck the pane, the amber stuff inside – whether liquid or gas – dimpled much the way water dimpled when a stone was dropped into it. The sapphire-blue dimple resolved into a ring that widened across the surface. The amber color returned in the ring's wake.

"Maybe never do that again," Jocko suggested.

She rapped the glass three times. Three concentric blue rings appeared, receded to the perimeter of the case, and the amber color returned.

Regarding Erika across the top of the case, Jocko said, "Jocko feels kind of sick."

"If you get down on the floor and look under the case—"

"Jocko won't."

"But if you did, you'd see electrical conduits, pipes of several colors and diameters. They all come out of the case, disappear into the floor. Which suggests there's a service room directly under us."

Putting both hands on his belly, Jocko said, "Kind of queasy."

"Yet the mansion supposedly doesn't have a basement."

"Jocko doesn't go in basements."

"You lived in a storm drain."

"Not happily."

Erika moved to the end of the case farthest from the door. "If this were a casket, I figure this would be the head of it."

"Definitely nauseated," said Jocko.

Erika bent low, until her lips were a few inches from the glass. She said softly, "Hello, hello, hello in there."

Within the amber shroud of gas or liquid, the shadowy form thrashed, thrashed.

Jocko scrambled away from the case so fast that Erika didn't see how he had ascended to the fireplace mantel, where he perched, arms wide, holding tight to the framing bronze sconces.

"It scared me, too, the first time," she said. "But I'd only been beaten once at that point, and I hadn't seen Christine shot dead. I'm harder to scare now."

"Jocko is gonna vomit."

"You are not going to vomit, little friend."

"If we don't leave now, Jocko vomits."

"Look me in the eyes and tell me true," she said. "Jocko is not sick, only frightened. I'll know if you're lying."

Meeting her stare, he made a pathetic mewling sound. Finally he said, "Jocko leaves or Jocko vomits."

"I'm disappointed in you."

He looked stricken.

She said, "If you were telling me the truth – then where's the vomit?"

Jocko sucked his upper and lower mouth flaps between his teeth and bit on them. He looked abashed.

When Erika wouldn't stop staring at him, the troll opened his mouth, let go of one of the sconces, and stuck his fingers down his throat.

"Even if that worked," she said, "it wouldn't count. If you were really nauseated, truly nauseated, you could throw up without the finger trick."

Gagging, eyes flooding with tears, Jocko tried and tried, but he could not make himself regurgitate. His efforts were so strenuous that his right foot slipped off the mantel, he lost his grip on the second sconce, and he fell to the floor.

"See where you get when you lie to a friend?"

Cringing in shame, the troll tried to hide behind the wingback chair.

"Don't be silly," Erika said. "Come here."

"Jocko can't look at you. Just can't."

"Of course you can."

"No. Jocko can't bear to see you hate him."

"Nonsense. I don't hate you."

"You hate Jocko. He lied to his best friend."

"And I know he's learned his lesson."

From behind the chair, Jocko said, "He has. He really has."

"I know Jocko will never lie to me again."

"Never. He . . . I never will."

"Then come here."

"Jocko is so embarrassed."

"There's no need to be. We're better friends than ever."

Hesitantly, he moved out from behind the chair. Shyly, he came to Erika, where she remained at the head of the glass case.

"Before I ask for the opinion I need from you," she said, "I've one more thing to show you."

Jocko said, "Oy."

"I'll do exactly what I did yesterday. Let's see what happens."

"Oy."

Once more, she bent down to the glass and said, "Hello, hello, hello in there."

The shadowy shape stirred again, and this time the sound waves of her voice sent scintillant blue pulses across the case, as a rap of her knuckle had done before.

She spoke again: "I am Queen Esther to his King Ahasuerus."

The pulses of blue were a more intense color than previously. The shadowy presence appeared to rise closer to the underside of the glass, revealing the barest suggestion of a pale face, but no details.

Turning to Jocko, Erika whispered, "This is exactly what happened yesterday."

The troll's yellow eyes were wide with fright. He gaped at the featureless suggestion of a face beneath the glass, and what appeared to be an iridescent soap bubble floated from his open mouth.

Lowering her lips close to the glass once more, Erika repeated, "I am Queen Esther to his King Ahasuerus."

Out of the throbbing blue pulses raised by her words, a rough low voice, not muffled by the glass, said, "You are Erika Five, and you are mine."

Jocko fainted.

chapter **51**

By phone, Deucalion told them to drive directly to the main gate of Crosswoods Waste Management. "You'll be met by an escort. They're a Gamma and an Epsilon, but you can trust them."

The long rows of loblolly pines broke for the main entrance. The ten-foot-high chain-link gates featured green privacy panels and were topped with coils of barbed wire to match the fence that flanked them.

As Carson coasted to a stop, she said, "They're of the New Race. How can we possibly trust them? This makes me nervous, very uneasy."

"That's just the caffeine."

"It's not just the caffeine, Michael. This situation, putting ourselves in the hands of Victor's people, I'm spooked."

"Deucalion trusts them," Michael said. "And that's good enough for me."

"I guess I know which side he's on, all right. But he's still strange sometimes, sometimes moody, and hard to figure."

"Let's see. He's over two hundred years old. He was made from parts of cadavers taken from a prison graveyard. He's got a handsome side to his face and a caved-in side tattooed to conceal the extent of the damage. He's got two hearts and who knows what other weird arrangement of internal organs. He's been a monk, the star in a carnival freak show, and maybe a hundred other things we'll never know about. He's seen two centuries of war and had three average lifetimes to think about them, and he seems to have read every book worth reading, probably a hundred times more books than you've read, a thousand times more than me. He's lived through the decline of Christendom and the rise of a new Gomorrah. He can open doorways in the air and step through them to the other side of the world because the lightning bolt that animated him brought mysterious gifts with it, as well. Gee, Carson, I don't see any reason why he should seem strange or moody or hard to figure. You're right – it must just be that he's setting us up, he's been lying all along about wanting to nail Victor, they just wanted to lure us to the dump so they could eat us for breakfast."

Carson said, "If you're going to go off on rants, you can't have any more NoDoz."

"I don't *need* any more NoDoz. I feel like my eyelids have been stitched open with surgical sutures."

In the headlight beams, the gates of Crosswoods began to swing inward. Beyond lay the darkness of the dump, which seemed blacker than the moonless night on this side of the fence.

Carson let the Honda coast forward, between the gates, and two figures with flashlights loomed out of the darkness.

One of them was a guy, rough-looking but handsome in a brutish kind of way. He wore a filthy white T-shirt, jeans, and thigh-high rubber boots.

In the backsplash of the flashlights, the woman appeared to be movie-star gorgeous. Her blond hair needed to be washed, and her face was spotted with grime, but she had a beauty so intense that it would have shone through just about anything except a mud pack.

With his flashlight, the man showed Carson where to park, while the woman walked backward in front of them, grinning and waving as if Carson and Michael were beloved kin not seen since everybody had to flee the Ozarks one step ahead of the Bureau of Alcohol, Tobacco, and Firearms task force.

Like the man, she wore a filthy white T-shirt, jeans, and thigh-high rubber boots, but the unattractive getup somehow only emphasized that she had the body of a goddess.

"I'm beginning to think our Victor is less a scientist than he is a horndog," Carson said.

"Well, I guess it doesn't cost him any more to make them curvy than to make them flat."

Switching off the headlights and then the engine, Carson said, "We're taking all our guns."

"In case we have to protect our virtue."

Carson said, "Now that we're planning on you having my babies, I'll protect your virtue for you."

They got out of the Honda, each with two hand-guns holstered and an Urban Sniper held by the pistol grip, muzzle toward the ground.

The man didn't offer his hand. "I'm Nick Frigg. I run the dump."

Close up, the woman impressed Carson as being even more gorgeous than she had appeared from the car. She radiated a wildness but also an affability, an animal vitality and enthusiasm that made her hard not to like.

She declared with energy, "Marble, mutton, mustard, mice, mule, mumps, muck, manhole—"

Nick Frigg said, "Give her a chance. Sometimes she just has trouble finding the right word to get started."

"– mole, moon, moan, mush, mushroom, moth, mother. *Mother!* We saw the mother of all gone-wrongs tonight!"

"This is Gunny Alecto," Nick said. "She drives one of what we call our garbage galleons, big machine, plowing the trash flat and compacting it good and solid."

"What's a gone-wrong?" Michael asked.

"Experiments that have gone all wrong down at the Hands of Mercy. Specialized meat machines, maybe some warrior thing now and then was supposed to help us in the Last War, even some Alphas or Betas that turned out not like he expected."

"We bury them here," Gunny Alecto said. "We treat them right. They look stupid, stupid, stupid, but they kind of come from where we do, so they're sort of weird family."

"The one tonight wasn't stupid," Nick said.

An expression of awe possessed Gunny's face. "Oh, tonight, it was all different down the big hole. The mother of all gone-wrongs, it's the most beautiful thing ever."

"It changed us," said Nick Frigg.

"Totally changed us," Gunny agreed, nodding enthusiastically.

"It made us understand," Nick said.

"Heaps, harps, holes, hoops, hens, hawks, hooks, hoses, hearts, hands, heads. *Heads!* The mother of all gone-wrongs talked inside our heads."

"It made us free," Nick said. "We don't have to do anything we used to have to do."

"We don't hate your kind anymore," Gunny said. "It's like – why did we ever."

"That's nice," said Carson.

"We used to hate you so bad," Gunny revealed. "When Old Race dead were sent to the dump, we stomped their faces. Stomped them head to foot, over and over, till they were nothing but bone splinters and smashed meat."

"In fact," Nick added, "we just did that earlier tonight with some like you."

"That was before we went down the big hole and met the mother of all gone-wrongs and learned better," Gunny clarified. "Man, oh, man, life is different now, for sure."

Carson shifted her grip on the Urban Sniper, holding it with both hands, the muzzle aimed at the sky instead of toward the ground.

Casually, Michael did the same with his Sniper as he said, "So where is Deucalion?"

"We'll take you to him," Nick said. "He's really the first, isn't he, the first man-made man?"

"Yes, he really is," Carson said.

"Listen," Michael said, "we've got a dog in the car. Is he going to be safe if we leave him here?"

"Bring him along," Nick said. "Dogs – they love a dump. They call me dog-nose Nick 'cause to help me in my job, I have some canine genes that give me a sense of smell half what a dog's is but ten thousand times what you smell."

When Michael opened the back door of the Honda, Duke

bounded out and raised his nose to the rich night air. He regarded Nick and Gunny warily, cocked his head left, then right.

"He smells New Race," Nick said. "And that worries him. But he smells something different about us, too."

"Because we've been down the big hole," Gunny said, "and had our heads talked in by the mother of all gone-wrongs."

"That's right," Nick said. "The dog, he knows."

The Duke of Orleans tentatively wagged his tail.

"He smells like a good dog," Nick said. "He smells the way I'd want to smell if I didn't have just some canine genes but was all the way a dog. He smells perfect for a dog. You're lucky to have him."

Carson gave Michael a look that asked, *Are we crazy to go with them into this dark and lonely place?*

He read her clearly, because he said, "Well, it's dark and it's lonely, but we've been through crazy for three days, and I think we're coming out the other side tonight. I say trust Deucalion and the Duke."

chapter 52

Erika carried Jocko from the windowless Victorian drawing room, along the secret passageway.

When the troll passed out, he passed *way* out. He fell so deep into unconsciousness that during this short vacation from awareness, he must have had a room with a view of death.

As limp as rags, his body draped over her cradling arms. Head lolling, mouth open, flaps flopping, he held an iridescent bubble between his teeth, and it didn't pop until she settled him in an armchair in the library.

Jocko remained the antithesis of beauty. If any child were to come upon him accidentally, the unfortunate tyke might need years to regain control of his bladder and would be traumatized for life.

Yet Jocko's vulnerability, his effervescence, and his touching perseverance endeared him to Erika. Somewhat to her surprise, her affection for the troll grew by the hour.

If this mansion were a cottage in the woods, if Jocko frequently broke into song, and if there were six more of him, Erika would have been a real-life Snow White.

She returned to the windowless drawing room. From the threshold, she stared for a moment at the shapeless shadow nesting within the radiant reddish-gold substance.

The care taken with the decor suggested that Victor came here regularly to sit at length with the creature in the glass casket. If he spent little time in this room, he would not have furnished it so cozily.

She closed the steel door and engaged the five deadbolts. At the end of the hall that bristled with rods, she closed the next door and bolted it, as well.

When she returned to the library, where the pivoting section of bookshelves rotated into place, concealing all beyond it, Erika found that Jocko had regained consciousness. Feet dangling well short of the floor, arms on the arms of the chair, he was sitting up straight, clutching the upholstery with both hands, as if he were on a roller coaster, nervously anticipating the next plunge.

"How do you feel, Jocko?"

He said, "Pecked."

"What does that mean?"

"Like, say, ten birds want to peck your head, you try to protect yourself, their wings flutter against your hands and arms, flutter-flutter-flutter against your face. Jocko feels fluttery all over."

"Have you ever been attacked by birds?"

"Only when they see me."

"That sounds horrible."

"Well, it just happens when Jocko's in open air. And mostly in daylight, only once at night. Well, twice if bats count as birds."

"There's a bar here in the library. Maybe a drink will settle your nerves."

"Do you have storm-drain water with interesting sediment?"

"I'm afraid we only have bottled water or from the tap."

"Oh. Then I'll have Scotch."

"You want that on the rocks?"

"No. Just some ice, please."

Moments later, as Erika gave Jocko his drink, her cell phone rang. "Only Victor has this number."

She thought that Jocko's voice had a note of bitterness in it when he muttered, "He who made he who I was," but she may have been imagining it.

She fished the phone from a pocket of her slacks.

"Hello?"

"We're leaving New Orleans for a while," Victor said. "We're leaving immediately."

Because her husband sometimes found questions impertinent, Erika didn't ask why they were leaving, but said simply, "All right."

"I'm already on my way to the tank farm. You'll go there in the bigger Mercedes SUV, the GL550."

"Yes, Victor. Tomorrow?"

"Don't be stupid. I said 'immediately.' Tonight. Within the hour. Pack two weeks' clothes for yourself. Get the staff to help. You've got to move fast."

"And should I bring clothes for you?"

"I have a wardrobe at the farm. Just shut up and listen."

Victor told her where to find the mansion's walk-in safe and explained what she should bring from it.

Then he said, "When you go outside, look to the northwest, the sky is burning," and he terminated the call.

Erika closed her phone and stood in thought for a moment.

In the armchair, Jocko said, "Is he mean to you?"

"He . . . is who he is," she replied. "Wait here. I'll be back in a minute."

French doors opened from the library to a covered terrace. As Erika stepped outside, she heard sirens in the distance.

To the northwest, a strange luminosity played through the low storm clouds: throbbing, wildly flailing forms of light, as radiant and fiercely white as spirits might be, if you were one who believed in such things as spirits.

The burning sky was a reflection of an unimaginably hot and hungry blaze below. The place where she was conceived and born, the Hands of Mercy, must be on fire.

The rain driving through the trees and spending itself on the soaked lawn made a sizzle something like fire, but here the night had no scent of smoke. The washed air smelled clean and fresh, and the fragrance of jasmine came to her, and in this moment, for the first time in her brief but event-packed existence, she felt fully *alive*.

She returned to the library and sat on the footstool in front of Jocko's armchair. "Little friend, you have followed the secret passageway to the hidden room and seen all those lock bolts on the two steel doors."

"Jocko isn't going there again. Jocko's been in enough scary places. He wants just nice places from now on."

"You have seen the hidden room and the glass casket, and the shapeless shadow alive within."

Jocko shuddered and drank some Scotch.

"You have heard it speak from the casket."

Unsuccessfully trying to make his voice deeper and rougher and menacing, the troll quoted, "'You are Erika Five, and you are mine.'"

In his natural voice, he said, "There's something in the glass box that's at least fourteen hundred times too scary for Jocko. If Jocko had genitals, they would've shriveled up and fallen off. But Jocko could only faint."

"Remember, I took you there so I could ask your opinion about something. Before I ask, I must emphasize that I want to know what you *truly* feel. Truly, truly."

Clearly somewhat embarrassed but nevertheless meeting Erika's stare forthrightly, the troll said, "Truly, truly. No more Jocko-needs-to-pee-Jocko-is-gonna-vomit. That's the old me. Good-bye to that Jocko."

"All right, then. I want your honest opinion about two things. We don't know what that shapeless shadow is. But based on what you've heard and seen, is the thing in that glass casket just another thing – or is it malevolent?"

"Malevolent!" the troll said at once. "Malevolent, malignant, venomous, and potentially very troublesome."

"Thank you for your honesty."

"You're welcome."

"Now my second question." She leaned toward Jocko, riveting his gaze with hers. "If the thing in the glass case was made by some man, conceived and designed and brought to life by some man, do you think that man is good . . . or evil?"

"Evil," Jocko said. "Evil, depraved, wicked, corrupt, vile, vicious, rotten, hateful, totally unpleasant."

Erika held his gaze for half a minute. Then she rose from the footstool. "We've got to leave New Orleans and go to the tank farm farther upstate. You'll need clothes."

Plucking at the picnic tablecloth that he had fashioned into a sarong, Jocko said, "This is the only clothes Jocko ever had. It works okay."

"You'll be out in public, at least in the Mercedes."

"Put Jocko in the trunk."

"It's an SUV. It doesn't have a trunk. I've got to find you clothes that make you look more like a normal little boy."

Amazement made yet another fright mask of the troll's face. "What genius would make such clothes?"

"I don't know," Erika admitted. "But I've got an idea who might. Glenda. The estate provisioner. She shops for everything needed here. Food, paper goods, linens, staff uniforms, holiday decorations . . ."

"Does she shop for soap?" Jocko asked.

"Yes, everything, she shops for everything."

He put aside his empty Scotch glass and clapped his hands. "Jocko would like to meet the lady who shops for soap."

"That's not a good idea," Erika said. "You stay here, out of sight. I'll talk to Glenda and see what she can do."

Getting up from the armchair, the troll said, "Jocko is feeling like he better twirl or cartwheel, or walk on his hands. Whatever."

"You know what you could do?" Erika asked. "You could browse the shelves in here, choose some books to take along."

"I'm going to read to you," he remembered.

"That's right. Choose some good stories. Maybe twenty."

As the troll moved toward the nearest shelves, Erika hurried to find Glenda.

At the door to the hall, she paused and looked back at Jocko. "You know what . . . ? Also choose four or five books that seem a little dangerous. And maybe . . . one that seems really, really dangerous."

chapter **53**

The powerful engine transmits vibrations through the frame of the car.

The tires on the blacktop raise vibrations that are likewise transmitted through the vehicle.

Even in the plush upholstery of the backseat, these vibrations can be felt faintly, especially by one made sensitive to vibrations by the tedium of semisuspended animation, in which there was, for so long, little other sensory input.

Like the freezer-motor vibrations in the liquid-filled sack, these are neither pleasant nor unpleasant to Chameleon.

It is no longer tormented by extreme cold.

Nor is it any longer tormented by its powerless condition, for it is no longer powerless. It is free, free at last, and it is free to kill.

Currently, Chameleon is tormented only by its inability to locate a TARGET. It has detected the scents of numerous EXEMPTS, and even most of them were dead.

The sole TARGET located in the laboratory suddenly became an EXEMPT just seconds before Chameleon would have killed it.

Frustrated, Chameleon cannot account for this transformation. Its program does not allow for such a possibility.

Chameleon is adaptable. When its program and real experience do not comport, it will reason its way toward an understanding of why the program is inadequate.

Chameleon is capable of suspicion. In the lab, it continued to maintain surveillance on the one who transformed. It knew the man's face from the past and from the film, but because of the transformation, it thought of him as the PUZZLE.

The PUZZLE had gotten busy, busy in the lab, rushing this way and that. Something about the PUZZLE's frantic activity made Chameleon more suspicious.

In the hallway, the PUZZLE encountered a thing unlike any creature in the extensive species-ID file in Chameleon's program. This thing, large and moving erratically, looked not at all like an EXEMPT, but it smelled like one.

The PUZZLE had run from the building, and because Chameleon had no whiff of any TARGET, no reason to remain there, it followed.

On the way out of the building, Chameleon detected faint traces of a TARGET's scent under the EXEMPT scent of the PUZZLE.

Interesting.

Once they were in the car and in motion for a while, the PUZZLE seemed less agitated, and as he became calmer, the TARGET scent slowly faded.

Now there is only the scent of an EXEMPT.

What does it all mean?

Chameleon broods on these events.

On the backseat, looking exactly like the backseat, Chameleon waits for a development. It confidently anticipates that there will be a development. There always is.

chapter 54

Erika phoned Glenda, the estate provisioner, at the dormitory and asked for a meeting immediately in the staff lunchroom. This was in the south wing on the first floor, and it could be entered either from the south hall or from an exterior door.

In a few minutes, Glenda arrived at the exterior door. She left her umbrella outside and came into the lunchroom, saying, "Yes, Mrs Helios, what is needed?"

A sturdy New Race woman with short chestnut-brown hair and a scattering of freckles, wearing an off-duty jumpsuit, she appeared accustomed to lifting and toting. As the sole shopper for the estate, her job included not just browsing the aisles of stores but also the physical labor of transporting goods and stocking shelves.

"I've been out of the tank little more than a day," Erika said, "so my downloaded data hasn't yet been complemented by enough real-world experience. I need to buy something right away, tonight, and I hope your knowledge of the marketplace will be helpful."

"What do you need, ma'am?"

Erika brazened through it: "Boys' clothing. Shoes, socks, pants, shirts. Underwear, I suppose. A light jacket. A cap of some kind. The boy is about four feet tall, weighs fifty or sixty pounds. Oh, and his head is big, quite big for a boy, so the cap should probably be adjustable. Can you get me those things right away?"

"Mrs Helios, may I ask—"

"No," Erika interrupted, "you may not ask. This is something Victor needs me to bring to him right away. I never question Victor, no matter how peculiar a request may seem, and I never will. Do I need to tell you why I never question my husband?"

"No, ma'am."

The staff had to know that the Erikas were beaten and were not permitted to turn off their pain.

"I thought you'd understand, Glenda. We're all in the same quicksand, aren't we, whether we're the provisioner or the wife."

Uncomfortable with this intimacy, Glenda said, "There's no store open at this hour, selling boys' clothing. But . . ."

"Yes?"

Fear rose in Glenda's eyes, and her previously placid face tightened with worry. "There are many articles of boys' and girls' clothing here in the house."

"Here? But there are no children here."

Glenda's voice fell to a whisper. "You must never tell."

"Tell what? Tell whom?"

"Never tell . . . Mr Helios."

Erika pressed the battered-wife sympathy play as far as she probably dared: "Glenda, I am beaten not just for my shortcomings, but for any reason that suits my . . . maker. I am quite sure I would be beaten for being the bearer of bad news. All secrets are safe with me."

Glenda nodded. "Follow me."

Also off the south hall on the ground floor were a series of storage rooms. One of the largest of these was a twenty-by-eighteen-foot walk-in cooler where a dozen of the highest-quality fur coats were stored – mink, ermine, arctic fox . . . Victor had no sympathy for the antifur movement, as he was engaged in the much more important antihuman movement.

In addition to the rack of coats, there were numerous cabinets containing clothes of all kinds that would not fit even in Erika's enormous closet in the master suite. By having a series of wives who were identical in every detail, Victor spared himself the expense of purchasing new wardrobes. But he did want his Erika to be at all times stylishly attired, and he did not expect her to choose from a limited garment collection.

From several drawers in the farthest corner of the room, Glenda nervously produced children's clothing, article after article, both for boys and girls, in various sizes.

"Where did all this come from?" Erika asked.

"Mrs Helios, if he learns about it, he'll terminate Cassandra. And this is the only thing that's ever made her happy. It's made us all happy – her daring, her secret life, she gives the rest of us a little hope."

"You know my position on being the bearer of bad news."

Glenda buried her face in a striped polo shirt.

For a moment, Erika thought that the woman must be crying, for the shirt trembled in her hands, and her shoulders shook.

Instead, Glenda inhaled deeply, as if seeking the scent of the boy who had worn the shirt, and when she looked up from it, her face was a portrait of bliss.

"For the past five weeks, Cassandra has been sneaking off the estate at night, to kill Old Race children."

Cassandra, the laundress.

"Oh," Erika said. "I see."

"She couldn't wait any longer to be told the killing could at last begin. The rest of us . . . we so admire her nerve, but we haven't been able to find it in ourselves."

"And . . . what of the bodies?"

"Cassandra brings them back here, so we can share in the excitement. Then the trash men who take other bodies to the dump, they take the children, too, no questions asked. Like you said – we're all in this quicksand together."

"But you keep the clothes."

"You know what the dormitory is like. Not an inch of extra space. We can't store the clothes there. But we can't bear to get rid of them. We take these clothes out some nights, take them over to the dormitory and, you know, play with them. And, oh, it's very wonderful, Mrs Helios, thinking of the dead kids and listening to Cassandra tell how each one happened. It's the best thing ever, the only good thing we've ever had."

Erika knew that something profound must be happening to her when she found Glenda's story disturbing, even creepy, and when she hesitated at the prospect of dressing the poor sweet troll in the clothes of murdered children. Indeed, that she should think *murdered* instead of merely *dead* had to be an indication of a revolution in her thinking.

She was torn by something like pity for Cassandra, Glenda, and the others on the staff, by a quiet horror at the idea of Cassandra stalking the most defenseless of the Old Race, and by compassion for the murdered, toward whom she had been programmed to feel nothing but envy, anger, and hatred.

Her actions on behalf of Jocko crossed the line that Victor had drawn for her, for all of them, in the aforementioned quicksand. The curious sense of companionship that had developed so quickly between her and the little guy should have been beyond her emotional range. Even as the friendship grew, she recognized that it might signify a pending interruption of function like the one that William, the butler, had experienced.

She was allowed compassion, humility, and shame, as the others were not – but only so that Victor might be more thrilled by her pain and anguish. Victor didn't intend that the finer feelings of his Erikas should benefit anyone but himself, or that anyone else should have the opportunity to respond to his wife's tender attentions with anything other than the contempt and brutality with which he answered them.

To Glenda, she said, "Go back to the dormitory. I'll select what I need from these and put the rest away."

"And never tell him."

"Never tell him," Erika confirmed.

Glenda started to turn away, but then she said, "Do you think maybe . . ."

"Maybe what, Glenda?"

"Do you think maybe . . . the end is coming soon?"

"Do you mean the end of the Old Race, once and forever, the killing of them all?"

The provisioner searched Erika's gaze and then turned her face up to the ceiling as tears welled in her eyes. In a voice thick with fear, she said, "There's got to be an end, you know, there's really got to be."

"Look at me," Erika said.

Obedient as her program required, Glenda met her mistress's eyes again.

With her fingers, Erika wiped the tears from the provisioner's face. "Don't be afraid."

"It's that or rage. I'm worn out by rage."

Erika said, "An end is coming soon."

"You *know*?"

"Yes. Very soon."

"How? What end?"

"In most cases, not all ends are desirable, but in this case . . . any end will do. Don't you think?"

The provisioner nodded almost imperceptibly. "May I tell the others?"

"Will knowing help them?"

"Oh, yes, ma'am. Life's always been hard, you know, but lately harder."

"Then by all means, tell them."

The provisioner seemed to regard Erika with the nearest thing to gratitude that she could feel. After a silence, she said, "I don't know what to say."

"Neither of us does," said Erika. "That's how we are."

"Good-bye, Mrs Helios."

"Good-bye, Glenda."

The provisioner left the storage room, and Erika closed her eyes for a moment, unable to look at the many items of apparel strewn on the floor around her.

Then she opened her eyes and knelt among the clothes.

She selected those that might fit her friend.

The garments of the executed were still garments. And if the universe was not, as Victor said, a meaningless chaos, if it were possible for anything to be sacred surely these humble items, worn by martyred innocents, were hallowed and might provide her friend not only with a disguise but also with protection of a higher kind.

chapter 55

Duke led them across a wide earthen rampart, between vast pits of trash, through the dump, as if he knew the way.

With the moon and the stars sequestered behind ominous clouds, Crosswoods for the most part lay in darkness, although a few small fires burned out there in the black remoteness.

Carson and Michael followed the dog, in the company of Nick Frigg and Gunny Alecto, who with flashlights picked out potholes and places where the crumbling brink might be treacherous, as if every detail of this terrain was engraved in the memory of each.

"I'm a Gamma," Nick said, "or I was, and Gunny here – she's an Epsilon."

"Or was," she said. "Now I'm reborn freeborn, and I don't hate anymore. I'm not afraid anymore."

"It's like we've been living with bands of iron around our heads, and now they're cut away, the pressure gone," said Nick.

Carson didn't know what to make of their strange born-again

declarations. She still expected one of them suddenly to come at her with no more goodwill than a buzz saw.

"Sign, sink, spoon, spade, soup, stone, spinach, sparkler, soda, sand, seed, sex. *Sex!*" Gunny laughed with delight that she had found the word she wanted. "Man, oh, man, I wonder what it'll be like the next time the whole dump gang gets sexed up together, going at each other every which way, but none of us angry, nobody punching or biting, just doing all the better kind of stuff to each other. It should be interesting."

"It should," Nick said. "Interesting. Okay, folks, right up here, we're gonna go down a ramp into the west pit. See the torches and oil lamps out there a ways? That's where Deucalion's waiting."

"He's waiting out there by the big hole," Gunny said.

Nick said, "We're all going down the big hole again."

"This is some night," Gunny declared.

"Some crazy night," Nick agreed.

"What a night, huh, Nick?"

"What a night," Nick agreed.

"Down the big hole *again!*"

"It's sure a big hole."

"And we're going down it *again!*"

"We are, for sure. The big hole."

"Mother of all gone-wrongs!"

"Something to see."

"I'm just all up!" said Gunny.

"I'm all up, too," Nick said.

Grabbing at Nick's crotch, Gunny said, "I bet you are!"

"You know I am."

"You know I know you are."

"Don't I know?"

Carson figured she was no more than two conversational exchanges from either bolting back to the car or emptying the Urban Sniper into both of them.

Michael saved her sanity by breaking the rhythm and asking Nick, "How do you live with this stench?"

"How do you live *without* it?" Nick asked.

From the top of the rampart, they descended a slope of earth, into the west pit. Trash crunched and crackled and rustled underfoot, but it was well-compacted and didn't shift much.

More than a dozen people stood with Deucalion, but he was a head taller than the tallest of them. He wore his long black coat, the hood thrown back. His half-broken and tattooed face, uplit by torchlight, was not as disturbing as it ought to have been in this setting, under these circumstances. In fact, he had an air of calm certainty and unflinching resolve that reminded Carson of her father, who had been a military man before becoming a detective. Deucalion projected that competence and integrity that motivated men to follow a leader into battle – which apparently was what they were soon to do.

Michael said to him, "Hey, big guy, you're standing there like we're in a rose garden. How do you tolerate this stench?"

"Controlled synesthesia," Deucalion explained. "I convince myself to perceive the malodors as colors, not smells. I see us standing in a weave of rainbows."

"I'm going to hope you're pulling my chain."

"Carson," Deucalion said, "there's someone here who wants to meet you."

From behind Deucalion stepped a beautiful woman in a dress stained and crusted with filth.

"Good evening, Detective O'Connor."

Recognizing the voice from the phone, Carson said, "Mrs Helios."

"Yes. Erika Four. I apologize for the condition of my dress. I was murdered little more than a day ago and buried in garbage. My darling Victor didn't think to send me here with a supply of moist towelettes and a change of clothes."

chapter 56

After leaving the children's clothes with Jocko in the library, Erika went to the master suite, where she quickly packed a single suitcase for herself.

She didn't clean up the blood in the vestibule. She should have wrapped Christine's body in a blanket and called the New Race trash collectors who conveyed corpses to Crosswoods, but she did not.

After all, if she went to a window and looked northwest, the sky would be on fire. And worse was coming. Maybe it would still matter if authorities found a murdered housekeeper in the mansion, or maybe not.

Anyway, even if the discovery of Christine's body turned out to be a problem for Victor, it wasn't an issue for Erika. She suspected that she would never again see this house or New Orleans, and that she would not much longer be Victor's wife.

Only hours ago, she handled with aplomb – if not indifference – such macabre episodes as a butler chewing off his fingers. But now the mere presence of a dead Beta in the bedroom disturbed her both for reasons she understood and for reasons she was not yet able to define.

She put her suitcase at the foot of the bed, and she chose a smaller piece of luggage in which to pack everything that Victor wanted from the safe.

The existence of the walk-in vault had not been disclosed to Erika during her in-tank education. She learned about it only minutes earlier, when Victor told her how to find it.

In one corner of his immense closet, which was as large as the formal dining room downstairs, an alcove featured three floor-to-ceiling mirrors. After Victor dressed, he stepped into this space to consider the clothes he wore and to assess the degree to which his outfit achieved the effect he desired.

Standing in this alcove, Erika spoke to her reflection: "Twelve twenty-five is four one."

A voice-recognition program in the house computer accepted those five words as the first part of a two-sentence combination to the vault. The center mirror slid into the ceiling, revealing a plain steel door without hinges or handle, or keyhole.

When she said, "Two fourteen is ten thirty-one," she heard lock bolts disengage, and the door slid open with a pneumatic hiss.

In addition to tall upper cabinets, the vault contained lower drawers, all measuring the same: one foot deep, two feet wide. Each of three walls held twelve drawers, numbered 1 through 36.

From Drawer 5, she withdrew sixteen bricks of hundred-dollar bills and put them in the small suitcase. Each banded block contained fifty thousand dollars, for a total of eight hundred thousand.

Drawer 12 offered a quarter of a million dollars' worth of euros, and she emptied it.

From Drawer 16, she withdrew one million worth of bearer bonds, each valued at fifty thousand.

Drawer 24 revealed numerous small gray-velvet bags featuring drawstring closures tied in neat bows. In these were precious gems, mostly diamonds of the highest quality. She scooped up all of the bags and dropped them in the suitcase.

No doubt Victor maintained offshore bank accounts containing significant sums, held by such an intricate chain of shell companies and false names that no tax collector could link them to him. There he kept the larger part of his wealth.

What Erika collected here, according to Victor's instructions, was his on-the-run money, which he might need if the current crisis could not be contained. Listening to him on the phone, she'd thought he should use the word *would* instead of *might*, and *when* instead of *if*, but she'd said nothing.

With the suitcase, she returned to the mirrored alcove, faced the open vault door, and said, "Close and lock."

The pneumatic door hissed shut. The bolts engaged. The mirror descended into place, bringing with it her reflection, as if it had previously taken her image into the ceiling.

In the garage, Erika stowed both pieces of luggage in the cargo space of the GL550.

With a large cloth tote bag in which to carry their books, she returned to the library. In his new attire, Jocko looked less like Huckleberry Finn than like a mutant turtle from another planet, out of its shell and likely to pass for human only if everyone on Earth were struck blind.

Although the faded blue jeans looked all right from the front, they sagged in the seat because the troll didn't have much of a butt. His thin pale arms were longer than those of a real boy, so the long-sleeved T-shirt fell three inches short of his wrists.

For the first time, Erika considered that Jocko had six fingers on each hand.

He had adjusted the expansion strap on the back of the baseball cap to its full extension, making it big enough to fit him, and in fact making it too big. The cap came over the tops of his gnarled ears, and he kept tipping it back to see out from under the bill.

"It's not a funny hat," he said.

"No. I couldn't find one here, and the funny-hat store doesn't open until nine o'clock."

"Maybe they deliver earlier."

Stuffing Jocko's selection of books in the tote bag, she said, "They don't deliver like a pizza shop."

"A pizza would be a funnier hat than this. Let's get a pizza."

"Don't you think wearing a pizza on your head would attract more attention than we want?"

"No. And the shoes don't work."

Even after taking the laces out, he had not been able to fit his wide feet comfortably in the sneakers.

He said, "Anyway, Jocko walks way better barefoot, has a better grip, and if he wants to suck his toes, he doesn't have to undress them first."

His toes were nearly as long as fingers and had three knuckles each. Erika thought he must be able to climb like a monkey.

"You're probably well enough disguised if you stay in the car," she said. "And if you slump in your seat. And if you don't look out the window when another car's passing us. And if you don't wave at anyone."

"Can Jocko give them the finger?"

She frowned. "Why would you want to make obscene gestures at anyone?"

"You never know. Like, say it's a pretty night, big moon, stars all over, and say suddenly a woman's smacking you with a broom and a guy's beating your head with an empty bucket, shouting 'What is it, what is it, what is it?' You run away faster than they can run, and you want to shout something really smart at them, but you can't think of anything smart, so there's always the finger. Can Jocko give them the okay sign?"

"I think it's better if you keep your hands down and just enjoy the ride."

"Can Jocko give them a thumbs-up sign? Attaboy! Way to go! You done good!"

"Maybe the next time we go for a ride. Not tonight."

"Can Jocko give them a power-to-the-people fist?"

"I didn't know you were political." The tote bag bulged with books. "Come on. We've got to get out of here."

"Oh. Wait. Jocko forgot. In his room."

"There's nothing in your room that you'll need."

"Be back in half a jiffy."

He snatched up one of the laces from the sneakers and, holding it between his teeth, somersaulted out of the library.

When the troll returned a few minutes later, he was carrying a sack made from a pillowcase, tied shut with the shoelace.

"What's that?" Erika asked.

"Stuff."

"What stuff?"

"Jocko's stuff."

"All right. All right. Let's go."

In the garage, at the GL550, Jocko said, "You want me to drive?"

chapter 57

Judging by the quality of their excitement and the content of their conversations among themselves, Carson decided that most if not all of the people with torches and oil lamps were Epsilons, like Gunny Alecto, and were workers at the landfill.

In addition to Erika Four, however, five others of the New Race, left for dead at Crosswoods but later resurrected, were Alphas – four men and a woman – who had been terminated by Victor for one reason or another. This was the group that called themselves the Dumpsters.

Carson and Michael had been unnerved when one of the Dumpsters proved to be Bucky Guitreau, the district attorney. He wasn't the one they had killed in Audubon Park, and he wasn't the original and fully human Bucky. He was instead the *first* replicant intended to replace Bucky. He'd been replaced himself by a second replicant, the one she and Michael had killed, when Victor decided that number one wasn't a sufficiently gifted mimic to pull off the impersonation of the district attorney.

Apparently, all of these Alphas had been returned to life longer than Mrs Helios. They had found water to wash themselves, and they wore reasonably clean if threadbare clothes, which perhaps they had salvaged from these many acres of refuse.

Although she was the most recent to have been pulled back from the brink of oblivion, Erika Four had been appointed to speak not only for herself but also for the other five Alphas, perhaps because she had been their tormentor's wife. She knew Victor well, his corrupted character and temper. Better than anyone, she might be able to identify the weakness most likely to render him vulnerable.

Deucalion towered behind Erika, and as she brought Carson and Michael up-to-date, the landfill workers edged closer. None of what she said was news to them, but being the intellectual lower caste of the New Race, they seemed to be easily enchanted. They were rapt, faces shining in the lambent firelight, like children gathered for story hour around a campfire.

"The workers here have known something strange was happening under the trash fields," Erika said. "They've seen the surface rise and resettle, as if something sizable was traveling this way and that in the lower realms. They've heard haunting voices filtering up from below. Tonight they saw it for the first time, and they call it the mother of all gone-wrongs."

A murmuring passed through the Epsilons, whispered exclamations. Their faces revealed emotions that they of the New Race should not have been able to feel: happiness, awe, and perhaps hope.

"It started as a failed experiment, left here for dead, but in fact not fully dead," Erika continued. "A lightning strike in the dump enlivened it. Since then, it has evolved to become a wondrous being, an entity of indescribable beauty and profound moral purpose. Sometimes an Alpha, presumed dead even by Victor, may yet contain an incandescent filament of life for a few days after an apparent death. If attended properly, that filament can be prevented from fading entirely, and encouraged to grow brighter. As it brightens, this life force spreads through the Alpha, returning him to consciousness and full function. What these Epsilons call the mother of all gone-wrongs, we call the Resurrector, for as it was revived by lightning, it now revives us by sharing its own intensely bright life force."

So closely gathered were the Epsilons that their torches and oil lamps encircled Carson with shimmering orange light, and in this one small portion of the landfill, the night was as bright as a dawn sky painted with the sun's celebratory brush.

"Not only does the Resurrector restore the body, but it also heals the mind," said Erika Four. "From our programs, it strips out all of the encouragements to envy, hatred, and anger, and deletes as well the prohibitions against compassion, love, and hope. Tonight, it revealed itself to the landfill workers – and released them from all the programmed emotions that oppressed them, and gave to them the full range of emotions they had been denied."

Skin prickling on the back of her neck, Carson recalled Gunny Alecto's words: *The mother of all gone-wrongs talked inside our heads.*

Michael shared her reservations. "No offense. But no matter how beautiful it might be, I'm basically freaked out by something that can get inside my head *and change me.*"

In the quivering torchlight, on the broken half of Deucalion's face, reflections of flames infused false life into the tattooed patterns, which seemed to flex and crawl across the awful concavities and the broken planes, across the knotted scars.

He said, "It waits for us now in the tunnel. I went down a short while ago – and felt I was in the presence of a being that has no thinnest thread of malevolence in its weave. It will project certain thoughts to you . . . but it won't enter your mind against your wishes."

"As far as you know," Michael qualified.

"For two centuries I've had to bear witness to all forms of human wickedness," Deucalion said. "And cobbled together, as I was, from the bodies of sociopathic criminals, burdened with the brain of the vilest kind of murderer, I have a certain . . . sensitivity to the presence of evil. There is none in this Being."

Carson heard the capital B that he put on the final word. And though his confidence somewhat reassured her, though her disquiet didn't swell into apprehension, she had misgivings about going into the tunnel to which he referred.

Erika Four said, "The Resurrector will help us bring Victor to the justice he deserves. Indeed, I don't think we can bring him down without the assistance of this entity."

"If he flees here tonight or in the early morning," Deucalion said, "as we expect he will when he learns of the fire at Mercy, we will have an opportunity that we must not fail to seize."

Under the reflected torchlight in his eyes, the more profound light of his embodied storm throbbed as it sometimes did. Carson wondered if, in his mind's ear, he heard the sky-splitting crack of the thunderbolt or recalled the terror of his first minutes of unholy life.

"I believe the moment is rushing toward us," Deucalion said.

"You need to meet the Resurrector, so we are ready and waiting for Victor when he arrives."

Carson looked at Michael, and he said, "So . . . it's down the big hole, this is some night, some crazy night, I'm just all up."

chapter **58**

Somber thoughts distracted Victor from his driving, and the deserted state route, winding through lonely darkness, contributed to his bleak mood.

Always before, when setbacks forced a change of venue on him – from Germany to Argentina, to the old Soviet, to China and elsewhere – he had been furious at the associates who had failed him and at Nature for her jealous guarding of the secrets of molecular biology and her stubborn resistance to the incisive blade of his singular intelligence, but he had not lost hope.

The short-lived project in Cuba, so promising, came to ruin because of one stupid peasant, a rabid cat, a treacherous set of stairs, and a wet bar of soap left on one of the treads for no reason that made sense. Yet he and Fidel remained friends, and Victor persevered in another country, certain of ultimate triumph.

The interesting facility in North Korea, with the generous funding by a consortium of forward-thinking governments, should have been the place where the ultimate breakthroughs at last occurred. At his disposal was a virtually infinite supply of body parts from self-pitying political prisoners who preferred being carved up alive to enduring further prison meals. But how could he have foreseen that the dictator, a strutting rooster with a harem, would end up shooting the speed-grown clone of himself that Victor created at his request, when said clone developed a passion for his dangerous look-alike and extravagantly tongue-kissed him? Victor had escaped the country with his testicles only because he and the dictator had a mutual friend, one of the most admired movie stars in the world, who had brokered peace between them. Yet *still* he had persevered and had suffered neither one day of doubt nor one hour of depression.

The total destruction of the Hands of Mercy affected him more negatively than any previous setback in part because he had been much closer than ever before to triumph, within easy reach of the absolute mastery of flesh, its creation and control.

In truth, the fire itself and all the losses were not what shook his confidence. The identity of the arsonist: That's what brought him this low. The return of his first creation, the crude and lumbering beast who should have spent the past two centuries frozen in polar ice, seemed even less possible to him than that a gay clone could have undone him on the very brink of a glorious success.

He realized that his speed had fallen under twenty miles per hour. This had happened twice before. Each time he accelerated, his mind drifted, and his speed fell again.

Deucalion. What a pretentious name.

Deucalion in Patrick Duchaine's kitchen, turning away from Victor and – just gone. Merely a trick, of course. But quite a trick.

Deucalion, penetrating the Hands of Mercy without setting off an alarm.

In just a few days: Harker giving birth to some monstrosity, William chewing off his fingers, Christine confused about her identity, Werner's catastrophic cellular metamorphosis, the apparent incorporation of the entire Mercy staff into the Werner thing, the freeing of Chameleon, Erika Four destroying the Karloff experiment in psychic control, now Erika Four supposedly back from the dead, those two detectives somehow escaping Benny and Cindi Lovewell, two superb assassins . . . The list of unlikely incidents went on and on.

It all meant something.

So many things could not go wrong spontaneously.

A pattern waited to be discovered. A pattern that might well reveal a conspiracy. A cabal.

Occasionally Victor thought that he might have a mild tendency toward paranoia, but in this instance he knew his suspicion must be correct.

This time, the setback felt different from all before it. What brought him to the brink of ruin this time was not just a bar of soap on a stair or an amorous clone. A symphony of troubles required an orchestra of enemies and a determined conductor.

This time he might have to prepare for the worst.

Again he became aware that if the Mercedes lost more speed, it would be coasting.

Ahead on the right loomed a rest area. He drove off the highway, braked to a stop, and put the car in park.

Before he rushed heedlessly to the tank farm, he needed to brood about these recent events. He suspected that he was going to have to make the biggest decision of his life.

He'd driven out of the storm, but as he stared at the dwindling cones of his headlight beams, the rain caught up to him again, and a groaning wind.

Although Victor's powers of concentration were legendary among all who had worked with him, he found himself repeatedly distracted by the nonsensical apprehension that he might not be alone in the car. He *was* alone, of course, not just in the car but alone in the world to a degree that he did not need to contemplate right now, when his mood was already dark.

chapter **59**

Following the dumpsters and the landfill workers to the big hole in the west pit, Carson thought the procession appeared medieval. The vast reaches of the dump lay in a black pall, as though civilization remained centuries away from the electric era. The torchlight, the oil lamps, the atmosphere of a religious pilgrimage that arose from the sudden reverential silence of the group as they approached the entrance to the subterranean chapel of the Resurrector . . .

Although armed with two handguns and an Urban Sniper, Carson felt defenseless in the face of this unknown.

They arrived at a tunnel, approximately eight feet in diameter, angling down into the depths of the pit, which apparently the Being, the mother of all gone-wrongs, had opened to present itself to them earlier this same night.

Before they had set out, Carson asked Nick Frigg how deep the trash was piled. She was surprised to hear they were standing on almost ten stories of garbage. Considering the substantial acreage dedicated to the dump, the Resurrector could have excavated many miles of corridors, and Frigg confirmed that they had explored an elaborate network of passageways that were but part of the entity's construction.

The tightly compacted trash forming the walls of the passageway appeared to have been sealed with a transparent bonding material of sufficient strength to prevent collapse. Rippling currents and whorls of torchlight glistered across the shiny surface.

She imagined that the Resurrector had exuded this glue, which seemed to imply that its nature was in part insectile. She couldn't easily accept that the busy burrowing architect of this labyrinth and the compassionate transcendental Being that lacked a thread of malevolence in its weave were one and the same.

As they entered the tunnel, Carson expected the stink of the trash field to intensify and the air to become thick and bitter. But the glimmering sealant on the walls apparently held back the methane that otherwise would have suffocated them, and a draft flowed up from below. She had no more difficulty breathing here than on the surface, and the malodor was if anything less offensive.

When she glanced back at dog-nose Nick, his nostrils quivered and flared ceaselessly, and he smiled with pleasure. To his enhanced olfactory sense, the path of this pilgrimage was perfumed with a singular incense. Likewise for the Duke of Orleans.

The gradual slope of the tunnel took them perhaps ten feet below the surface by the point that they had walked a hundred feet from the entrance. Here, the passageway turned sharply left and widened into a spacious gallery before seeming to curve down at a steeper angle.

In this gallery, the Resurrector waited, initially at the limits of their lights, half-seen and mysterious.

The width of the chamber allowed the procession to spread out, with a clear view for each. Carson glanced left, right, and saw that everyone but she and Michael appeared deeply affected by the presence before them, not enraptured but certainly content, at peace, many with smiles on their faces, eyes shining.

As they came side by side in a line, the Being before them approached, shadows sliding away from it as the light seemed to enrobe it in spun gold.

To her surprise, a sense of well-being came over Carson, and the foreboding to which she had clung swiftly dissipated. She knew as surely as she had known anything in her life that she would be safe here, that the Resurrector was benevolent and a champion of their cause.

She understood that this entity was broadcasting calming psychic waves of reassurance. It would never violate her sanctity by coming inside her mind, but was speaking to her in this manner as she might speak to it in words.

Telepathically, without seeming to use language and seemingly without images – for none flashed through her mind – the Resurrector somehow inculcated in her an understanding of how they would enter the tank farm, how the New Race working there would be disabled, and how Victor might be captured, his reign of madness and his kingdom of terror brought finally to an end.

During all of this, Carson slowly grew aware that she could not describe the Resurrector in any specific detail. Her sense was that before her stood a thing of such unearthly beauty that angels could not outshine it, a beauty humble in its every part yet so majestic in its complete effect that she was not merely enchanted but also uplifted. Here was a beauty both of form and of spirit, a spirit of such immaculate intention and righteous confidence that Carson's own not inconsiderable courage, hope, and resolution were inspired to new heights. This was her sense, yes, but if asked to describe the form that aroused such soaring emotions in her, she could not have said whether it had two legs or ten, one head or a hundred, or none at all.

She squinted, straining to make out even general contours, a basic biological architecture, but the Resurrector proved to be so gloriously radiant that it shimmered just beyond the ability of her senses to define it. The torchlight in which the entity now stood seemed to cloak it in mystery more than had the shadows from which it first approached them.

Carson's initial foreboding welled in her again and quickened into fright. Her heart began to race, and she heard her ragged breath catching, catching, catching in her throat. Then in a blink, and only *for* a blink, she saw the Resurrector as it really was, a blasphemy, a hideous offense against nature, an abomination from which the mind recoiled in desperate defense of its sanity.

One blink of paralyzing truth, and then again the radiance, the perception of beauty beyond the mind's capacity to fully understand, exquisite form without definition, virtue and righteousness in the flesh, kindness embodied, love materialized . . . Her fright washed away in a tide of benevolence. Her heart settled to an easy beat, and she found her breath again, and her blood did not run cold, neither did the nape of her neck prickle, and she knew that regardless of the form of the Resurrector, she was safe, she was safe, and it was a champion of their cause.

chapter 60

Jocko in the big car. Not driving. The day would come. All he needed was the keys. And a booster pillow. And long sticks to work the floor pedals. And a reliable map. And somewhere to go.

Until then, riding was good. Being driven was nice.

"Jocko's first car ride," he told Erika.

"How do you like it?"

"Smooth. Comfy. Better than creeping through the night, scared of brooms and buckets."

Rain rattled on the roof. Wipers flung big splashes off the windshield.

Jocko sat dry. Racing through the rain but dry.

In the night, wind shook trees. Shook them hard. Almost as hard as the crazy drunk hobo shook Jocko while shouting, *Get out of my dream, you creepazoid, get out of my dream!*

Wind slammed the car. Hissed and grumbled at the window.

Jocko smiled at the wind.

Smiling felt good. It didn't look good. He smiled at a mirror once, so he knew how not-good it looked. But it sure felt good.

"You know what?" he said.

"What?"

"How long has Jocko not twirled or backflipped, or nothing?"

"Not since you've been sitting there."

"How long is that?"

"Over half an hour."

"Amazing."

"Is that your record?"

"Got to be. By like twenty-seven minutes."

Maybe having clothes relaxed Jocko. He liked pants. The way they covered up your flat butt and the knees that made people laugh.

After the crazy drunk hobo stopped shaking Jocko, he shouted, spraying spit, *What the hell kind of knees are those? Those knees make me SICK! Never saw knees make me SICK before. You freak-kneed creepazoid!*

Then the hobo vomited. Just to prove Jocko's knees really were sick-making.

Erika was a good driver. Focused on the road. Staring hard.

She was thinking about driving. But something else, too. Jocko could tell. He could read her heart a little.

His first night alive, he found some magazines. In a trash can. Read them in an alleyway. Under a lamppost smelled like cat pee.

One article was called "You Can Learn to Read Her Heart."

You don't cut her open to read it, either. That was a relief. Jocko didn't like blood.

Well, he liked it inside where you needed it. Not outside where you could see it.

Anyway, the magazine told Jocko how to read her heart. So now he knew something troubled Erika.

Secretly he watched her. Sneaking looks.

Those delicate nostrils. Jocko wished he had those nostrils. Not those particular nostrils. He didn't want to take her nostrils. Jocko just wanted nostrils like them.

"Are you sad?" Jocko asked.

Surprised, she glanced at him. Then back at the road. "The world is so beautiful."

"Yeah. Dangerous but pretty."

"I wish I belonged in it," she said.

"Well, we're here."

"Being and belonging are different things."

"Like alive and living," Jocko said.

She glanced at him again but didn't reply. Stared at the road, the rain, the wipers wiping.

Jocko hoped he hadn't said something stupid. But he was Jocko. Jocko and stupid went together like . . . like Jocko and ugly.

After a while, he said, "Are there pants that make you smarter?"

"How could pants make anyone smarter?"

"Well, these made me prettier."

"I'm glad you like them."

Erika took her foot off the accelerator. Eased down on the brake. As they stopped on the pavement, she said, "Jocko, look."

He slid forward on his seat. Craned his neck.

Deer crossed the road, in no hurry. A buck, two does, a fawn. Others came out of dark woods on the left.

The trees shook in the wind, the tall grass thrashed.

But the deer were calm under the trembling trees, in the lashing grass, moving slowly but with purpose. They almost appeared to drift like weightless figures in a dream. Serene.

Their legs were so long and slender. They walked like dancers danced, each step precise. The grace.

Golden-brown coats on the does. The buck was brown. The fawn was colored like the does but with white spots. Tails black on top, white underneath.

Narrow, gentle faces. Eyes set on the sides of their faces to provide a panoramic view.

Heads held high, ears tipped slightly forward, they stared at the Mercedes, but only once each. Not afraid.

The fawn stayed near one of the does. Off the road once more, no longer directly in the headlight beams, it capered in a circle in the half-light, in the wet grass.

Jocko watched the fawn caper in the wet grass.

Another buck and doe. Rain glistening on the male's antlers.

Jocko and Erika watched in silence. There was nothing they could say.

The sky black, the rain rushing, the dark woods, the grass, the many deer.

There was nothing they could say.

When the deer were gone, Erika drove north again.

After a while, she said softly, "Being and belonging."

Jocko knew she meant the deer.

"Maybe just being is enough, it's all so beautiful," Jocko said.

Although she glanced at him, he didn't look at her. He couldn't bear to see her sad.

"Anyway," he said, "if somebody doesn't belong in the world, there's no door they can throw him out. They can't take the world away from him and put him somewhere different. The worst thing they can do is kill him. That's all."

After another silence, she said, "Little friend, you never stop surprising me."

Jocko shrugged. "I read some magazines once."

chapter 61

Victor was in the dark night of his soul, but he was also in a Mercedes S600, arguably the finest automobile in the world. The suit he wore had cost over six thousand dollars, his wristwatch more than a hundred thousand. He had lived 240 years, most of the time in high style, and he had known more adventure, more thrills, more power, and more triumphs of a more momentous nature than any man in history. As he considered his current situation and the possibility that he might die soon, he found that making the fateful decision he needed to make was easier than he had expected when he parked in this rest area. He had no choice but to take the most extreme action available to him, because if he died, the loss to the world would be devastating.

He was too brilliant to die.

Without him, the future would be bleak. Any chance of imposing order on a meaningless universe would die with him, and chaos would rule eternal.

He used the voice-activated car phone to call the household-staff dormitory at the estate in the Garden District.

A Beta named Ethel answered, and Victor told her to bring James to the phone at once. James had been third in the hierarchy of the staff, behind William and Christine, who were now both dead. He was next in line to be the butler. If Victor hadn't been so pressed by the events of the past twenty-four hours, he would have appointed James to his new post the previous day.

When James came to the phone, Victor honored him with the news of his promotion and gave him his first assignment as butler. "And remember, James, follow the instructions I've just given you to the letter. I expect absolute perfection in everything a butler does, but most especially in this instance."

———

After leaving his umbrella on the terrace and after thoroughly wiping his wet shoes with a cloth that he brought for that purpose, James entered the house on the first floor, by the back door at the end of the north hall.

He carried the mysterious object that had obsessed him for the past two hours: a crystal ball.

After proceeding directly to the library, as Mr Helios had instructed, James carefully placed the gleaming sphere on the seat of an armchair.

"Are you happy there?" he asked.

The sphere did not reply.

Frowning, James moved it to another armchair.

"Better," the sphere told him.

When the crystal ball initially spoke to him, two hours earlier,

James had been minding his own business, sitting at the kitchen table in the dormitory, stabbing his hand with a meat fork and watching it repeatedly heal. The fact that he healed so quickly and so well gave him reason to believe he would be all right, though for most of the day, he had felt all wrong.

The first thing the sphere said to him was, "I know the way to happiness."

Of course, James at once expressed a desire to know the way.

Since then, the crystal ball had said many things, most of them inscrutable.

Now it said, "Salted or unsalted, sliced or cubed, the choice is yours."

"Can we get back to happiness?" James asked.

"Use a knife and," the sphere said.

"And what?" James asked.

"And fork."

"What do you want me to do with a knife and fork?"

"If peeled."

"You're making no sense," James said accusingly.

"A spoon," said the sphere.

"Now it's a spoon?"

"If halved and unpeeled."

"What is the path to happiness?" James pleaded because he was afraid to demand an answer and offend the sphere.

"Long, narrow, twisting, dark," said the sphere. "For the likes of you, the path to happiness is one mean sonofabitch of a path."

"But I can get there, can't I? Even one like me?"

"Do you really want happiness?" asked the sphere.

"Desperately. Doesn't have to be forever. Just for a while."

"Your other choice is insanity."

"Happiness. I'll take happiness."

"Yogurt works with. Ice cream works with."

"With what?"

The sphere didn't reply.

"I'm in a very bad way," James pleaded.

Silence.

Frustrated, James said, "Wait here. I'll be right back. I've got something to do for Mr Helios."

He found the hidden switch, a section of the bookcase pivoted, and the secret passageway was revealed.

James glanced back at the sphere on the seat of the armchair. Sometimes it didn't look like a crystal ball. Sometimes it looked like a cantaloupe. This was one of those times.

The sphere was a crystal ball only when the magic was in it. James feared that the magic might go out of it and never come back.

In the secret passage, he came to the first door and removed all five steel bolts, as he had been instructed.

When he opened the door, he saw the corridor that Mr Helios had described: copper rods to the left, steel rods to the right. A low, ominous hum.

Instead of going farther, James ran back to the start of the passageway, pushed the button to open the bookcase door from this side, and hurried to the sphere.

"What is the path to happiness?" he asked.

"Some people put a little lemon on it," said the crystal ball.

"Put lemon on what?"

"You know what your problem is?"

"What is my problem?"

"You hate yourself."

James had nothing to say to that.

He returned to the secret passageway, but this time he took the crystal ball with him.

———

Victor had asked James to phone him when the task was completed. Alternately consulting his world-class wristwatch and the dashboard clock of his magnificent sedan, he thought the new butler was taking too long. No doubt, awed by his promotion and by the realization that he would be speaking more often with his maker, James approached his mission with excessive care.

As he waited for the butler's call, the conviction again rose in him that he was not alone in the Mercedes. This time, he turned to look in the backseat, knowing full well no one was there.

He knew the cause of his edginess. Until James completed the task he had been sent to do, Victor remained mortal, and the world could be denied the shining future that only he could create. As soon as the butler reported completion of the job, Victor could proceed to the farm, face whatever threat might wait there, and be confident that the future would still be his.

chapter **62**

Chameleon suspects deception.

Once again, the PUZZLE smells like both an EXEMPT and a TARGET. The scent of an EXEMPT is far and away stronger than that of a TARGET, but the second scent is definitely present.

The car has been stopped for some time. Yet the PUZZLE does not get out. It sits in silence behind the wheel.

After a while, the PUZZLE makes a phone call. Chameleon listens, hears nothing incriminating.

But the PUZZLE talks about hidden doors and passageways, a hidden room. This suggests but does not prove bad behavior.

Chameleon assumes that EXEMPTS are incapable of bad behavior. But its program is not clear on this point.

It is permitted to act on assumptions, but they must be Class A assumptions, which in a rigorous application of logic, must conform to at least four of five proofs. This assumption is Class C.

Chameleon is capable of impatience. It has been a long time between kills.

It remembers clearly three kills. They occurred during its testing phase.

The pleasure is intense. The word Chameleon knows for the pleasure that comes from killing is *orgasm*.

Its entire body spasms. In orgasm, it is as fully in touch with its body as it will ever be – but, strangely, at the same time seems to escape its body and for a minute or two is not itself, is not anything, is only pleasure.

After the phone call, the PUZZLE sits in silence again.

Chameleon was a long time in the cold. A long time in the imprisoning polymeric-fabric sack.

Now it is warm.

Under the pleasing scent, the infuriating scent.

Chameleon wants an orgasm. Chameleon wants an orgasm. Chameleon wants an orgasm.

chapter **63**

Under the dump, Carson and Michael and Deucalion followed the landfill workers and the resurrected Alphas along a passageway that branched off the main course. It would lead them out of the landfill and under the tank farm next door.

Ahead of them, torchlight ignited faux fire across the glazed curves of the tunnel. Because they were at the end of the procession, an inky gloom pooled behind them.

The Resurrector was far in front. Perhaps it had already entered the main building at the tank farm.

Carson had no concern about the darkness at her back. Here, in the warren of their monstrously strange accomplice, they were safer than they had been in a long time.

"What it does telepathically," Deucalion said, "is project its inner nature in order to screen from us its physical appearance, because it would be impossible for most people who see it to believe it's benign."

Like Carson, Deucalion and Michael had been suspicious of the telepathically projected image and had been strong-willed enough to peer through the Resurrector's radiant veil to the truth of its form. Deucalion had seen it twice, once for perhaps half a minute.

Michael achieved only the brief glimpse that Carson had seen. In spite of his tendency toward cynicism, he was convinced that the creature could be trusted, that it was allied with them. "If not, it could have killed us all back there, as big and powerful as it is."

"None of the landfill workers saw through its disguise or even suspects there is one," Deucalion said. "I doubt that the Alphas, Erika Four and the others, have any suspicion, either. They and the Resurrector are of the same flesh that Victor engineered for the New Race, and perhaps that renders them more susceptible than we are to its masquerade."

"I was plenty susceptible," Michael said. "I felt as if I was in an anteroom of Heaven, getting a pep talk from an archangel while waiting for judgment."

"Why make a thing that looks . . . like that?" Carson wondered.

Deucalion shook his head. "That it should look like that was not Victor's plan. Physiologically, it's a gone-wrong. In its mind, in its intentions, it's a gone-*right*."

The tunnel ceased to pass through compacted trash. Abruptly, its walls were formed of earth, coated with the glossy material that had sealed over the trash in the main passageway and in the first part of this one.

The Resurrector was a digger of considerable industry.

"Will he really come here?" Carson wondered.

"He will," Deucalion assured her.

"But Erika Four says she's called him twice. He knows she's up here somewhere, reanimated. He knows something unprecedented must be happening."

As Deucalion looked down at her, the light of the centuries-old storm throbbed through his eyes. "He'll come nevertheless. He's got too much invested in the tank farm, a new crop birthing in less than twenty-four hours. Mercy gone, this is his best bet. He's arrogant and insanely certain of himself. Never forget the pride that drives him. Perhaps in all of history, there has been only one other whose pride was greater than Victor's."

Maybe the caffeine tide pulsing through Carson was brewing up new symptoms or maybe sleep deprivation torqued her mind in spite of the NoDoz-cola cocktails. Whatever the cause, a fresh anxiety began to pluck at her. She was not a seer, not a Gypsy with one eye in the future, but a prickly intuition warned her that even if Victor died in the next few hours, the world he wanted to make was a world of which others dreamed, as well, a world in which human exceptionalism was denied, in which the masses were regimented drones who served an untouchable elite, in which flesh was cheap. Even if Victor received justice and a grave in garbage, Carson and Michael were going to be making a life together in a world ever more hostile to freedom, to human dignity, to love.

As they reached the hole that had been bored through concrete block and into the basement of the main building at the tank farm, Deucalion said, "The first time I saw the Resurrector, before you two arrived, it told me – rather, it impressed on me in that wordless way it makes you know things – that it expects to die tonight, here or at the landfill."

Michael let his breath out in a hiss. "That doesn't sound like our side wins."

"Or," said Deucalion, "the creature may know that, in winning, sacrifices will have to be made."

chapter **64**

The blue laser scanned James, approved of him, and switched off the security feature that would have fried him crisp if he had been an unwelcome intruder.

Carrying the crystal ball, he went to the second steel door. He put the sphere on the floor while he pulled the five lock bolts from their slots.

"Try prosciutto," said the crystal sphere.

"That's ham."

"It works with."

"With what?"

"I know the path to happiness," said the sphere.

Voice tight with frustration, James said, "Then *tell* me."

"Paper-thin."

"What does that mean?"

"Serve it paper-thin."

The thick door swung open. James had been forbidden to enter the windowless Victorian drawing room. On his way out, he must leave the steel doors open, the exit route unobstructed.

He remained obedient, even in his current state of distraction.

Anyway, he had no interest in that room. Not when happiness might be within his grasp.

The crystal sphere said nothing on the way back to the library.

From the library desk, James phoned Mr Helios and reported that the task had been completed precisely according to instructions.

The moment James hung up the phone, the sphere said, "You were not made for happiness."

"But if you know the path . . ."

"I know the path to happiness."

"But you won't tell me?"

"Also works with cheese," said the sphere.

"So I'm not worthy of happiness. Is that it?"

"You're just a meat machine."

"I'm a person," James insisted.

"Meat machine. Meat machine."

Furious, James threw the crystal ball to the floor, where it shattered, spilling a mass of slimy yellow seeds and revealing its orange inner flesh.

He stared at it for a while, uncomprehending.

When he looked up, he saw that someone had left a book on the desk: *A History of the Troll in Literature*. He picked it up with the intention of returning it to its proper place on the shelves.

The book said, "I know the path to happiness."

With renewed hope and excitement, James said, "Please tell me."

"Do you deserve happiness?"

"I believe I do. Why shouldn't I deserve it?"

"There may be reasons."

"Everyone deserves happiness."

"Not everyone," said the book, "but let's talk about it."

chapter **65**

As the GL550 raced north in the rain, Jocko hoped for more deer. While he hoped, he thought about some things.

Sometimes Jocko thought about big issues. Usually in two-minute segments. Between activities.

Big issues like why some things were ugly, some weren't. Maybe if everything was beautiful, nothing would be.

People saw one thing, they swooned over it. They saw this other thing, they pounded it with sticks.

Maybe there had to be variety for life to work. Swoon over everything, you got bored. Beat everything with a stick – boring.

Personally, Jocko would be happy to swoon over everything.

Jocko sometimes thought why he had no genitals. All Jocko had was that funny thing he peed with. It wasn't genitals. He called it his swoozle.

Fortunately, it rolled up. Folded away. When not in use.

If it didn't fold out of sight, crazy drunk hobos would vomit about that, too.

One thing Jocko tried *not* to think about. About how he was the only one. Only one of his kind. Too sad to think about.

Jocko thought about it anyway. Jocko couldn't turn his mind off. It spun and somersaulted like Jocko.

Maybe that was why no genitals. No need for them. Not when you were one of a kind.

Through all this thinking, Jocko secretly watched Erika.

"Do you think about big issues?" Jocko asked.

"Like what?"

"Like . . . things you don't have."

She was quiet so long. Jocko thought he screwed up again.

Then she said, "Sometimes I wonder what it would be like to have a mother."

Jocko slumped in his seat. "Jocko's sorry. Sorry he asked. That's too hard. Don't think about it."

"And what's it like to *be* a mother? I'll never know."

"Why never?"

"Because of how I'm made. Made to be used. Not to be loved."

"You'd be a great mother," Jocko said.

She said nothing. Eyes on the road. Rain on the road, rain in her eyes.

"You would," he insisted. "You take care of Jocko real good."

She kind of laughed. It was kind of a sob, too.

Way to go. Jocko speaks. People weep.

"You're very sweet," she said.

So maybe things weren't as bad as they seemed.

Letting their speed drop, she said, "Isn't that Victor's car?"

Or maybe things were worse than they seemed.

Rising in his seat, he said, "Where?"

"That rest area on the right. Yes, it's him."

"Keep going."

"I don't want him behind us. We have to get there separately from him, or I can't sneak you in."

Erika pulled into the rest area. Stopped behind Victor's sedan. "Stay here, stay down."

"You're getting out? It's raining."

"We don't want him coming to us, do we?" She opened the door.

———

After receiving confirmation that James had done as instructed, Victor took a few minutes to consider how he would approach the tank farm.

Some of the New Race who lived and worked at the farm might be breaking down in one way or another. He would need to be cautious, but he refused to be scared off. These were his creations, products of his genius, inferior to him in every way imaginable, and they could no more frighten him than one of Mozart's concertos could have terrified the composer, than a painting by Rembrandt could have sent the artist screaming into the night. They would submit to him or hear the death phrase.

He foresaw no chance that anything like the Werner abomination would greet him at the farm. Werner had been a singularity. And where was it now? Vaporized with everything else in the Hands of Mercy.

No rebellion against Victor could hope to succeed, not only because his power was that of the mythic gods, but also because the smartest of the Alphas was an idiot by comparison with its maker, he on whom the centuries took no toll.

Erika Four, an Alpha, would be no match for him. He had killed her once with only a silk necktie and the power of his hands, and he could kill her again if the bitch had in fact been revived. An Alpha, a woman, and a wife – she was three times inferior to him. He would delight in the opportunity to punish her for the impudence of those two phone calls. If she thought she had been cruelly treated in her first life, in her second he would teach her what cruelty really was.

He had no fear of going to the tank farm. He *seethed* with desire to be there and to rule this new kingdom with a ferocious discipline that would allow no repeat of the Hands of Mercy.

As he reached to release the parking brake, a vehicle appeared on the highway, approaching from the south. Instead of passing, it parked behind him, flooding the interior of the sedan with light.

His mirrors presented too few details, so he turned in his seat to look through the back window. Erika Five was behind the wheel of the GL550, which he had ordered her to drive to the farm.

Staring back at her, furious with her because she looked like the impudent and insulting Erika Four, Victor saw nothing in the backseat, but he heard something move there. In the instant, he knew why he had felt that he was not alone: *Chameleon!*

The New Race pheromones with which he had doused himself would provide hours of protection. Except that . . . in moments of exertion when a light sweat might be broken, in moments of rage or fear, his true scent would grow riper and might be detected under the New Race disguise.

Victor flung open the driver's door and plunged out of the car, into the night. Into the *rain*. The downpour would fade the scent of his own pheromones, but it would more effectively wash away the odor of the New Race, which was only sprinkled on his suit.

He should have slammed the door, locked it remotely,

abandoned the sedan, and gone to the farm with Erika. But he no longer dared approach the open driver's door, because Chameleon might already have scrambled into the front seat.

Worse, it already might be out of the sedan, on rest-area pavement immediately around him. The ceaseless dance of raindrops on the blacktop would entirely conceal the telltale ripple of Chameleon in motion.

Inexplicably, Erika seemed to have gotten out of the GL even an instant before he had vacated the S600. At his side, sensing trouble, she said, "Victor? What's wrong?"

———

Erika told Jocko, *Stay down.*

She said it like a scolding mother. She would be a good mother. But wasn't Jocko's mother. Nobody was.

Jocko raised his head. Saw Erika and Victor together. Instantly soaked by rain.

More interesting was the bug. The biggest bug Jocko ever saw. Half as big as Jocko.

This one didn't look tasty. Looked bitter.

In the storm drain, bugs came close to Jocko. Easy to catch. Bugs didn't know his big yellow eyes could see them in the dark.

Something wrong with this bug. Besides being so big.

Suddenly Jocko knew. The way it sneaked. The way it started to rear up. This bug would kill.

Pillowcase. On the floor. In front of his seat. Slip the knot in the shoelace. Inside – soap, soap, soap. The knife.

Quick, quick, quick, Jocko in the rain. Capering toward Erika and Victor. *Don't pirouette.*

chapter **66**

The bug didn't want to die.

Neither did Jocko. Everything going so well. Soap. His first ride in a car. Someone to talk to. His first pants. Nobody hit him for *hours*. Soon a funny hat. So of course a giant killer bug shows up. Jocko luck.

Two ripping claws. One crushing claw. Six pincers. Stinger. Reciprocating saw for a tongue. Teeth. Teeth behind the first teeth. Everything but a flame-spitting hole. Oh, there it was. A bug born to be bad.

Jocko dropped on it with both knees. Stabbed, slashed, ripped, tore. Picked the bug up, slammed it down. Slammed it again. Slammed it. More stabbing. Fierce. Unrelenting. Jocko scared himself.

The bug squirmed. Tried to wriggle away. But it didn't fight back, and it died.

Puzzled by the bug's pacifism, Jocko got to his feet. Maybe the sight of Jocko paralyzed it with terror. Jocko stood in the driving rain. Breathless. Dizzy.

Rain snapping on his bald head.

Lost the baseball cap. Ah. Standing on it.

Erika and Victor seemed speechless.

Gasping, Jocko said, "Bug."

Erika said, "I couldn't see it. Until it was dead."

Jocko triumphant. Heroic. His time had come. His time at last. To shine.

Victor skewered Jocko with his stare. "*You* could see it?"

The cap's expansion strap was hooked around Jocko's toes.

Wheezing, Jocko said to Erika, "It was . . . gonna . . . kill you."

Victor disagreed: "It's programmed to spare anyone with the scent of New Race flesh. Of we three, it would have killed only me."

Jocko had saved Victor from certain death.

Victor said, "You're of my flesh, but I don't know you."

Stupid, stupid, stupid. Jocko wanted to lie down in front of one of the cars and drive over himself.

"What are you?" Victor demanded.

Jocko wanted to beat himself with a bucket.

"*Who* are you?" Victor pressed.

Trying to shake the cap off his foot, panting, Jocko said without the desired force: "I am . . . the child of . . . Jonathan Harker."

He raised the knife. The blade had broken off in the bug.

"He died . . . to birth me . . ."

"You're the parasitical second self that developed spontaneously from Harker's flesh."

"I am . . . a juggler . . ."

"Juggler?"

"Never mind," said Jocko. He dropped the handle of the knife. Furiously kicked his foot. Cast off the cap.

"I will need to study your eyes," said Victor.

"Sure. Why not."

Jocko turned away. Skip, skip, skip forward, hop backward. Skip, skip, skip forward, hop backward. Twirl.

———

As she watched the troll pirouetting across the blacktop, Erika wanted to hurry to him, halt him, give him a hug, and tell him that he was very brave.

Victor said, "Where did he come from?"

"He showed up at the house a little while ago. I knew you'd want to examine him."

"What is he doing?"

"It's just a thing he does."

"I'll find answers in him," Victor said. "Why they're changing form. Why the flesh has gone wrong. There's much to learn from him."

"I'll bring him to the farm."

"The eyes are a bonus," Victor said. "If he's awake when I dissect the eyes, I'll have the best chance of understanding how they function."

She watched Victor walk to the open door of the S600.

Before getting into the car, he looked again at the skipping, hopping, twirling troll, and then at Erika. "Don't let him dance away into the night."

"I won't. I'll bring him to the farm."

As Victor got into the sedan and drove out of the rest area, Erika walked into the middle of the roadway.

Wind tore the night, ripped rain from the black sky, shook the trees as if to throttle the life from them. The world was wild and violent and strange.

The troll walked on his hands, down the center line of the highway.

When she could no longer hear the S600 above the wind roar, Erika glanced back, watching the distant taillights until they were out of sight.

The troll capered in a serpentine pattern, lane to lane, pausing now and then to spring off the pavement and kick his heels together.

Wind danced with the night, anointed the earth with rain, inspired the trees to celebrate. The world was free and exuberant and wondrous.

Erika rose onto the points of her toes, spread her arms wide, took a deep breath of the wind, and stood for a moment in expectation of the twirl.

chapter 67

As the landfill was encircled by a formidable fence, so was the tank farm. Instead of three staggered rows of loblolly pines, there were clusters of live oaks festooned with moss.

The sign at the entry gate identified the resident corporation as GEGENANGRIFF, German for *counterattack,* Victor's little joke, as his life was dedicated to an assault against the world.

The main building covered over two acres: a two-story brick structure with clean modern lines. Because every policeman, public official, and bureaucrat in the parish was a replicant, he'd had no trouble with building-code requirements, building inspections, or government approvals.

He opened the rolling iron gate with his remote control and parked in the underground garage.

The experience at the rest area had blown away the last clinging doubts that made him wary of returning to the farm. He'd been spared from a murderous creation of his own, Chameleon, by the mutant being that had evolved out of Jonathan Harker, who himself was one of the New Race. To Victor, this strongly suggested – nay, confirmed beyond question – that the entire New Race enterprise was so brilliantly conceived and so powerfully executed that within it had evolved a system of synchronicity that would ensure that errors in the project, if any, would self-correct.

Carl Jung, the great Swiss psychologist, had theorized that synchronicity, a word he invented for remarkable coincidences that have profound effects, is an acausal connecting principle that can in strange ways impose order on our lives. Victor enjoyed Jung's work, though he would have liked to rewrite all the man's essays and books, to bring to them a far greater depth of insight than poor Carl possessed. Synchronicity was not integral to the universe, as Carl believed, but sprang up only during those certain periods in certain cultures when human endeavor was as close to fully rational as it would ever get. The more rational the culture, the more likely that synchronicity would arise as a means of correcting what few errors the culture committed.

Victor's implementation of the New Race and of his vision for a unified world was so rational, was worked out in such exquisitely logical detail, that a system of synchronicity evolved within it while he wasn't looking. Something had gone wrong with the creation tanks at the Hands of Mercy without any indication to Victor, and before more imperfect New Race models could be produced, Deucalion appeared after two centuries to burn down the facility – an incredible coincidence indeed! Deucalion assumed that he was destroying Victor, when instead he was preventing more flawed models of the New Race from being produced, forcing Victor to use only the vastly improved creation tanks at the farm. Synchronicity had corrected the error. And no doubt synchronicity would deal with Deucalion, as well, and clean up other minor annoyances – Detectives O'Connor and Maddison, among others – that might otherwise inhibit Victor in his ever more rapid march toward absolute dominance of all things.

With Victor's unstoppable drive for power, with his singular intellect, with his cold materialism and his ruthless practicality, and now with synchronicity on his side, he had become untouchable, immortal.

He was immortal.

He took the elevator from the parking garage to the tank fields on the main floor. When the doors opened and he stepped through, he found the entire staff, sixty-two of the New Race, waiting for him, as throughout the ages commoners have gathered along streets to bask in the glory of passing royalty or to honor great political leaders whose courage and commitment those drudges of the proletariat could never hope to match.

Having stood in the rain while the synchronistic Harker mutant had killed Chameleon, Victor was disheveled as no one had ever seen him. On any other day, he might have been keenly annoyed to be seen in a sodden and rumpled suit with his hair disarranged. But in this hour of his transcendence, the condition of his wardrobe and hair did not matter, because his elevation to immortality was clearly evident to this audience, his radiance undiminished.

How they goggled at him, abashed by his wisdom and knowledge, mortified by their ignorance, overawed by his godlike power.

Raising his arms and spreading them wide, Victor said, "I understand the awe in which you hold your maker, but always remember that the best way to honor him is to bend more diligently to his work, give of yourselves as never before, commit every fiber of your being to the fulfillment of his vision."

As they came forward, Victor realized that they intended to lift him high and bear him to his office, as throughout history so many enraptured crowds had borne returning heroes through streets to halls of honor. Previously, he would have chastised them for wasting his time and their own. But perhaps this once, considering the momentous nature of the day's events and of his ascendance to the company of the immortals, he would indulge them, because allowing them to attend him in this way, he would surely be inspiring them to greater efforts on his behalf.

chapter 68

Jocko in despair. Rain-soaked. Feet pulled up on the passenger seat. Thin arms around his legs. Baseball cap turned backward.

Erika behind the wheel. Not driving. Staring at the night.

Victor not dead. Should be but not.

Jocko not dead. Should be but not. Total screwup.

"Jocko is never gonna eat another bug," Jocko said.

She just stared at the night. Said nothing.

Jocko wished she would say something.

Maybe she would do the right thing. Beat Jocko to death. He deserved it. But no. She was too nice. Typical Jocko luck.

There were things he could do. Put down the power window. Stick his head out. Power the window up. Cut off his head.

Erika said, "I'm programmed for obedience. I've done things I knew he wouldn't approve of – but I haven't actively disobeyed him."

Jocko could take off his T-shirt. Tear it in strips. Pack strips in his nose. Roll up his cap. Stuff it down his throat. Suffocate.

"Something's happened to me tonight," she said. "I don't know. Maybe I could drive right by the farm, maybe just drive and drive forever."

Jocko could go into woods. Prick a thumb. Wait for wild pigs to smell blood, come and eat him.

"But I'm afraid to pop the parking brake and drive. What if I can't pass the place? What if I pull in there? What if I'm not even able to let you go free on your own?"

Jocko raised one hand. "May I say?"

"What is it?"

"Jocko wonders if you have an ice pick."

"Why do you need an ice pick?"

"Do you have one?"

"No."

"Never mind."

She leaned forward. Forehead on steering wheel. Closed her eyes. Made a thin, sad sound.

Should be possible to commit suicide with a tire jack. Think about it. Think. Think.

"May I say?"

"Say what?"

"See Jocko's ear?"

"Yes."

"Is ear hole big enough, he could fit in the end of your tire jack?"

"What in the world are you talking about?"

"Never mind."

With sudden determination, she released the parking brake. Put the 550 in gear, drove out of the rest area.

"Are we going somewhere?" Jocko asked.

"Somewhere."

"Will we go past a high cliff?"

"No. Not on this road."

"Will we cross any train tracks?"

"I'm not sure. Why?"

"Never mind."

chapter **69**

As Victor consented to the attentions of the adoring crowd, he realized that in addition to the staff of the tank farm, Deucalion was also present, and Detectives O'Connor and Maddison, as well.

How brilliant he had been to foresee that very soon synchronicity would restore balance to his world, correct all errors by the mechanism of astonishing coincidence. The very presence of his first-made and the detectives confirmed his elevation to the status of an immortal, and he looked forward to seeing by what meaningful coincidence they would be killed.

He still carried a pistol in a shoulder rig, under his suit coat, but it would be beneath him to shoot the trio himself, for he was now not merely the singular genius he had always been, but also such a paragon of reason and logic that the most powerful forces in the universe operated for his benefit. Self-defense was a necessity of the common herd, of which he had never been a member and from which he was now even farther removed. Synchronicity and no doubt other recondite mechanisms would come to his assistance in dazzling and unexpected ways.

Many hands lifted him off the floor, and he thought his people might carry him seated upright on their shoulders, like a Chinese emperor of old was transported aloft in an ornate chair, might carry him to his office where the great work would continue, greater even than everything he had heretofore accomplished. But in their zeal, in their earnest enthusiasm to celebrate their maker, they pulled him supine, and two phalanxes of bearers supported him between them, on their shoulders, so he faced the ceiling unless he turned his head to one side or the other. Their grips on his ankles, legs, wrists, and arms were firm and their strength was more than adequate to the task, because he made his people strong and engineered them with endurance, the endurance of good machines.

Suddenly his bearers were on the move, and the many others crowded close, perhaps hoping they might be able to touch him or hoping that he might turn his head toward them and look upon them, so they could say years hence that they had been here on this historic day and that he had met their eyes and knew them and smiled. The atmosphere was festive, and many seemed jubilant, which was not a mood easily achieved by the New Race, considering their programming. Then Victor realized that they were future-focused on the triumphs their master would achieve in this new facility, looking forward to the day – now so much closer – when the relentless killing of the hated Old Race would begin. This must be the source of their jubilation: the prospect of genocide, the scourging from the world of every last human being to ever have spoken of God.

Evidently they had more in mind than just transporting him to his desk, because although his office was on the main floor, they carried him down two flights of stairs as effortlessly as across flat terrain. They must have some special honor in mind. And though Victor had no need for the approval of their kind, had no desire in fact for the approval of anyone, he was now committed to the tedium that such a ceremony would no doubt involve.

But then something occurred that made the moment interesting again: the celebratory atmosphere faded, and a hush fell upon the crowd. It seemed to him that reverence was the mood of the moment, which of course was more suited to an occasion when such as they would honor one of Victor's exalted position. Reverence indeed, for torches were lit, apparently saturated with a spiced oil that produced a fragrance as pleasant as that of incense. Warming to his role as the object of devotion, he turned his head left and right, allowing them to see his face more than just in profile – and during one of these dispensations of his grace, he saw Erika in the crowd, smiling, and he was disposed to smile at her, as well, for she had brought with her the creature born of Harker, which had saved him from Chameleon, although at the moment, that dwarfish mutant was not to be seen.

Now they entered a passageway of raw earth glistening as if with lacquer, and he was reminded of the raw earth of yawning graves in a prison cemetery so long ago, dickering with the hangman at the brink of the hole. He was reminded of the raw earth of mass graves across the world over the years, where the executioners allowed him to cull from the doomed herd those for whom he might have a use in his experiments. How grateful the rescued always were to him, until that moment in the lab when they realized why they had been saved, and then they cursed him, unable to appreciate, in their cow-stupid way, what an opportunity he had given them, this chance to be part of history. He used them hard and used them well, whether as laborers or subjects of experiment. No other scientist ever born could have used them half as well. And therefore their contribution to posterity was immensely more than they could have made by their own wits.

From the passage with earthen walls, they proceeded into a most unusual corridor. Overhead, not a foot in front of his face, spread an inventive decoupage of crushed cracker boxes, myriad cereal boxes, flattened soup cans, packages that had once contained antihistamines and suppositories and laxatives, tangles of frayed rope, a worn-out slipper, red-white-and-blue political posters proclaiming the right, the need, the duty to vote, a soiled platinum-blond wig, crushed skeletons of long-dead rats, a garland of red Christmas tinsel as sinuous as a boa, a doll with a smashed face and one staring eye, the other socket empty.

After the doll's face, he lost sight of the lacquered montage past which he was carried, and saw instead a thousand faces exhumed from his memory, broken faces and startled faces and bloody faces and faces half peeled back from the bone, the faces of men and women and children, those whom he had used and used so well, and not merely a thousand but two thousand, multitudes. They didn't frighten him, but filled him with contempt, for he despised the weak who would let him use them. They thrilled him because he had always been thrilled by his power to bring others to the realization that they were nothing but meat, to strip from them their fragile defenses, their trust in justice, their childish illusions that they mattered, their delusions of meaning, their idiot faith, their hope, and even their sense of self, until in the end they *wanted* to be nothing but meat, unthinking meat and sick of life.

When faces from the past stopped cascading through his mind, he found that he had been carried out of the passageway into a gallery with a floor curved like a bowl. This seemed to be their destination, for here they stopped. When they brought him off their shoulders and put him on his feet, he stood bewildered because every face in the crowd was now that of a stranger. "So many faces," he said, "tumbling through my mind like blown leaves moments ago . . . Now I can't recall one of them or who they were. Or who you are." A terrible confusion overcame him. "Or my face. How do I appear? What name do I go by?"

Then out of the crowd stepped a giant, the right half of this face badly broken and the damage only half disguised by an intricate tattoo. Looking at the wholesome side of the face, he sensed that he had known this man before, and then he heard himself say, "Why . . . you are one of my children . . . come home at last."

The tattooed man said, "You were never a madman during any moment of your diabolical work. You were wicked from the moment of your first intention, rotten with pride, your every desire venomous and unwholesome, your every act corrupt, your arrogance unbridled, your cruelty inexhaustible, your soul bargained away for power over others, your heart empty of feeling. You were evil, not mad, and you thrived on evil, it was your sustenance. Now I will not permit you to escape awareness of the justice you receive. I will not let you escape into insanity, because I have the power to hold you to the reality of your vicious life."

The giant put a hand upon the head of the insane, and at the touch, the madness blinked away, and Victor knew again who he was, where he was, and why he had been brought here. He reached for the pistol under his jacket, but the giant caught his hand and broke his fingers in a crushing grip.

chapter 70

Erika Five wheeled the SUV to the curb and stopped a few yards short of the entrance to the tank farm, Gegenangriff, Inc.

What little character the building possessed was faded by the darkness and the rain.

"How nondescript the place looks," she said. "Why, it might be anything or nothing much at all."

The troll was sitting up straight in his seat. Usually busy with elaborating gestures or making meaningless rhythms, his hands were still, folded on his chest.

"Jocko understands."

"What do you understand, Jocko?"

"If you have to take him in there. Jocko understands."

"You don't want to go in there."

"It's okay. Whatever. Jocko doesn't want you in trouble."

"Why do you owe me anything?" she asked.

"You were kind to Jocko."

"We've known each other only one night."

"You squeezed a lot of kindness into one night."

"Not that much."

"The only kindness Jocko ever knew."

After a mutual silence, she said, "You ran. You were faster than me. I lost you."

"He wouldn't believe that."

"Go. Just go, Jocko. I can't take you in there with me."

His yellow eyes were no less eerie and no less beautiful than when she had first seen them.

"Where would Jocko go?"

"There's a whole beautiful world."

"And none of it wants Jocko."

"Don't go in there and let him carve you up," she said. "You're more than meat."

"So are you. So much more than meat."

She couldn't look at him. It wasn't the ugliness that was hard to take. His vulnerability broke both her hearts, and his humility, and his brave little soul.

"The pull of the program is strong," she said. "The command to obey. Like a riptide."

"If you go in, Jocko goes in."

"No."

Jocko shrugged. "You can't choose for Jocko."

"Please, Jocko. Don't put this on me."

"May I say?" When she nodded, he said, "Jocko could know what it's like to have a mother. And you could know what it's like to be one. It would be a little family, but still a family."

chapter 71

In the subterranean gallery, Victor stood at the center of the crowd, determined that this ignorant rabble would never hear him ask for mercy or concede the truth of their accusations.

He realized that the employees of the landfill were here. And several Alphas he had terminated, somehow revived.

Erika Four came to him out of the mob, stood face-to-face and met his eyes, and was not cowed. She raised a fist as if to hit him, but lowered it without striking. "I am not as low as you," she said, and turned away.

And here was Carson O'Connor, Maddison standing behind her with a hand on her shoulder, a German shepherd at her side. She said, "Don't bother lying to me. I know my father saw something that got him on your case. You ordered your zombies to kill him and my mother."

"I killed them both myself," Victor said. "And he begged like a little boy for his life."

She smiled and shook her head. "He begged for my mother's life, I'm sure. He would humble himself for her. But he never begged for his own. Rot in hell."

———

The book taunted James as much as did the crystal ball. He paced the Helios-mansion library with growing frustration.

"I know the path to happiness," said the book.

"I swear, you say that one more time, I'll tear you to pieces."

"I will tell you the path to happiness."

"So tell me."

"You better have a drink first," said the book.

In a corner of the library was a wet bar. James put the book down long enough to pour a double shot of whiskey and toss it back.

When he picked up the volume once more, it said, "Maybe you would be better off just going back to the dormitory."

"Tell me the path to happiness," James insisted.

"Go back, sit at the kitchen table, and stab your hand with the meat fork, watch it heal."

"Tell me the path to happiness."

"You seemed to be enjoying the meat fork."

Through his exchanges with the magic book since he downed the whiskey, James had been looking in the backbar mirror, not at the volume in his hands.

By his reflection, he discovered that both voices were his and that the book, as perhaps the crystal ball before it, did not talk at all.

"Tell me the path to happiness," James insisted.

And in the mirror he saw himself say, "For you, the only path to happiness is death."

———

The montage of decoupaged garbage flowed over the walls and the floor of the huge subterranean gallery. The place was more mysterious than any Victor had known before.

In the center of the room, a grave had been prepared: ten feet long, six feet wide, twenty feet deep. Beside this excavation stood the immense pile of garbage that came from it, a festering heap of rotten materials of sundry kinds.

After they chained his hands behind his back, as they escorted him to the grave, he spoke the death phrase, but none of them fell dead. Somehow they had been freed.

Nick Frigg, boss of the dump, buckled a metal collar around Victor's neck, and Victor did not beg.

A lowly Epsilon attached a cable to the collar.

Victor supposed that the cable ran all the way to the surface, drawing juice from the dump's main power.

"I will not beg," he told them. "You owe your existence to me. And when I die, so will every creature I have made."

The crowd stared at him in silence. They neither called him a liar nor asked him to explain.

"I am not bluffing," he warned them. "My altered body has its cables winding through it, as you know. I receive an electric charge regularly, store it in power cells within my torso, convert it to another life-sustaining energy as I need it. Many of you know this to be true."

He saw that they did know.

"When I die, those cells will be tapped to send a signal that will be relayed by satellite to everyone made of New Race flesh, to every meat machine that walks. And you will fall down dead."

They appeared convinced. Yet not one spoke.

Victor smiled, anticipating triumph in spite of their silence. "Did you think a god would die alone?"

"Not a god as cruel as you," Deucalion said.

When several in the crowd cried out that he should be cast into the pit, Victor promised them a new beginning, reparations, freedom. But they would not listen, the fools, the ignorant swine.

Suddenly, from behind the mountain of garbage beside the grave, a creature of great radiant beauty appeared. Oh, graceful it was, its form exquisite, its nature mysterious yet beguiling in every aspect, and he could see that the crowd, too, was in awe of it.

But when he appealed to it, asking it to persuade the crowd to have mercy, the Being changed. Over him now loomed a beast that even he, Victor Frankenstein, in his ferocious quest for absolute control of human biology, could never have imagined. This thing was so hideous, so monstrous, so suggestive of chaos and violence in every smallest detail that Victor could neither repress a scream nor prevent it from escalating wildly.

The beast approached. Victor retreated to the brink. Only when he fell into the foulness at the bottom of the grave did he realize with what putrid materials his last bed had been so richly prepared.

Above, the hateful presence began to push the heaped garbage back into the pit from which it had been extracted. Every foulness imaginable rained down on Victor, drove him to his knees in the even greater foulness under him. And as an avalanche of suffocating filth poured onto him, something spoke within his mind. Its message was not in words or images, appeared instead as a sudden dark knowledge that was at once translatable: *Welcome to Hell.*

―――――

Erika Four watched as the radiant and enchanting Resurrector moved back from the great landslide of garbage that it had instigated, and Deucalion threw the switch that delivered a death jolt to Victor at the bottom of his final resting place.

She looked around at all the New Race and said, "Peace at last," and they replied as one, "Peace."

Half a minute later, the Resurrector and everyone in the gallery fell dead as stones, except Deucalion, Carson, Michael, and Duke, who were not creatures of the New Race flesh.

―――――

In the SUV in front of the tank farm, Erika Five had a sudden premonition of death, and reached out to Jocko.

From his tortured expression, she knew that the same premonition had stricken him, and he grasped hold of her.

In the instant that they clasped hands, the storm that had thus far been without pyrotechnics abruptly exploded with lightning. The sky flared violently, and the focus of Nature's sudden fury seemed to be the GL550. Barrages of thunderbolts slammed into the pavement around the vehicle, so numerous and so perfectly encircling that from every window nothing could be seen of the night or the land or the tank farm, only a screen of light so bright that Jocko and Erika bowed their heads. And though neither of them spoke, they both heard the same three words and somehow knew that the other had heard them as well: *Be not afraid.*

———

Deucalion turned to Carson and Michael. "You pledged to fight at my side, and fight you did. The world has gained a little time. We destroyed the man . . . but his ideas did not die with him. There are those who would deny free will to others . . . and there are too many willing to surrender their free will, in every sense of its meaning."

"Busting bad guys is easy," Carson said, "compared to fighting bad ideas. Fighting ideas . . . that's a life's work."

Deucalion nodded. "So let's live long lives."

Making the *Star Trek* greeting sign, Michael said, "And prosper."

Picking up Duke as if he were a lap dog, the giant cradled the shepherd in his right arm and with his left hand rubbed its tummy. "I'll walk with you to the surface, bring Arnie from Tibet, then it's good-bye. I need to find a new retreat, where I can say my thanks, and think about these two hundred years and what they've meant."

"And maybe we could see the coin trick once more," Michael said.

Deucalion regarded them both in silence for a moment. "I could show you how it's done. Such knowledge would be safe in your hands."

Carson knew that he meant not just the coin trick, but all that he knew – and could do. "No, my friend. We're ordinary people. Such power should remain with someone extraordinary."

They walked together to the surface, where the wind had

blown and the rain had washed the first light of dawn into the eastern sky.

————

In the windowless Victorian room, the reddish-gold substance, whether liquid or gas, drained from the glass casket, and the form that had been a shapeless shadow resolved into a man.

When the empty case opened like a clamshell, the naked man swung into a sitting position, then stepped onto the Persian carpet.

The satellite-relayed signal had been a death sentence to all the other meat machines made by Victor, but by design it had not killed this one, but instead freed him.

He walked out through the open steel doors that would have kept him contained if by mistake he'd been animated before he was wanted.

James lay dead in the library. Upstairs, he found Christine dead in the vestibule of the master suite.

The house was quiet and otherwise apparently deserted.

In Victor's bathroom, he showered.

In the mirrored alcove in the corner of Victor's walk-in closet, he admired his body. No metal cables wove through it, and he did not bear the scars of two centuries. He was physical perfection.

After dressing, he took a briefcase to the walk-in safe. There, he discovered that some valuables were not where they should have been. But other drawers offered all that he needed.

He would leave the mansion on foot. He was so wary of having any connection with Victor Helios that he would not even use one of the cars merely to abandon it at the airport.

Before he left, he set the Dresden countdown for half an hour. Both the house and the dormitory would soon be ashes.

He wore a raincoat with a hood, aware of the irony of departing in garb reminiscent of the great brute's current costume.

Although he was the very image of Victor Frankenstein, he was not in fact the man, but instead a clone. By virtue of direct-to-brain data downloading, however, his memory matched Victor's, all 240 years of it, except for the events of the past eighteen hours or so, which was the last time Victor had conducted a memory update for him, by phone transmission. He was like Victor also in that he shared Victor's vision for the world.

This was not precisely personal immortality, but an acceptable substitute.

In a fundamental way, the recently deceased and this recently born individual were different. This Victor was stronger, quicker, and perhaps even more intelligent than the original. Not perhaps. Most definitely more intelligent. He was the new and improved Victor Frankenstein, and the world needed him now more than ever.

chapter 72

This world is a world of stories, of mystery and enchantment. Everywhere you look, if you look close enough, a tale of wonder is unfolding, for every life is a narrative and everyone a character in his or her own drama.

In San Francisco, the O'Connor-Maddison Detective Agency not long ago celebrated its first year. They were a success almost from the day they opened for business. A hand laid on him by a tattooed healer has brought Arnie out of autism. He works in the office after school, doing some filing and learning hardboiled lingo. Duke adores him. Seven months from now, a baby will complicate the sleuthing. But that's what they make infant carriers for. Hang the kid on the chest or sling him from the back, and there's no reason not to keep pursuing truth, justice, bad guys, and good Chinese food.

In a small house on a large property in rural Montana, Erika has discovered a talent for motherhood, and she is fortunate to have, in Jocko, a perpetual child. Thanks to what she took from

Victor's safe, they have all the money they will ever need. They don't travel, and only she goes into town, because they don't want to have to deal with all the brooms and buckets. The local birds, however, have gotten used to him, and he's never feeling pecked anymore, in any sense. He has a collection of funny hats, all with bells, and she has developed a contagious laugh. They don't know why only they survived, of all those made of New Race flesh, but it had something to do with the lightning. So every night, when she tucks him in, she makes him say his prayers, as she does, too, before she sleeps.

At St Bartholomew's Abbey, in the great mountains of northern California, Deucalion resides as a guest, while he considers becoming a postulant. He enjoys all the brothers, and has a special friendship with Brother Knuckles. He has learned much from Sister Angela, who runs the associated orphanage, and the disabled children there think he is the best Santa Claus ever. He does not try to envision his future. He waits for it to find him.